I0654142

PRIVATEER, LLC

A Florida Crime Novel

J.L. Block Enterprises

PRIVATEER, LLC

A Florida Crime Novel

Copyright © 2025 by J.L. Block Enterprises.

All rights reserved. This is a work of fiction. Names, characters, places, and incidents are products of the authors' imaginations or are used fictitiously, except where real-life analogs have been rendered so unflattering as to invite litigation, in which case please consult our attorneys, who are themselves fictitious.

Any resemblance to actual persons, living or dead, is coincidental.

Any resemblance to actual legislation is regrettable.

First Edition

Printed in the United States of America

Paperback ISBN: 978-1-969709-38-8

For anyone who has ever filled out federal paperwork

and wondered if anyone else would read it.

(No one did.)

INTERNAL MEMORANDUM—PRIVILEGED
FROM: Legal
TO: Reader
RE: The Following Novel

This is a work of satire. It takes place in the state of Florida, which is itself a work of satire that is somehow also a state.

The Lee Bill does not exist. The privateer program does not exist. Half the Booty, Global does not exist. Any resemblance to actual American policy, past or present, is a failure of our imagination to keep pace with reality.

Senator Richard Lee is not based on any specific United States Senator. He is based on approximately thirty-seven of them, averaged.

Trevor Kline is not a real person. He has been a real person, however, several times, at several different companies, and will be again.

The cartels are real. We've changed their names. They know who they are.

Please enjoy responsibly.

—Counsel

"Authorized by Congress. Funded by cocaine."

"When piracy goes corporate, morality becomes optional."

—Congressional testimony, redacted

Privateer, LLC

PART ONE

ASSEMBLY

INTERNAL MEMORANDUM—CONFIDENTIAL

FROM: Trevor Kline, CEO, Half the Booty, Global
TO: Board of Directors
RE: Q1 Privateer Market Landscape Assessment
DATE: [REDACTED]

Team,

Exciting developments in the maritime asset recovery space.

As many of you know, the Lee Bill has now been active for approximately ninety days, and I'm pleased to report that market conditions are exceeding our most optimistic projections. The competitive landscape is, frankly, embarrassing. Most licensed operators appear to have been recruited from a casting call for "people who peaked in high school" and their operational sophistication is roughly equivalent to a middle school paintball team with a boat loan.

This is excellent news for us.

I've attached a competitive analysis prepared by our strategy team. Key highlights:

— The Coastal Compliance (our primary benchmark for "what not to do") was recently machine-gunned by a Guatemalan trawler. Their captain has since become a motivational speaker. His fee is $500. I've included a clip. It's devastating.

— Black Flag Group continues to operate in ways that are, diplomatically speaking, "robust." They are useful to us. I would not invite them to dinner. I would not invite them to anything that required cutlery.

— A new entrant has filed under the name "Privateer, LLC." Led by a former Coast Guard commander named Marcus Hale. Twenty-two years of service. Honorable discharge. His crew includes a convicted drug trafficker, a weapons designer under ATF surveillance, and a man whose background check reads like a Florida Man article generated by artificial intelligence. Initial reports suggest he intends to operate with complete transparency and accurate seizure reporting.

I know. I laughed too.

But I want us to monitor this closely. Honest operators, however naive, can create uncomfortable benchmarks. If his numbers are clean and ours are "optimized," the optics become complex.

Action items: Legal to prepare competitive countermeasures. PR to develop "concerned colleague" narrative. Finance to identify pressure points.

The ocean is big enough for everyone. But only if everyone plays the same game.

And we decide what game that is.

—TK

"Excellence is not an act, but a margin."

PROLOGUE

COMPLIANCE

Seventy-two hours before Captain Marcus Hale received his privateer license, a man named Darren Holcomb learned an important lesson about liability.

The lesson arrived at 3:47 AM in the form of a Guatemalan fishing trawler that was not, technically speaking, a fishing trawler.

Darren Holcomb was thirty-four years old, recently divorced, and the proud captain of the Coastal Compliance, a fifty-two-foot former pleasure yacht that his crew had spray-painted tactical gray because someone said it looked "more official." He had seventeen hours of maritime experience, a laminated federal authorization card, and approximately four hundred thousand dollars in projected revenue if he could just seize one goddamn boat before his investors started asking questions.

The investors were his ex-wife's new boyfriend and two guys he'd met at a CrossFit gym.

"Target acquired," said Darren into the radio, trying to sound like someone who had ever acquired anything other than a variable-rate mortgage and a drinking problem.

His first mate, a former Applebee's manager named Todd, squinted at the radar. "That's definitely a boat."

"Can you confirm cartel affiliation?"

Todd shrugged. "It's in the ocean. At night. That's suspicious, right?"

Darren consulted the Lee Bill's Official Guidelines for Authorized Maritime Interdiction, a forty-seven-page document he had skimmed exactly once while sitting on the toilet. Section 3.2.1 stated that probable cause could be established through "reasonable suspicion of illicit activity based on observable behavioral indicators."

"They're being evasive," Darren announced.

"They're moving in a straight line," Todd observed.

"Evasively."

This was good enough for Darren. He grabbed the loudspeaker.

"ATTENTION VESSEL. THIS IS THE COASTAL COMPLIANCE, OPERATING UNDER FEDERAL AUTHORIZATION NUMBER—" he checked his laminated card— "SEVEN-FOUR-SEVEN-BRAVO-NINE. YOU ARE ORDERED TO HEAVE TO AND PREPARE FOR BOARDING."

The fishing trawler did not respond.

It did, however, open fire.

The thing about cartel gunners is that they practice.

Darren Holcomb's crew did not practice. Darren Holcomb's crew had done a single afternoon of "tactical training" at a paintball facility in Sarasota run by a man who claimed to be ex-Special Forces but was actually ex-Cinnabon.

The first burst of automatic weapons fire shattered the Coastal Compliance's windshield and killed the radar immediately. The second burst caught Todd in the shoulder, which was unfortunate because Todd had been holding a flare gun at the time and his reflexive trigger pull sent a burning phosphorus projectile directly into the cabin, where it ignited a pile of tactical vests that someone had ordered from Amazon and never properly stored.

"FUCK," screamed Darren, which was reasonable.

"FUCK," screamed Todd, which was also reasonable, given the circumstances.

"FUCK," screamed Kevin, the third crew member, a twenty-three-year-old who had joined because his uncle told him it would be "like the Coast Guard but you get to keep the money."

Kevin had also been promised equity.

The cartel trawler, which was carrying approximately eight hundred kilos of cocaine and was crewed by men who had been shooting people since the Clinton administration, swung alongside with professional efficiency. Two men with AK-47s positioned themselves at the rail. A third man, older, with a face like a leather bag left in the sun, stepped forward and looked down at the burning pleasure yacht with something like pity.

"Privateers?" he asked in accented English.

Darren, on his back, bleeding from glass cuts, surrounded by fire and screaming, managed to hold up his laminated card. "Federal authorization."

The cartel leader studied it for a moment.

Then he laughed.

It was not a cruel laugh, exactly. It was the laugh of a man who had seen many stupid things in his life and had just added to the collection. "You know," he said, almost conversationally, "we hear about this law. The pirate law. We think, this is crazy, yes? America is making pirates legal. But then we think, okay, it will be professionals. Navy men. Killers." He gestured at the Coastal Compliance. "Not this."

"We're authorized," Darren insisted weakly.

"You're on fire," the cartel leader observed.

The leader sighed and turned to his men. In Spanish, he said, "Put them out. Take their fuel. Leave them the radio."

One of the gunners looked surprised. "We're not killing them?"

"Why?" The leader shrugged. "They'll do more damage to this program alive. Let the Americans see what their law creates."

He looked back at Darren one more time. "Tell your investors," he said pleasantly, "that the ocean has rules. Your Congress doesn't make them. We do."

Twenty minutes later, the Coastal Compliance sat dead in the water, her fuel tanks drained, her cabin gutted by fire, her crew alive but comprehensively humiliated.

Todd had stopped screaming. Kevin had thrown up twice.

Darren sat against the rail, laminated card still clutched in his hand, and stared at the horizon where the cartel trawler had disappeared.

"I want my equity back," Kevin whispered.

Darren didn't respond.

He was calculating, in the numb way of a man whose entire business model had just been machine-gunned, how he was going to explain this to the CrossFit guys.

Seventy-two hours later, the story hit local news.

By the time it reached national coverage, Darren Holcomb had been repackaged. The burning yacht became a "firefight." The humiliating mercy became a "tactical withdrawal." The cartel leader's contempt became "proof that the cartels are scared."

The Lee Bill's sponsors pointed to the incident as evidence that the program was working. "Our brave privateers are engaging the enemy," said Senator Richard Lee, author of the bill, standing in front of a flag he had never served. "This is exactly the kind of disruption we intended."

Senator Lee had been a personal injury attorney before entering politics. His maritime experience consisted of a booze cruise in Cabo San Lucas that he had once described, in a moment of creative autobiography, as "an extended naval operation." He wore boat shoes to press conferences. He kept a decorative anchor on his desk. He had used the phrase "anchor's aweigh" in seventeen separate speeches, and mispronounced it every single time.

Three cable networks ran segments on "The New Pirates of the Caribbean."

Applications for privateer licenses increased four hundred percent.

And somewhere in Tampa, a former Coast Guard commander named Marcus Hale watched the coverage with the expression of a man who had just seen his worst fears validated and also somehow made his decision easier.

Because if idiots like Darren Holcomb were going to do this anyway—

Maybe it was time for someone competent to try.

This was, in retrospect, an error in judgment.

But it was also the beginning.

CHAPTER ONE

THE GOOD ONES QUIT

Six months earlier

Commander Marcus Hale had seen some shit.

Twenty-two years in the Coast Guard will do that. You pull bodies from the water. You watch hurricanes eat towns. You intercept boats full of people so desperate they've paid their life savings to float across open ocean in vessels held together by prayers and duct tape. You do this for two decades and you either go numb or you go crazy or you find something to believe in that keeps you human.

Marcus had believed in the law.

Not in some abstract, philosophical sense. He believed in it the way an engineer believes in physics—as a set of rules that, if followed correctly, produced predictable outcomes. The law said you couldn't traffic drugs. The law said you couldn't smuggle people. The law gave him authority to stop these things, and when he stopped them, the system processed the results and justice, in its slow and imperfect way, occurred.

It wasn't pretty. It wasn't fast. But it worked.

And it was so much easier than everything else.

The night his marriage ended, Marcus was fifty-three years old and sitting in a Denny's parking lot at 2 AM, unable to make himself go home.

He'd just finished a thirty-six-hour operation. A container ship out of Cartagena, tip from DEA, coordinated intercept with three agencies. They'd found two hundred kilos hidden in a false compartment behind frozen fish.

Clean bust. Good work. The kind of thing that would show up in reports and make someone's quarterly numbers look impressive.

His phone showed eleven missed calls from Laura.

He knew what they were about. He knew because it was their anniversary—seventeenth—and he'd known three days ago that the operation would run long, and he'd said he'd figure something out, and then he hadn't figured anything out because there was always something more urgent than figuring things out.

The restaurant reservation had been at 7 PM. It was now 2:14 AM.

He could go home. Face it. Have the conversation that had been building for years, the one where she'd say "you're never here" and he'd say "the job requires—" and she'd say "the job is an excuse" and he'd say "people are dying, Laura" and she'd say "so is this marriage" and he'd feel righteous because he was out saving the world while she was upset about a dinner reservation.

That was the thing about righteousness. It was a fortress. You could hide inside it and feel good about yourself while everything around you burned.

Marcus sat in the Denny's parking lot for another forty-five minutes. At one point a waitress came out for a cigarette break, saw him sitting in the dark, and asked if he was okay. He said yes. She gave him the look you give someone who is obviously not okay and is lying about it in a Denny's parking lot at 2 AM, which is a very specific look that Denny's waitresses have perfected through generations of witnessing human decline.

Then he drove to the base and slept on the cot in his office.

The divorce papers arrived three months later.

He signed them without argument. Laura got the house. He didn't fight for custody of Sarah because Sarah was nineteen and in college and had stopped returning his calls somewhere around her sixteenth birthday, and fighting for custody of an adult who didn't want to see you was just another way of avoiding the question of why she didn't want to see you.

Laura called him one last time, after the papers were finalized.

"I want you to understand something," she said. Her voice was calm. She'd moved past anger somewhere in year twelve, into something worse—clarity. "I don't hate you. I don't even blame you anymore. But I need you to know what you did."

"I worked. I provided—"

"You hid." She cut him off. "Every time things got hard—with us, with Sarah, with anything that required you to be a person instead of a commander—you hid in the job. You hid in being right. You let yourself believe that catching criminals was more important than being a husband or a father because catching criminals was easier."

"That's not—"

"You know what's hard, Marcus? Sitting with a teenage girl who's crying because she doesn't understand why her father looks through her like she's a stranger. You know what's easy? Giving a speech about duty and sacrifice and then leaving before anyone can ask follow-up questions." Marcus said nothing.

"You're not a bad person," Laura continued. "You're not cruel. You're just... absent. You've been absent for twenty years. And the worst part is, I don't think you even know it. I think you genuinely believe you were doing the right thing."

"I was doing my job."

"Your job was your favorite hiding spot. That uniform, that authority, that moral clarity—it let you feel like a hero while your daughter grew up wondering why her father didn't seem to see her."

"I saw her. I—"

"You saw a problem to be solved. A schedule to optimize. A commitment to fulfill when convenient." Laura's voice cracked, just slightly. "You never saw her, Marcus. You never saw me. You just saw yourself, reflected in our disappointment, and somehow convinced yourself that our disappointment was proof of your virtue."

The line was quiet for a long moment.

"Goodbye, Marcus," Laura said. "I hope you figure it out. I really do. But I'm not going to wait anymore." She hung up.

Marcus sat in his quarters with the phone in his hand. Outside his window, the base was quiet, the ocean dark.

He waited for the grief to come. The regret. The desperate need to call her back and fight for what they'd had. Nothing came.

Just a loosening in his chest. A lifting of weight he hadn't realized he'd been carrying.

He could focus on the work now without distraction.

Instead, it felt like permission.

The day Marcus Hale lost his faith was a Tuesday.

He was thinking about his daughter's latest sigh—she'd called that morning, first time in four months, to remind him that her wedding was in three months and he still hadn't confirmed his plus-one situation; the call lasted ninety seconds—when the intercept call came in.

Suspected drug vessel, forty miles offshore. Fast boat, radar contact intermittent. The kind of intercept he'd done a thousand times.

They caught it clean. His crew was good—Lieutenant Park on tactical, Petty Officer Dominguez on the fifty-cal, a boarding team that had trained together for three years. They lit up the target with spotlights, issued commands in English and Spanish, and watched the go-fast boat cut its engines and drift to a stop without a single shot fired.

Professional. Textbook. Exactly how it was supposed to work.

The boat was carrying six hundred kilos of cocaine and three dead bodies.

The cocaine was standard—pressed bricks, cartel stamps, wholesale value around eighteen million. The bodies were not standard. Two men and a woman, bound, gagged, shot in the head. Not smugglers. The boat captain, a skinny Honduran with gang tattoos and dead eyes, explained it readily: "Witnesses. They saw us load in Cartagena. What were we supposed to do?"

Marcus looked at the bodies.

The woman was maybe thirty. Dark hair matted with blood. She wore a thin gold necklace with a small cross.

"Commander?" Lieutenant Park was looking at him. "You okay?"

"Fine," Marcus said. "Document everything. Chain of custody. I want this one airtight."

He had the captain processed, documented, handed over to DEA.

Three weeks later, he learned the captain had been released.

Not acquitted. Not mistried. Released. Charges reduced, testimony excluded on a technicality, cooperation agreement signed with an agency Marcus had never heard of. The six hundred kilos went into evidence. Eighteen months later, Marcus found out that "evidence" had somehow become four hundred kilos by the time it reached trial, and no one could explain where the other two hundred had gone.

The three bodies were never identified.

And the captain—the man who had executed them as casually as swatting flies—was back on the water within six months, working for a different cartel, doing exactly the same thing.

Marcus requested a meeting with his commanding officer to discuss what he called, in careful bureaucratic language, "systemic failures in the interdiction-to-prosecution pipeline."

His commanding officer, a rear admiral named Patterson who had never once gotten his dress whites wet, listened politely for twenty minutes and then said: "Commander, the system processes what the system processes. Your job is interdiction. What happens after is not your concern."

"Sir, with respect, if interdiction has no consequences—"

"Has excellent consequences," Patterson interrupted. "We seized eighteen million in product. That's a win. That goes in the report. That's what Congress sees."

"The people who did this are free."

Patterson smiled the smile of a man who had made admiral by understanding that some things were not meant to be said out loud. "The people who did this are assets now, Commander. They provide intelligence. They enable future operations. They are, in their way, working for us."

"They murdered three people."

"They allegedly murdered three people. And the value of their cooperation outweighs—" he paused, searching for the right euphemism— "historical considerations."

Marcus stood up.

"I need to think about my future in this organization," he said.

Patterson nodded like he'd been expecting this. "Take some leave, Marcus. You've earned it. Come back fresh. The system works. You just need to remember what part of it you're responsible for."

Marcus walked out.

He thought about the woman with the gold cross. He thought about his daughter's sigh.

He thought about twenty-two years of believing that following the rules meant something, and how comfortable that belief had been, and how easy it was to confuse comfort with purpose.

He never walked back in.

CHAPTER TWO

ASSEMBLY REQUIRED

Bo "Gator" Wilkes was drunk at 10 AM on a Wednesday, which was actually an improvement.

On Tuesdays, he was usually drunk by 8.

The bar was called The Rusty Anchor, which was generous because there was nothing rusty about it—the rust would have implied historical character. This was a cinder block rectangle off Route 41 with a hand-painted sign, a parking lot that was fifty percent potholes, and a clientele that made the phrase "day drinking" redundant because most of them hadn't stopped from the night before. Gator liked it.

He was forty-one years old, built like a fire hydrant wrapped in sun damage, and had spent his entire life within a hundred miles of where he was born. He'd been a shrimper, a gator hunter (hence the name), a fishing guide, a boat mechanic, and for one memorable summer, a "marine consultant" for a reality TV show about swamp people that never aired because three of the cast members got arrested for something involving an alligator, a county commissioner, and a profound misunderstanding of consent laws.

He had never left Florida.

He had never wanted to.

Florida was perfect. Florida had swamps and boats and women who made bad decisions and alcohol that cost four dollars a drink. Florida had heat that made you mean and humidity that made you crazy and a general atmosphere of lawlessness that Gator found spiritually nourishing.

He was nursing his third Budweiser and explaining to no one in particular why manatees were "basically just sea cows and sea cows ain't endangered, they're just slow" when the man in the polo shirt walked in.

Gator knew immediately he wasn't local.

The polo shirt was the first tell—clean, tucked in, the kind of thing someone wore when they wanted to look casual but didn't know how. The posture was the second tell—straight, balanced, military. The way his eyes swept the room before he sat down was the third.

Cop, Gator thought automatically. Or ex-cop. Or military. Same thing, basically.

The man sat down two stools away and ordered a coffee.

Coffee. At The Rusty Anchor. Where the coffee machine had been broken since the Bush administration—the first one—and "coffee" meant instant Folgers heated in a microwave that had witnessed things no microwave should witness. The microwave had a sticker on it that said WORKS GREAT and below that, in different handwriting, NOT TRUE.

The bartender, a woman named Sheila who had been divorced three times and had the tattoos to prove it, raised an eyebrow but poured it anyway.

The man took a sip. His face didn't change, which told Gator everything he needed to know about this person's pain tolerance.

"You Bo Wilkes?" the man asked.

Gator considered lying. Lying was usually the smart play when someone you didn't know used your full name. But there was something about this guy—the tiredness behind the discipline, the sense that he was here because he'd run out of better options—that made Gator curious.

"Depends on who's asking and what he did."

"I'm asking. And I'm hoping he hasn't done anything recently because I need someone who can pass a background check."

Gator laughed. "Mister, I got background. Check ain't the word I'd use."

The man reached into his pocket and placed a laminated card on the bar.

Federal authorization. Privateer license. Official seal and everything.

Gator stared at it for a long moment.

"The pirate thing," he said slowly. "That's real?"

"It's real."

"And you want me to... what? Be a pirate?"

"Privateer," the man corrected. "There's a legal distinction."

"What's the distinction?"

"Paperwork."

Gator grinned. This was already the most interesting thing that had happened to him since the alligator incident.

"I'm Marcus Hale," the man said. "I spent twenty-two years in the Coast Guard. I know boats, I know interdiction, and I know that this program is going to be a complete shitshow unless someone professional gets involved."

"And you came to me?" Gator took a long drink. "Mister, I don't know what you heard, but 'professional' ain't exactly my brand."

"I heard you can fix any engine with duct tape and profanity. I heard you once navigated through a storm that killed six other boats using nothing but a compass and spite. I heard you know every waterway between here and Cuba and half of them aren't on any map."

Gator shrugged modestly. "That last part's true. The other parts are mostly true."

"I also heard you have a… flexible relationship with firearms regulations."

"I prefer 'creative.'"

Marcus leaned forward. "I need someone who can keep a boat running in conditions it wasn't designed for. I need someone who knows these waters better than the people we'll be chasing. And I need someone who won't panic when things go sideways."

"Things always go sideways."

"Exactly."

Gator studied the laminated card again. Fifty percent of seized assets. That was a lot of money, floating around in those waters. Cartel money. Drug money. The kind of money that changed lives.

Also the kind of money that ended them.

"What's the catch?" Gator asked.

"The catch is that we do this right. No skimming drugs. No planting evidence. No selling what we seize back to different cartels. Clean operations, clean numbers, clean conscience."

Gator squinted at him. "You're telling me you want to be honest pirates?"

"Privateers."

"Whatever. You want to be honest?"

"I want to prove it's possible."

Gator laughed again, but there was something different in it this time. Something that might have been respect, or might have been the recognition of a man who'd found a purpose stupid enough to be worth dying for.

"Mister Hale," Gator said, "you are either the dumbest smart person I ever met or the smartest dumb person. I can't tell which yet."

"Does it matter?"

Gator finished his beer.

"Nah," he said. "Either way, I'm in."

He stuck out his hand. Marcus shook it.

"One condition," Gator added. "I know people. All kinds of people. Some of 'em are useful, some of 'em are criminals, most of 'em are both. You want to operate in these waters, you're gonna need local knowledge. Relationships. Trust."

"That's fine."

"I mean it. I'm a friendly guy. I talk to people. Buy 'em drinks. Remember their birthdays. That's how I know what I know." Gator's grin was easy, open. "People tell me things because they like me. You start telling me I can't be friendly, this ain't gonna work."

Marcus noticed a man at the end of the bar watching them. Weathered face, fishing shirt, a deep, permanent tan earned by decades on the water. When Marcus looked at him, the man raised his beer in a casual salute—but his eyes didn't match the gesture. They were cataloging. Measuring.

Gator waved back without looking. "That's Eddie. Good people."

The man called Eddie smiled and returned to his drink. But Marcus caught him glancing their way twice more before they left.

"Just be careful," Marcus said. "The people we'll be dealing with aren't the kind who forgive loose lips."

"Mister Hale," Gator said cheerfully, "I've been loose-lipping my whole life and I ain't dead yet. That's gotta count for something."

It did count for something.

Just not what either of them expected.

Click came second. Luis came fourth. They arrived by different roads and for different reasons, but the pattern was the same: Marcus found broken people in broken places and asked them to do something that sounded insane.

Click—real name Elliot Harrow, age thirty-one, formerly of MIT until MIT proved "insufficiently practical"—was living in a modified shipping container in Homestead surrounded by razor wire and devices that were not, technically speaking, illegal. The sign outside read: HARROW TECHNICAL SOLUTIONS. Beneath it, smaller: "If you can't prove it's illegal, it isn't."

Marcus stood at the gate and said, "That's not how the law works."

A camera swiveled. A speaker crackled.

"That's exactly how the law works," said the voice inside. "The law is words on paper. Words require interpretation. If there's no precedent that specifically prohibits my exact methodology, I am—legally speaking—pioneering."

"You're pioneering prison time."

"I prefer to think of it as accelerated judicial education."

The interior was a mad scientist's fever dream organized by someone with OCD. Weapons, modifications, and unidentifiable devices lined the walls in perfect rows. A massive orange tabby named Mr. Whiskers sat on a shelf of what Click described as "mostly inert" detonators and watched Marcus with the disinterest of an apex predator who had already eaten.

Click had googled Marcus before the meeting, run a background check before the conversation, and correctly identified his branch, rank, and reason for leaving the Coast Guard before Marcus finished his first cup of shipping-container coffee.

"You want weapons that can disable cartel vessels without violating maritime law, international treaty, or the Lee Bill's proportional force provisions," Click said, as if reading a menu. "I can do better than that. I can make it look legal."

"What do you want out of this?"

"Field data. Purpose. A reason to build things that matters." His eyes were pale blue and burned with an intensity of a person who saw the world as an infinite series of problems, regardless of whether anyone had asked for solutions. "Also, Mr. Whiskers requires a litter box station with proper ventilation on any vessel. He's essential personnel."

"The cat is not essential personnel."

"The cat detected ATF surveillance three times. The cat has a better operational track record than most humans."

Marcus shook his hand and left, wondering if "professional" had ever been a realistic criterion.

Luis Calderón came from farther away—from nine years in federal prison, from twenty years of cartel logistics before that, from a world where spreadsheets and violence were the same skill set. Gator found him through a chain of connections that involved at least three people currently incarcerated.

They met at 2 AM in a diner outside of Opa-locka. Luis was already there—a man in his late forties with graying hair, calm eyes, and the quiet self-possession of someone who had long ago made peace with what he was.

"I know what you're going to ask," Luis said before Marcus could speak. "Why would a convicted drug trafficker want to help catch drug traffickers?"

"Is there a good answer?"

"There's an honest one." Luis's expression didn't change. "I want to do damage. I want to hurt the people who do what I used to do. I want to make their operations more expensive, more difficult, more dangerous."

"That sounds like revenge."

"Call it what you want. The point is, I know how they think. Their routes, their methods, their vulnerabilities. I know how to read a shipment from a mile away. I spent twenty years learning the drug trade from the inside." He leaned forward. "Let me use that knowledge to burn it down."

Marcus studied him. There was no desperation in Luis's face. No hope. Just a cold, patient purpose that was either exactly what the crew needed or exactly what would destroy them.

"Why?" Marcus asked. "Not the professional reasons. The real reason."

Something moved behind Luis's eyes. Something he kept locked in a room he didn't open for strangers.

"I have my reasons," Luis said. "They're personal. They're permanent. And they're the only thing keeping me alive."

He extended his hand.

Marcus shook it, understanding that some doors opened later, or not at all.

Dana Kessler came third, and she didn't come easily.

Marcus found her through military contacts—a former Navy security specialist who had done three tours in places that didn't officially exist, protecting people whose names were classified, doing work that would never appear on any record.

Her service file was a masterpiece of redaction. Entire paragraphs blacked out. Commendations from agencies that used only acronyms. A discharge that was "honorable" in the official sense and "complicated" in every other sense.

She agreed to meet him at a coffee shop in Fort Lauderdale. Public place. Neutral territory.

She was already there when Marcus arrived. Sitting in the corner. Back to the wall. Eyes on every entrance. The coffee in front of her was untouched and positioned exactly where it wouldn't interfere with a quick draw from her right hip. Beside it, a small pair of compact binoculars and a dog-eared paperback titled *Pelagic Birds of the Western Atlantic.*

Marcus noticed the book. Decided not to ask.

Dana Kessler was thirty-eight years old, Black, built like a distance runner, with close-cropped hair and a practiced stillness that came from years of waiting for things to go wrong. She wore civilian clothes—jeans, a plain gray t-shirt—but everything about her screamed operator.

Through the window behind her, a brown pelican had landed on the railing of the outdoor seating area. Dana's eyes flicked toward it, and Marcus caught something he didn't expect: a flash of pure, irrational discomfort. Her hand twitched toward her coffee cup. The pelican cocked its head and stared at her with the vacant malevolence that only seabirds can achieve.

Pelecanus occidentalis, Dana thought, involuntarily, the Latin arriving the way some people's grandmother's prayers arrived—automatic, unbidden, more instinct than thought. Wingspan two meters. Bill capacity three gallons. Known to kill pigeons whole. She dragged her eyes back to Marcus.

"Commander Hale," she said, pulling her attention back. A statement, not a question.

"Ms. Kessler."

"Dana." She gestured to the seat across from her. "Sit." He sat.

"I read your proposal," she said. "Privateer operations. Clean numbers. Legal interdiction." She tilted her head. "You actually believe that's possible?"

"I believe it's worth trying."

"Why?"

Marcus had prepared a simple answer—something about honor and duty and proving that the system could work if good people engaged with it.

Instead, he said: "Because I spent twenty-two years doing it the right way and watching the wrong people win. Because I have a daughter who won't return my calls and an ex-wife who was right about everything and a career that looked impressive on paper and meant nothing in practice. Because I'm fifty-three years old and I've never done anything that actually mattered, and I'd like to try before I die."

Dana studied him for a long moment.

"That's more honest than I expected," she said.

"I'm told I have a problem with honesty. It makes people uncomfortable."

"I'm not uncomfortable." Dana leaned back. "I'm curious. You're building a crew of criminals, lunatics, and damaged people. What makes you think that collection of liabilities can function as a unit?"

"They're not liabilities. They're people the system failed." Marcus met her gaze. "You're on that list too."

Something flickered in Dana's expression.

"I wasn't failed by the system," she said quietly. "I worked for the system. I was very good at it. I protected people who didn't deserve protection. I looked the other way when I should have looked directly."

"What changed?"

Dana was quiet for a moment. Her hand moved to a thin silver chain around her neck—a small pendant Marcus couldn't quite see.

The pelican outside flapped against the window. Dana flinched—the full-body jerk of someone confronting a primal fear—then immediately recovered, her face resetting to professional neutrality so fast you'd miss it if you blinked.

Marcus noticed but didn't comment.

"My brother," she said finally. "David. Marine. Two tours in Afghanistan. Came back with a Purple Heart and a prescription for OxyContin that turned into heroin when the prescription ran out." Marcus said nothing.

"I was stationed overseas when he overdosed. I didn't even know he was using. Our parents were dead, and I was the only family he had left, and I was in a concrete room somewhere in—" she stopped, shook her head—"somewhere. While my little brother died alone in a bathtub in Tallahassee with a needle in his arm."

"I'm sorry."

"Don't be. I'm not looking for sympathy." Dana's voice was flat, controlled. "I'm looking for something to do with this anger. It's been three years and it hasn't faded. It just sits there. Waiting."

"Anger at who?"

"Everyone. The cartels. The system. The doctors. The military that broke him." She looked at Marcus directly. "Myself, mostly. For not being there. For choosing the mission over my family."

Marcus felt something turn in his chest.

"I know that feeling," he said.

"I imagine you do." Dana's eyes were sharp. "That's why I'm here, Commander. Not because I believe in your clean numbers. Because I recognize the look of someone trying to outrun guilt by doing good."

"Does it work?"

"I'll let you know."

She stood and extended her hand.

"I'm in," she said. "But I have conditions. I run security. My calls on safety are final. And when I tell you someone is dangerous, you listen."

"Agreed." They shook.

"One more thing," Dana said. "The people you're recruiting—they're broken in obvious ways. Easy to see, easy to manage. I'm broken in ways that aren't obvious. Ways I've spent years learning to hide. If I start to slip, if this work becomes about revenge instead of justice… I need someone to tell me."

"I will."

"Promise."

"I promise."

Dana nodded once, turned, and walked out.

Through the window, the pelican tracked her departure with its horrible beady eyes. Dana gave it a wide berth that was almost certainly unconscious.

Marcus watched her go and thought about all the different ways people carried their damage—some of them loud, some of them silent, and some of them so well-hidden that by the time you found them, it was already too late.

Frank Mulligan came last, and he came drunk.

Marcus found him at a bar in Hialeah at 4 PM on a Monday, which was apparently Frank's natural habitat. The bartender didn't even look up when Marcus walked in—just pointed at the corner booth where a man in his late fifties sat hunched over a glass of whiskey like it was the only thing keeping him anchored to the earth.

Former homicide detective. Thirty years MDPD. Decorated, respected, destroyed.

The drinking had started after his second divorce. The suspension had come after his third IA complaint. The forced retirement had arrived like a mercy killing for a career that had been dying for years.

"Frank Mulligan," Marcus said, sliding into the booth across from him.

"That's the name." Frank didn't look up from his drink. "You're Marcus Hale. Coast Guard. Retired. Starting some kind of pirate thing."

"How did you—"

"Gator told me. Gator tells everyone everything. It's his whole deal." Frank finally raised his eyes. They were bloodshot, weary, and sharper than they had any right to be. "He said you're looking for a cop. Former cop. Someone who knows how investigations work from the other side."

"I'm looking for someone who can interrogate, investigate, and identify threats before they become problems."

"You're looking for a drunk." Frank smiled humorlessly. "Let's be honest, Hale. I know what I am. I know what you're hoping I can be. The question is whether what I am is close enough to what you need."

Marcus leaned back. "Are you functional?"

"Define functional."

"Can you do the job?"

"Depends on when you need me to do it." Frank took a long drink. "Before 2 PM, I'm usually pretty sharp. After 6 PM, I'm unreliable. In between is

27

negotiable." He set down the glass. "I'm not going to lie to you and say I've got it under control. I don't. I haven't for years. But I'm still the best investigator you're going to find who's desperate enough to say yes to whatever this is."

"What if I need you sharp at 6 PM?"

"Then you'd better give me something worth being sharp for." Frank's eyes held a challenge. "I've spent the last three years drinking myself to death because I couldn't find a reason not to. My wife left. My kids don't call. My career was a joke that stopped being funny. Give me something that matters and I'll be whatever you need me to be."

"And if I can't?"

"Then I'll still probably be better than your other options." Frank shrugged. "Look, Hale. I know cops. I know criminals. I know how to read a room, work a witness, and find the lie in a story. I've been doing it for three decades. The booze hasn't taken that away. It's just... dulled the edges."

Marcus thought about it.

A drunk detective with sharp instincts and a death wish. Another broken person looking for a reason to keep going.

"I have one rule about the drinking," Marcus said.

"Only one?"

"When we're operational, you're sober. Not 'mostly sober.' Not 'functional.' Sober. Can you do that?"

Frank was quiet for a moment.

"I can try," he said finally. "I won't promise more than that. Promising more would be a lie."

"Trying is enough." Marcus extended his hand. "Welcome to Privateer, LLC."

Frank shook it.

"Privateer, LLC." Frank laughed, and it was a sound that had once been genuine but had soured somewhere along the way. "Jesus Christ. My mother wanted me to be a priest."

"Too late for that."

"Too late for a lot of things." Frank finished his drink in one long swallow. "When do we start?"

"Tomorrow. 8 AM. Marina on the causeway. Try to be vertical."

"I'll try to be conscious. Vertical is negotiable."

Marcus stood to leave.

"Hey, Hale," Frank called after him. Marcus turned.

"This clean numbers thing. This honest piracy bullshit." Frank's eyes were unreadable. "You really believe in it?"

Marcus thought about the three bodies on the go-fast boat. The woman with the gold cross. The captain who walked free.

"I believe in trying," he said.

"Yeah." Frank nodded slowly. "I guess that's all any of us got left."

Marcus walked out into the afternoon heat.

He had his crew.

God help them all.

CHAPTER THREE

CERTIFIED

The Federal Privateer Licensing Facility was located in a strip mall between a nail salon and a Subway. This seemed appropriate.

The sign out front read: U.S. MARITIME ASSET RECOVERY LICENSING OFFICE. Beneath it, in smaller letters: "Appointments Required / Walk-ins Welcome." This contradiction was never explained. A third sign, handwritten and taped to the door, read: "Air conditioning is aspirational."

Marcus had made an appointment. The appointment was for 9:00 AM. He arrived at 8:45 with his complete crew, all of them dressed in what they apparently considered "business casual."

For Gator, this meant jeans without visible stains and a shirt with buttons.

For Click, this meant all black, because he'd read somewhere that it was "professional."

For Luis, this meant exactly what he always wore, which was already more professional than everyone else.

For Frank, this meant a wrinkled blazer over a t-shirt that said "I VOID WARRANTIES."

For Dana, this meant looking like the only adult in a room full of children dressed by their drunk uncles.

The facility itself was exactly what Marcus had expected: a room that had clearly been something else before (dentist's office, based on the still-visible marks where chairs had been bolted to the floor), hastily converted with cubicles, flags, and a counter staffed by people who had that unmistakable look of federal employees assigned to offices no one had expected to actually need.

A woman at the counter smiled the smile of someone who had been smiling for so long it had become a medical condition.

"Privateer licensing?"

"Yes, ma'am," Marcus said.

"Wonderful. Please take a number and have a seat. You'll be called."

There was no one else in the waiting area. There were thirty-seven chairs. The number dispenser showed "47." The sign above the counter read "NOW SERVING: 43."

"We're the only ones here," Marcus observed.

"Policy is policy," the woman said, still smiling. "Please take a number."

They waited eleven minutes.

During this time, Gator discovered that the vending machine had been unplugged but still accepted coins (he lost two dollars before figuring this out), Click began sketching what he called "improvements" to the fire suppression system, Frank found a way to fall asleep in a plastic chair that shouldn't have been physically possible, and Luis read every word of a pamphlet titled "So You Want to Be a Privateer! Frequently Asked Questions" with the quiet horror of a man watching a car accident unfold in slow motion.

"Question seven," Luis read aloud. "'Can I keep souvenirs from seized vessels?' The answer is 'Consult your regional compliance officer.'" He looked at Marcus. "They think people are going to keep souvenirs."

"People are definitely going to keep souvenirs."

"Question twelve: 'What if the pirates I'm trying to catch are also licensed privateers?' The answer is—" Luis turned the page— "'This situation is unlikely.'"

"It's already happened twice," Dana said. "I checked."

Dana leaned over to Marcus. "Tell me again why I said yes to this."

"Because you were bored."

"I wasn't that bored."

"You were doing security for a mall."

"It was a nice mall."

"Number forty-seven," the woman called.

They approached the counter as a group.

The woman's smile flickered. "Is this… all one application?"

"One crew. One license. Multiple backgrounds."

"I see." She typed something into a computer that was at least fifteen years old. The computer made a sound like it was thinking about dying. "And you have the required documentation?"

Marcus placed a folder on the counter. It was three inches thick.

"Articles of incorporation for the LLC. Federal tax ID. Maritime insurance certificates. Individual background check authorizations. Liability waivers. Equipment manifests. Training certifications—"

"Training certifications?" The woman frowned. "I don't see that on our requirements list."

"It's not required. I added it anyway."

"That's... unusual."

"I prefer thorough."

The woman began flipping through the folder. Her frown deepened with each page like a geologist discovering increasingly alarming fault lines.

"Mr. Wilkes," she read. "You have seventeen... let me count... eighteen moving violations in the past five years."

Gator shrugged. "They were all on land."

"You also have two arrests for—" she squinted— "'reckless discharge of novelty ordnance.'"

"Acquitted."

"Both times?"

"Look, the first one was a Roman candle, which technically ain't—"

"Moving on." The woman turned pages. "Mr. Harrow. You've been raided by ATF three times."

"Visited," Click corrected. "They visited. We had coffee. They didn't find anything."

"Because there was nothing to find?"

"Because I have an excellent lawyer and an even better understanding of what constitutes a 'destructive device' under 26 U.S.C. § 5845."

The woman stared at him. Click smiled.

It was not a reassuring smile.

"Mr. Calderón." The woman's voice had gone flat. "You served nine years in federal prison for drug trafficking."

"Yes."

"You were a high-level cartel operative."

"Distribution and logistics, primarily. I was never directly involved in—"

"Sir, you were convicted of conspiracy to distribute over ten thousand kilograms of cocaine."

Luis nodded. "The prosecution was very thorough."

The woman looked at Marcus.

"You're aware that your crew includes a convicted drug trafficker."

"I'm aware."

"And you still want to proceed."

"Ma'am, the Lee Bill doesn't prohibit former felons from participating in licensed privateering operations. I checked. Twice. I also had a lawyer check. The specific language excludes only individuals with active warrants or ongoing supervised release conditions."

"Mr. Calderón completed his supervised release?"

Luis produced a document. "Eighteen months ago. I have the paperwork."

The woman took the document, examined it, and added it to the growing pile.

"Mr. Mulligan." She was now speaking with the careful tone of someone defusing a bomb. "Former detective. Forced retirement. Multiple IA complaints."

Frank opened his eyes—Marcus hadn't even realized he'd woken up. "Sustained?"

"What?"

"The complaints. How many were sustained?"

The woman checked. "None."

"Then they were complaints, not findings. Big difference." Frank leaned forward, suddenly sharp-eyed in a way that caught the woman off guard. "Also, your computer screen is reflecting in the window behind you. I can see you've been playing FreeCell for the last ten minutes. I don't judge—that's a solid game—but you might want to minimize it before your supervisor walks by. She's in the hallway. I can hear her shoes."

The woman looked at the window. At her screen. At the hallway. She minimized FreeCell.

"You were still forced to retire," she said, slightly shaken.

"'Encouraged' is the word they used. And the encouragement came with a full pension and a non-disclosure agreement that I'm technically violating right now, so let's maybe speed this along."

The woman turned finally to Dana.

Her expression softened slightly. "Ms. Kessler. Former Navy. Security specialist. Honorable discharge. No criminal record."

"That's correct."

"Why are you here?"

Dana glanced at Marcus, then back at the woman. "Poor life choices."

The physical examination took place in a back room that had definitely been the dentist's x-ray area.

A man in a white coat who introduced himself as "Dr. Martinez, contractor" checked their blood pressure, vision, and ability to stand on one leg for thirty seconds. The last test was apparently meant to assess "maritime balance readiness."

Gator failed it three times before Dr. Martinez marked him as "adequate."

"I got inner ear problems," Gator explained. "From this one time with a airboat and some fireworks and a slight miscalculation regarding wind speed."

"I don't need to know," Dr. Martinez said.

"It was real pretty though. Like, 'til the part where it wasn't."

"I really don't need to know."

The psychological evaluation was conducted by a woman named Dr. Chen who looked like she had been pulled from a university psychology department and was still trying to figure out how she'd ended up in a strip mall interviewing aspiring pirates.

She asked each of them the same questions:

"Have you ever experienced thoughts of self-harm?"

"Have you ever been diagnosed with a personality disorder?"

"How do you typically respond to high-stress situations?"

"Have you ever killed anyone?"

The last question was delivered with the same casual tone as the others, which Marcus found impressive.

Gator's answer: "Not on purpose. Well, mostly not on purpose. There was this one situation with a propeller, but the judge said—"

Click's answer: "Define 'killed.' If we're talking about direct causation versus contributing factors in a Rube Goldberg sequence of events that I may or may not have initiated—"

Luis's answer: A long silence, followed by "I prefer not to answer." Another silence. "The number is not small."

Frank's answer: "In the line of duty, three times. Off duty, none. That I know of." He paused. "I've blacked out a lot, though, so I can't be a hundred percent."

Dana's answer: "Yes." Nothing more.

Marcus's answer: "I've been in situations where people died. Whether I killed them or the circumstances killed them is a philosophical distinction I try not to think about."

Dr. Chen wrote something on her clipboard.

"You all passed," she said.

"Really?" Marcus couldn't hide his surprise.

"The threshold is… adjusted… for this program."

"What does that mean?"

Dr. Chen looked at him with the expression of someone who had given up trying to make sense of her professional situation. "It means Congress wanted results, not standards. I've approved eleven crews this month. One of them was led by a man who answered 'Have you ever been diagnosed with a personality disorder?' with 'Which one?' and then listed four." She rubbed her temples. "I have a PhD from Johns Hopkins. I used to treat anxiety in adolescents. Now I'm rubber-stamping pirates in a Subway parking lot. Life is a journey."

The final step was the Oath of Compliance.

They gathered in a room that had been decorated with flags, a podium, and a framed copy of the Lee Bill that no one had dusted in what appeared to be months. The frame was slightly crooked. Nobody had corrected it. This felt like a metaphor.

A man in a suit entered. He was the platonic ideal of a strip-mall oath administrator—government bland, professionally forgettable, the human equivalent of beige.

"Please raise your right hands," he said. They did.

"Do you solemnly swear to uphold the laws and regulations governing private maritime interdiction operations, to conduct yourselves with honor and integrity in the pursuit of authorized asset recovery, and to submit accurate and complete reports within the specified timeframes as required by federal statute?"

"I do," Marcus said.

"I do," Dana said.

"I do," Luis said.

"Sure," Frank said.

"Legally speaking, yes," Click said.

"Hell yeah," Gator said.

The man in the suit sighed.

"Close enough." He stamped something. "Congratulations. You are now federally authorized privateers. Your licenses will be mailed within six to eight weeks. In the meantime, here are your temporary authorizations."

He handed Marcus six laminated cards.

They were still warm from the printer.

Marcus looked at his card. His photo—taken ten minutes ago against a white wall—stared back at him. Beneath it: CAPTAIN MARCUS HALE.

PRIVATEER, LLC. FEDERAL AUTHORIZATION NUMBER 747-BRAVO-12.

The man in the suit shook his hand. "Good luck out there," he said. "Try not to start a war."

He did not sound like he was joking.

They walked out into the Florida sunshine, licensed and legal.

Gator held his card up to the light like it was a rare gem. "I'm a pirate," he said, wonder in his voice.

"Privateer," Marcus corrected automatically.

"Whatever. I'm official."

Click was already on his phone. "I need to update my LinkedIn."

"You have LinkedIn?" Dana asked.

"I have seven. Different names. It's complicated."

Luis looked at his card without expression. "I spent nine years in prison for what we're about to do."

Frank clapped him on the shoulder. "Welcome to America, buddy. Crime's only crime if you don't have a license."

Marcus watched his crew—this collection of misfits, criminals, and broken people—celebrating in a strip mall parking lot with laminated federal authorizations that made everything they were about to do technically legal.

He thought about the Coastal Compliance, burning on the water.

He thought about Admiral Patterson, talking about processing.

He thought about the three bodies in the go-fast boat, never identified, never mourned.

This was going to be a disaster.

But at least it would be his disaster.

Marcus looked at his card one more time. Federal authorization. Official seal. A laminated rectangle that turned six people into something the law recognized.

Somewhere, three bodies on a go-fast boat had never been identified. Somewhere, those families were still waiting.

The laminated card didn't fix that. Nothing fixed that.

But maybe it was a start.

"Alright," Marcus said. "Let's go buy a boat."

CHAPTER FOUR

SECOND CHANCE

The boat was named Second Chance, which Marcus refused to see as symbolic.

She was fifty-four feet of former Coast Guard patrol vessel that had been decommissioned, sold at auction, bought by a man who planned to turn her into a party boat, abandoned when that man went to prison for tax fraud, and eventually acquired by Privateer, LLC for a price that Luis accurately described as "suspicious."

"She's ugly," Dana observed.

This was true. The Second Chance had the aesthetic appeal of a shoe box that had been left in the rain and then kicked. Her paint was peeling. Her hull was scarred. Her deck looked like it had lost a fight with a very angry forklift.

"She's functional," Marcus said.

"She's a tetanus shot waiting to happen," Frank added.

"She's ours."

Gator was already aboard, crawling into spaces that shouldn't have fit a human, making approving noises that sounded vaguely sexual.

"Twin diesels!" he shouted from somewhere below. "Caterpillar 3406s! Someone took real good care of these babies!"

"The engines are good?"

Gator's head appeared through a hatch, grinning. "The engines are beautiful. The rest of her's dog shit, but the engines…" He kissed his fingers. "Poetry."

Click was examining the radar array with the expression of a man who had just found a new project.

"This is military surplus," he said. "Outdated. I can upgrade it."

"Legally?"

"…Mostly."

"Click."

"Fine. Entirely legally. But I'm going to be very annoyed about it."

Luis walked the deck slowly, hands in his pockets, saying nothing. Marcus knew that look—he was calculating. Running scenarios. Thinking about how this boat would perform in a chase, a fight, an escape.

Dana was doing a security assessment of the perimeter when a pelican landed on the bow rail approximately four feet from her face. She drew her sidearm before catching herself, then holstered it with the forced casualness of someone pretending they had not just almost shot a bird.

"Problem?" Marcus asked.

"No problem." Her voice was perfectly controlled. The pelican stretched its enormous throat pouch and made a sound like a garbage disposal processing wet leather. Dana took three deliberate steps backward. "I'm going to inspect the stern."

She inspected the stern for a very long time.

Frank, who had observed the entire exchange from a folding chair on the dock, raised his flask in a toast that no one asked for.

"Fun fact," he said. "Brown pelicans can store up to three gallons in that pouch. Three gallons. Of anything. Fish, water, the hopes and dreams of everyone who's ever trusted a government program." He took a drink. "I used to work a case where a pelican ate a man's Chihuahua whole. Right off the leash. The bird didn't even slow down. Just—" he made a gulping motion— "gone. The man sued the city."

"Frank," Marcus said. "Why do you know that?"

"Because I know everything that's terrible. It's a gift." Frank looked at Dana's retreating back with something like understanding. "Ornithophobia's more common than people think. The Pentagon did a study."

"They did not."

"They might have. I read a lot of weird shit when I can't sleep. Which is always."

From the stern, without turning around, Dana's voice carried back in the clipped cadence of someone correcting the record against her will.

"Two gallons. Not three. And the Chihuahua thing is urban legend—there are no verified cases of a brown pelican consuming a mammal over two pounds. They'll try. They can't swallow it. The pouch dislocates their jaw."

Silence.

Marcus looked at Frank. Frank looked at Marcus.

"How," Frank said slowly, "do you know that."

"I don't." Dana was still not turning around. "Stop talking about the birds."

"You absolutely just corrected me on—"

"*Stop talking about the birds,* Frank."

Frank held up his flask in surrender. Marcus filed the moment, quietly, in the folder he kept for things he would never mention out loud. The file in that folder, labeled DANA, was beginning to have interesting subheadings.

The renovation took three weeks.

It should have taken two, but the crew spent the first four days arguing about priorities.

"We need a grill," Gator said.

"We need a weapons locker," Dana said.

"We need a signal amplification array with redundant—"

"We need a grill," Gator repeated, louder, as if volume were the problem. "You can't run a boat without a grill. It's maritime law."

"It is absolutely not maritime law," Marcus said.

"It should be. I'm writing a letter."

"To whom?"

"The maritime law people. Whoever they are." Gator was already sketching something on a napkin. "Look, I got it all figured out. Propane grill, port side, with a windscreen so the burgers don't taste like salt. We put the weapons locker starboard. Balance. It's physics."

"That's not physics," Click said.

"It's close enough to physics."

Frank, who had been sitting in a deck chair drinking since 9 AM, raised a hand. "I need a space for interrogation."

"A what?" Marcus asked.

"Interrogation. We're going to catch people. I'm going to need to talk to them. I need a room. A good room. Uncomfortable chair, one light source, no windows." He took a drink. "I've been doing this for thirty years. The room matters. A bad interrogation room is like a bad therapist's office—people clam up."

"You want us to build a tiny scary room inside a boat."

"I want us to build an effective operational interview facility inside a maritime vessel." Frank paused. "Also, it should be near the head. Nothing makes a person cooperative like needing to pee and not being able to."

"That's inhumane," Dana said.

"That's Interrogation 101. They teach it at Quantico."

"They definitely don't teach 'put people near the toilet' at Quantico."

"They teach it between the lines."

Luis had been silent throughout this exchange. He now spoke for the first time.

"A cooler."

Everyone looked at him.

"A large cooler. Industrial. For storing seized product at proper temperature." He paused. "Cocaine degrades in heat. If you want accurate weights at processing—and we do—the product must be stored at a consistent temperature from seizure to handoff."

"You want a cocaine fridge," Gator said.

"I want a temperature-controlled evidence storage unit."

"That's a cocaine fridge."

"The terminology is irrelevant. The product integrity is not."

Marcus pinched the bridge of his nose. "Here's what's going to happen. Dana gets the weapons locker. Click gets the communications array. Luis gets his cooler. Gator does not get a grill."

"Cap—"

"No grill."

"What if it's a small grill?"

"No grill of any size."

"What about a hot plate?"

"Gator."

"A MICROWAVE? Can a man have a MICROWAVE on a BOAT?"

"Fine. A microwave."

Gator pumped his fist. "That's basically a grill."

"It is nothing like a grill."

"You can make nachos in a microwave. Nachos are grill food. Transitive property. Basically a grill."

Marcus looked at Dana. Dana looked at Marcus. They shared the silent communication of two people who had independently concluded that this crew was going to be the death of them and had decided to proceed anyway.

Click raised a hand. "For the record, Mr. Whiskers requires a litter box station with proper ventilation. He's coming aboard for extended operations."

"The cat is not coming aboard."

"The cat is essential personnel."

"The cat is a cat."

"The cat detected ATF surveillance three times. The cat has a better operational track record than most of the people in this conversation."

The microwave arrived two days later. Gator immediately attempted to make nachos. The nachos caught fire. The fire set off the smoke detector Click had just installed. The smoke detector, which Click had modified "for sensitivity," emitted a sound that could be heard from three docks away and caused a pelican colony on the adjacent pier to launch into the air in a shrieking mass of prehistoric fury.

Dana, who had been doing push-ups on the foredeck, dove behind the weapons locker and didn't emerge for four minutes.

"I hate this boat," she said when she finally stood up. "I hate everyone on this boat. I hate the microwave. I hate the pelicans. And I especially hate nachos."

"The nachos weren't that bad," Gator said, scraping charcoal off a plate. "Just a little crispy."

"They were on fire, Gator."

"Crispy and on fire are a spectrum."

Gator practically lived aboard after that, rebuilding systems that hadn't been touched in years, replacing parts that had been held together by hope and corrosion. He slept in the engine room more often than not, surrounded by tools and empty beer cans and the unmistakable smell of a man who had stopped caring about conventional hygiene.

Click transformed the communications array into something that probably shouldn't have been possible with civilian equipment. Marcus didn't ask questions. The less he knew, the less he could be prosecuted for.

Dana and Frank handled weapons acquisition, which turned out to be easier than expected. The Lee Bill allowed privateers to "maintain appropriate armaments for self-defense and interdiction operations," which Congress had helpfully failed to define.

"So we can have anything?" Frank asked, reading the relevant section for the third time.

"Anything that isn't explicitly prohibited by other federal law," Dana confirmed.

"What about a fifty-cal?"

"Legal."

"Grenades?"

"Technically legal with the right paperwork."

Frank's eyes widened. "What about—"

"No tanks," Marcus interrupted. "No missiles. No nuclear devices."

"I wasn't going to say nuclear devices."

"You were building up to it."

Frank shrugged. "I was building up to it."

Luis handled logistics—fuel contracts, supply lines, the boring necessities that kept an operation running. He also, to everyone's surprise, cooked. His arroz con pollo, made from ingredients he sourced from locations Marcus didn't ask about, was, according to Gator, "the best thing I've eaten since my grandmother died, and I include the food at her funeral." He did it with the quiet efficiency of a man who had once managed the movement of hundreds of kilos of cocaine across international borders and now applied those same skills to marine diesel and MREs.

One afternoon, Dana found Gator at the fuel dock, chatting with a dockworker she didn't recognize. By the time she got close, Gator was already laughing, slapping the man on the shoulder like an old friend.

"—so the captain figures we can run clean numbers, right? Actually report what we seize. None of this skimming bullshit the other crews pull." Gator was practically glowing with enthusiasm. "Gonna be the first honest privateers in the whole damn program."

The dockworker nodded along, eyes too interested.

Dana waited until the man left, then grabbed Gator's arm.

"What the hell was that?"

"What? That's just Paulie. Works the pumps. Good guy."

"You just told him our entire operational philosophy."

Gator's face creased in confusion. "So? It ain't a secret. Clean numbers is the whole point."

"It's information. About us. About how we operate. About what makes us different." Dana kept her voice low, aware of other people on the dock. "You don't know who Paulie talks to. You don't know who's listening. You don't know what information is valuable to people who might want to hurt us."

"You're being paranoid."

"I'm being professional." She released his arm. "There's a difference."

Gator watched her walk away, genuinely puzzled. He'd been talking to people his whole life. It was who he was. The idea that friendliness could be a weapon used against him simply didn't compute.

He'd learn. They all would.

The first shakedown cruise was a disaster.

Not a big disaster—no one died, nothing exploded, the boat didn't sink—but a disaster in the way things that go wrong when six people who have never worked together try to coordinate under pressure.

It started with the engine.

Gator had sworn the Caterpillars were "ready to purr like kittens who fuck." Within twenty minutes of leaving the dock, the port engine began making a noise that sounded less like a kitten and more like a garbage disposal attempting to process a brick.

"That's normal!" Gator shouted over the grinding. "That's just her clearing her throat!"

"Engines don't have throats," Dana pointed out.

"Everything's got a throat if you believe hard enough!"

Then the radar went down.

Click had promised his upgrades were "field-ready," a phrase that apparently meant "will work until exposed to actual saltwater." The screen flickered, showed static, and then displayed what appeared to be a Portuguese weather forecast.

"That's not right," Click admitted.

"You think?"

"I can fix it. I just need…" He looked around frantically. "Does anyone have a capacitor and maybe some ferrite beads?"

"What kind of boat do you think this is?" Marcus demanded.

"The kind with a prepared crew?"

Luis, to everyone's surprise, produced a small case from his jacket. "I have components."

Click stared at him. "Why do you have components?"

"I learned very early in my career that the ability to improvise repairs is worth more than the ability to shoot straight." He opened the case. "Shooting is easy. Fixing things is power."

Click took the case like he was receiving a religious artifact. "I think I love you."

"You're not my type."

Meanwhile, Frank had gotten into the weapons locker and was having what he called "a moment of appreciation" and Dana called "an alarming display of arousal toward firearms."

"This is beautiful," Frank murmured, running his hands along a tactical shotgun. "Who loaded these?"

"I did," Dana said.

"Buckshot?"

"Alternating slugs and buck. First round is buck for spread, second is slug for penetration, third is buck again for—"

"Follow-up." Frank nodded approvingly. "You've done this before."

"More than I'd like."

"Yeah." Frank's voice went quiet. "Me too."

By sunset, they had traveled forty-three miles, repaired three separate system failures, discovered that the head (maritime for "toilet") backed up when anyone over two hundred pounds used it (Gator was offended), and learned that Click was violently seasick but refused to admit it.

"I'm not seasick," Click insisted, green-faced, gripping the rail with white knuckles. "I'm experiencing a mild vestibular disagreement with the ocean's interpretation of wave frequency."

"You just threw up on a seagull," Gator observed.

"The seagull had it coming."

They anchored in a cove to regroup.

"That was a clusterfuck," Dana announced.

"Language," Marcus said automatically, then realized how ridiculous that sounded given that he was commanding a privateer crew. "Actually, no. Fair assessment. That was a clusterfuck."

"We're gonna die," Frank said cheerfully.

"We're not going to die."

"We're probably going to die."

"Frank—"

"I'm not scared or anything. Just being realistic. Most people who go up against cartels die. We're people. Math isn't hard."

Gator emerged from the engine room, covered in grease. "She'll run now. I fixed the thing."

"What thing?"

"The thing that was broke."

"Be more specific."

"The thing in the engine that makes the engine go. It wasn't going. Now it goes."

Marcus was quiet for a moment. "Gator, I need you to understand that when we file reports—and we will file reports—'the thing that makes the engine go' is not going to satisfy federal auditors."

Gator scratched his head, leaving a streak of grease. "The... fuel injector linkage assembly?"

"Was that so hard?"

"I don't like fancy words. They make simple things complicated."

Luis had been sitting quietly throughout this exchange. Now he spoke.

"We're not ready."

Everyone looked at him.

"For a real engagement," Luis continued. "We're not ready. The equipment is unstable. The crew is unpracticed. The communications are—" he glanced at Click, who was still looking green— "temperamental."

"You're right," Marcus admitted. "We need more time."

"We don't have time." Luis looked at the horizon. "Half the Booty filed their first seizure report yesterday. Three hundred kilos. The Coastal Compliance—the crew that got shot up—they're being rebuilt with private equity money. Black Flag Group isn't even pretending to follow protocols."

"How do you know all this?"

"I listen." Luis's expression didn't change. "Old habits."

Dana leaned forward. "What are you saying?"

"I'm saying that by the time we're ready, the map will already be drawn. The other crews will have established territories, relationships, agreements. We'll be late to a game that's already in progress."

"So what do you suggest?"

Luis was quiet for a moment.

"We go out. Tomorrow. We find something small. We make mistakes where the consequences are survivable. And we learn."

"That's reckless," Dana said.

"Yes. But it's also how cartels train their people. You don't learn to swim by reading about water."

Marcus looked around at his crew—exhausted, dirty, completely unprepared for what they were about to do.

"Tomorrow," he said. "We hunt."

That night, Marcus couldn't sleep.

He sat on deck, watching the stars and thinking about all the ways this could go wrong. The boat could fail. The crew could break. They could encounter something they couldn't handle and die stupidly in the water, another cautionary tale for the evening news.

Or worse—they could succeed. They could intercept drugs, seize assets, taste the money and the power that came with it. And then the real test would begin: whether they could stay honest in a system designed to corrupt.

Luis appeared beside him, silent as smoke.

"Can't sleep either?"

"I don't sleep much."

They sat in silence for a while.

"Can I ask you something?"

"Yes."

"Why are you really here? Don't give me the redemption speech. I've heard the redemption speech. What's the real reason?"

Luis was quiet for so long Marcus thought he wasn't going to answer.

"Damage," he said finally. "I want to do damage to the people who do what I did. Not to save anyone. Not to make up for anything. Just to hurt them the way they hurt—"

He stopped.

"That's not noble," Marcus said.

"No. It's not."

"It might be enough."

The corner of Luis's mouth moved, barely. "We'll see."

They sat together until dawn, watching the water turn from black to gray to gold.

Then they went to war.

CHAPTER FIVE

FIRST BLOOD

The first target was a mistake.

Not their mistake—the cartel's mistake. Someone had gotten sloppy, run a route that was too predictable, loaded a boat that was too heavy, hired a crew that was too inexperienced.

Marcus didn't know any of this at the time.

All he knew was that Click's temperamental radar had picked up a contact moving at twenty-three knots on a heading that made no commercial sense, and Luis had looked at the data and said, very quietly: "That's cocaine."

"How can you tell?"

"Speed says smuggler. Heading says stupid smuggler. Time of day says overconfident stupid smuggler." Luis studied the blip. "They're probably new. Running their first load. Told the route was safe."

"Is it?"

"It was. Until us."

Marcus felt the familiar surge of pre-mission adrenaline—the sharpening of senses, the quickening of thought. Twenty-two years of training screamed at him to follow protocol, call for backup, establish communication with relevant authorities.

But there was no protocol for this.

There was no backup coming. They were it.

"Battle stations," Marcus said.

The phrase felt ridiculous. They weren't a navy vessel. They weren't even a proper crew. They were six people on a boat held together by spite and duct tape, about to intercept a drug shipment because Congress had passed a law that said they could.

But everyone moved.

Gator hit the engines. The Caterpillars roared to life—the grinding noise was gone, replaced by a deep, satisfying growl that promised violence and speed.

Click took his position at communications—he called the array "Dr. Singh," a name nobody asked about—headset on, fingers dancing across equipment that looked like it belonged in a museum or possibly an evidence locker. He was also, Marcus noticed, slightly green. The seasickness medication he'd taken had apparently not survived the encounter with the breakfast burrito he'd eaten against Luis's advice.

"I'm fine," Click said preemptively.

"I didn't ask."

"Your face asked."

Dana distributed weapons the way other people distributed place settings—each person got what fit them, adjusted for their grip, their stance, their particular form of reckless courage. She'd zeroed Frank's rifle for his slight left-eye dominance without telling him, because Frank would argue and then shoot worse.

Frank checked his weapon twice, nodded, and found a position with good sightlines. He was, Marcus noticed, stone sober. Not because he'd stopped drinking—he'd finished his flask twenty minutes ago—but because the prospect of violence had a clarifying effect on Frank that therapy never had. His hands were steady. His eyes were sharp. He looked like a completely different person from the wreck Marcus had found in the Hialeah bar.

"Focus," Frank murmured to himself. Then, louder: "Their helm is drifting left. Periodic. Every thirty to forty seconds."

"So?"

"So their pilot's checking something to his left. A phone, a radio, or another person. He's distracted. If we approach from the right, we've got a longer window before he spots us." Frank paused. "Also, the way they're riding—bow high, stern dragging—they've loaded from the back forward. That means the cockpit is light. One good wave and they'll lose helm control."

Marcus stared at him.

"What?" Frank said. "I worked maritime homicide for three years. You learn boat stuff."

Luis simply watched the radar, his calm never wavering.

"Intercept in twelve minutes," he said. "They haven't seen us yet."

"How do you know?"

"If they had, they'd be running."

The go-fast boat came into view at 0547 hours.

It was exactly what Marcus expected—a low-slung cigarette boat with oversized engines and a deck loaded with cargo wrapped in black plastic. Three men visible: one at the helm, two watching the horizon with the tense alertness of people who expected trouble but hoped it would come from a different direction.

Marcus grabbed the loudspeaker.

He'd rehearsed this. He'd practiced the words until they felt natural. He'd prepared for this moment for weeks.

And then Gator did something unexpected.

"YEEEEEHAWWW!" Gator screamed, hitting the throttle so hard the Second Chance practically leaped out of the water. "LET'S GET 'EM, BOYS!"

The element of surprise was, in retrospect, lost.

The go-fast boat reacted instantly. Engines screamed. The bow lifted. They were running before Marcus could get a single word of official authorization out of the loudspeaker.

"Gator!" Marcus shouted. "What the hell?"

"Instinct!" Gator shouted back, grinning like a maniac. "Chase instinct! It's a Florida thing!"

"We had the advantage—"

"We still got the advantage! They're heavy and we ain't! Simple physics!"

This was, Marcus realized with horror, technically true. The go-fast boat was carrying enough weight to significantly reduce its speed advantage. The Second Chance, while not built for racing, had clean engines and an enthusiastic lunatic at the helm.

They were actually gaining.

"Contact is attempting to flee," Click announced formally into his headset, apparently recording for posterity. "Engaging pursuit per Lee Bill Section 4.7.2, authorization of necessary force to prevent—" He paused, leaned over the rail, and vomited. Then he returned to the mic. "—escape. Disregard ambient audio."

"Was that on the recording?" Dana shouted.

"The recording captures everything. It's comprehensive."

"Great. Federal evidence of you puking."

"Seasickness is a physiological response, not a professional failing. The Pentagon—"

"If you say 'the Pentagon did a study,' I will throw you overboard."

The chase lasted eleven minutes.

Eleven minutes of screaming engines and salt spray and Marcus's heart trying to exit his chest through his throat. Eleven minutes of Gator howling like a demon and Dana taking position at the bow and Frank watching the target boat with the predatory calm of a man who had found, after years of drowning, something to be sober for.

Luis stood perfectly still, watching, calculating.

"They're going to dump," Luis said suddenly.

"What?"

"The cargo. They're going to dump it. Lose the evidence, claim they're just fishermen."

Even as he spoke, Marcus saw movement on the go-fast boat. One of the crew was cutting the plastic-wrapped bundles free, preparing to throw them overboard.

"Warning shot," Marcus ordered.

Click raised something that looked like a rifle but had been modified so extensively it barely resembled its original form.

"Define warning," Click said.

"A shot. That warns them."

"How much warning?"

"Click, for the love of—" Click fired.

The round hit the water approximately three feet from the go-fast boat's hull. It did not explode. It did not ignite. It did emit a sound—a screaming, whistling, genuinely terrifying sound that made Marcus's teeth vibrate and caused a pelican resting on the water nearby to launch itself skyward with a shriek of prehistoric outrage.

The pelican, apparently deciding that the Second Chance was the source of its distress, banked hard and flew directly at Dana.

What happened next occurred in approximately 1.3 seconds: Dana, who had been calmly sighting down her rifle at the go-fast boat, saw four pounds of angry seabird hurtling toward her face. She ducked. The rifle fired. The round, which had been aimed at the water near the go-fast boat's hull, instead clipped the boat's antenna array, which shattered in a shower of sparks and fiberglass.

"BIRD!" Dana shouted—the first time anyone had heard anything approaching panic from her.

"What?" Marcus turned.

"NOTHING. I SAID 'HEARD.' AS IN I HEARD YOUR ORDER." Dana straightened up, face composed, as though she had not just been terrorized by a pelican. "Continue."

The man who had been about to dump the cargo froze.

The boat's helm jerked hard to the right.

And then, in what Marcus would later describe in his official report as "an unexpected navigational failure," the go-fast boat's pilot lost control and the vessel spun out, catching a wave wrong and flipping in a spectacular cartwheel of fiberglass and cocaine.

Everyone on both boats stared.

"Huh," Gator said.

"That wasn't supposed to happen," Click muttered.

"Bodies," Dana said, already moving, professionalism fully restored. "We need to check for bodies." Two survivors.

The third man had gone under and hadn't come back up.

The survivors were young—early twenties, maybe. Terrified. Bleeding from cuts and scrapes but nothing serious. They scrambled aboard the Second Chance with the desperate energy of people who had just discovered that the ocean wanted to kill them.

Marcus zip-tied their hands. Standard procedure. He read them something that approximated rights, though the legal status of Miranda in a maritime privateer context was, as Click had noted, "an unexplored area of jurisprudence."

"Please," one of them said in accented English. "Please, we are just fishermen—"

"You're fishermen," Luis said flatly, appearing beside them like a ghost. "Who happened to be carrying approximately four hundred kilos of cocaine."

He crouched down to their level.

"I know your organization," Luis continued, his voice almost gentle. "I know who you work for. I know what route you were running. I know you're both very young and very stupid and thought this would be easy money."

The survivors went pale.

"I also know," Luis said, "that if we let you go, you'll be dead within a week. Your employers don't accept failure. So here's what's going to happen." He stood.

"You're going to answer Captain Hale's questions. You're going to tell us everything you know about the operation. And when we hand you over to the authorities, you're going to cooperate fully, because federal prison is significantly better than what's waiting for you otherwise."

The two men looked at each other.

Then they started talking.

The haul was better than expected.

Three hundred and seventy-two kilos of cocaine, most of which had stayed bundled despite the crash. Street value: approximately fifteen million dollars. Privateer cut: fifty percent. After expenses, split six ways: just under one point two million each.

If they were honest about the numbers.

This was, as Marcus understood, the moment of truth.

They stood on deck, surrounded by plastic-wrapped wealth, and Marcus watched his crew.

Gator was looking at the bundles with an expression Marcus couldn't read.

Frank was deliberately not looking at them.

Click was taking photographs, documenting everything with methodical precision.

Dana was at the stern with the .308, tracking the horizon in the systematic sweep pattern she'd learned in places she couldn't name—fifteen degrees left, hold, fifteen degrees right, hold, repeat until the ocean either produced a threat or put you to sleep.

And Luis was counting.

He counted the way he did everything—with a patience that suggested he had been doing this exact thing, in some form, for a very long time. His hands moved over the bundles without hesitation, sorting, stacking, calculating weights by feel before confirming with the scale.

He was too good at this.

"Three hundred seventy-two kilos," Luis announced. "I counted twice."

Marcus looked at him. "You sure?"

"I'm sure."

"Not three hundred fifty? Not three-sixty? Not some nice round number that might've fallen overboard during the confusion?"

Luis met his eyes. His hands were still resting on the cocaine. The product. The same pressed bricks, same cartel stamps, same chemical smell that Marcus had encountered a thousand times in the Coast Guard.

But Luis was looking at them differently.

"Three hundred seventy-two kilos, Captain. That's what we recovered. That's what we report."

"Luis." Marcus lowered his voice. "Twenty kilos overboard and nobody would ever know. That's a lot of money for a crew that can barely afford fuel."

"I would know." Luis's voice was quiet. Absolute. "I spent twenty years counting product for people who skimmed. I never skimmed. Not once. Not a gram. I was known for honest weights."

"You were also known for moving ten thousand kilos of cocaine."

"Yes." Luis pulled his hands away from the bundles. He looked at them—his hands—as though seeing something on them that soap and time and prison hadn't washed away. "You want to know why I'm here. The real reason. Not the professional reasons I gave you at that diner." Marcus waited.

"My daughter's name was Maria." Luis's voice didn't waver, but something behind it shifted, like a door opening onto a room he kept dark. "She had her mother's laugh. She wanted to be a veterinarian. She wrote me letters every week for the first two years I was inside."

The deck was silent. Even the ocean seemed to quiet.

"Then the letters stopped. I thought she was angry. I thought she'd given up on me." Luis paused. "She was already dead. She'd been dead for three months before anyone thought to tell me. They found her in an apartment in Tampa with a needle in her arm and my name in her wallet." Nobody spoke.

"I moved ten thousand kilos of this." Luis touched one of the bricks, gently, the way you'd touch something that had hurt someone you loved. "Maybe more. I knew what it did. I knew where it went. I told myself it was business. Supply and demand. I wasn't making anyone use it."

He pulled his hand back.

"Maria got hooked on pills after a car accident. Nothing dramatic—a fender bender, some back pain, a doctor who wrote prescriptions like candy. The pills ran out. The pain didn't. So she found other sources." His eyes moved across the bundles. "Sources like this. Sources like me."

Gator had stopped looking at the cocaine. He was looking at Luis.

Frank had closed his eyes.

"Three hundred seventy-two kilos," Luis said again, and now Marcus understood the precision wasn't professionalism. It was penance. Every gram accounted for was a gram that wouldn't reach another Maria. Every honest number was a small, insufficient act of atonement by a man who knew that atonement was impossible but chose it anyway.

"I'm not looking for redemption," Luis said. "Redemption is for people who did something wrong by accident. I knew what I was doing." He looked at Marcus directly. "But I can count. I can count accurately. And I can make sure that every single gram we seize is reported, documented, and destroyed. That's not redemption. That's the minimum." The silence stretched.

Then Gator spoke.

"Well shit," he said quietly. "I guess we really are the honest pirates."

"Privateers," Marcus said. But his voice was rough.

"Whatever." Gator looked at the bundles, then at Luis, then at the bundles again. "We're the weird ones either way."

The paperwork took four hours.

Federal forms. Coast Guard notifications. DEA liaison reports. Evidence chain of custody documentation. Prisoner transfer requests. Incident summaries in triplicate.

Marcus did it all himself, typing with two fingers on a laptop that Click had "improved" in ways that made the keyboard occasionally spark.

By the time he finished, the sun was setting.

"First seizure," Dana said, appearing beside Marcus with two beers. "Congratulations."

Marcus took the beer. "We got lucky."

"We got competent. Lucky would have been no chase at all."

"One of them died."

Dana was quiet for a moment. "Yeah. That happens."

"It's not supposed to happen."

"With respect, Captain—nothing about this is supposed to happen. We're privateers. Legal pirates. We just chased down a drug boat and seized fifteen million dollars' worth of cocaine because a Senator from Florida thought it would play well in the midterms." She took a long drink. "'Supposed to' stopped meaning anything a long time ago."

Marcus couldn't argue with that.

That night, Marcus dreamed about the third man—the one who went under and didn't come back up.

In the dream, the man was floating just below the surface, eyes open, watching. Not angry. Not sad. Just watching, with a patience of the dead.

When he woke up, the Second Chance was moving through calm water, engines humming, heading back to port with evidence and prisoners and paperwork and the beginning of a reputation.

The first seizure was done.

The first death was logged.

And somewhere out there, other boats were moving, other crews were hunting, and the ocean was filling with people who had licenses that made everything they did technically legal.

Marcus looked at his laminated authorization card.

PRIVATEER, LLC.

FEDERAL AUTHORIZATION NUMBER 747-BRAVO-12.

PART TWO

THE GAME

INTERNAL MEMORANDUM—CONFIDENTIAL

FROM: Trevor Kline, CEO, Half the Booty, Global
TO: Senior Leadership Team
RE: Competitive Threat Assessment Update—Privateer LLC
DATE: [REDACTED]

Team,

I'll be brief.

Privateer LLC filed their first seizure report. 372 kilograms. Reported weight matches processing weight to the gram. Chain of custody documentation is, and I say this with genuine bewilderment, flawless.

They reported honest numbers.

I need everyone to understand how dangerous this is. Not because 372 kilograms matters—we moved that last Tuesday before breakfast. It's dangerous because their numbers are accurate and ours are "accurate," and if anyone with a calculator and a grudge ever compares the two, questions will be asked that we do not want answered.

I've spoken with Anton. He shares my concerns, though he expressed them in his usual way, which is to say he stared at me for forty-five seconds without blinking and then said "handle it." I love working with Anton. He really makes you feel like a valued partner and not at all like a man standing in front of a wood chipper trying to explain why the wood isn't chipping fast enough.

Action items:

- PR: Begin seeding narrative that "overly precise reporting" is a red flag for data manipulation. Yes, I'm aware this is the opposite of true. That's what makes it PR.

- Legal: Research whether there's a way to file a complaint about someone being *too* honest. I'm told there isn't, but I pay you people to find ways around "isn't."

- Operations: Monitor their routes. I want to know where they go, when they go, and what they have for breakfast. Especially that Click person. He concerns me. Anyone who lives in a shipping container by choice has either figured something out or lost something fundamental, and I'm not sure which is worse.

- Finance: Model the impact of one clean crew on our quarterly optics. If the answer is "nothing," great. If the answer is "something," find me a different answer.

On a lighter note, Chad Bryson has applied for privateer certification. You may know him as @SentItChad from TikTok. His application video included a backflip. He has 1.2 million followers. I am going to kill myself.

Just kidding. I'm going to monetize him.

Related: the Block Enterprise crew has now been cited three times this quarter for bringing their tiger to the dockmaster meetings. Their attorneys continue to argue that Tootsie is an "emotional support animal" and I continue to argue that is not what those words mean. We are losing. Tootsie remains credentialed.

—TK

"The market corrects everything. Even virtue."

CHAPTER SIX

THE MARINA

Privateer Marina was what happened when you gave yacht club aesthetics to people who solved problems with violence.

The facility sprawled across forty acres of prime Florida waterfront, a monument to the speed at which capital could transform legal ambiguity into infrastructure. Six months ago, it had been a derelict commercial fishing dock. Now it featured a clubhouse with a full bar, a tactical gear outlet, a weapons maintenance shop, and a Starbucks that had somehow gotten a franchise license despite the fact that its customers regularly showed up covered in blood and cocaine residue.

The barista had seen some shit.

The dockmaster, a woman named Esperanza Ruiz who had run commercial fishing operations out of Key West for thirty years before the privateer program turned her dock into a circus, waved them toward their assignment with the exhausted efficiency of someone who had cataloged every variety of maritime stupidity and was no longer capable of surprise.

Marcus guided the Second Chance into their assigned slip—berth 47, which put them between a converted shrimp trawler called the Tax Write-Off and an aggressive-looking catamaran with "CIVIL FORFEITURE" painted on the hull in letters you could read from space.

Dana took in the scene without comment: crews loading equipment, forklifts moving seized goods, a group of men in matching polo shirts conducting what appeared to be a team-building exercise involving zip-ties and mannequins. Someone had set up a taco truck near the fuel depot. The banner above the window read EL PIRATA, with a smaller slogan underneath: *You Seize 'Em, We Season 'Em.* A pelican colony had established itself on the dockmaster's office roof, a development that Dana registered with the careful awareness of a soldier cataloging enemy positions.

A man walked past the taco truck leading what was, unambiguously, a Siberian tiger on a leash.

Nobody reacted. Not the crews, not the pelicans, not the taco truck operator, who accepted the man's order for three carnitas without interrupting eye contact.

"That's a tiger," Click said.

"That's Tootsie," Esperanza called, without looking up from her clipboard. "Emotional support animal. His paperwork is in order."

"Whose emotional support animal?"

"A gentleman named Justin. Or Erik. I honestly cannot tell them apart and I have stopped trying. They co-captain the Block Enterprise. She's in slip eleven. Don't feed the tiger."

"I wasn't planning to," Click said.

"People say that. Then they plan to."

Dana watched the tiger accept a carnita with the polite dignity of a creature who had long ago made peace with being the weirdest thing in any given marina. She filed this image in a mental folder labeled FLORIDA and resolved never to open it again.

"Is that a gift shop?" Click asked, pointing, determinedly changing the subject.

It was indeed a gift shop. PRIVATEER PROVISIONS, the sign read. Through the window, Marcus could see t-shirts, coffee mugs, and stuffed animals dressed in tactical gear.

"They're selling merch," Frank observed flatly. "Pirate merch."

"Privateer merch," Gator corrected. "There's a legal distinction."

"Paperwork," everyone said in unison.

Frank wandered into the gift shop and emerged with a coffee mug that read "SEIZED MY COFFEE," a bumper sticker that said "My Other Boat Is Your Boat," and a keychain shaped like a miniature laminated federal authorization card. He seemed genuinely pleased.

"These are terrible," he said. "I love them."

Senator Richard Lee arrived an hour later in a motorcade that was aggressive for a state senator—three black SUVs, a communications van, and a trailing vehicle that his chief of staff described as "security" and everyone else recognized as the hair-and-makeup team.

The Senator emerged wearing boat shoes, a blazer with brass buttons, and the quiet confidence of a man who had never questioned his own competence because no one around him was paid enough to do it for him.

"Marit-time!" he announced to the gathered press, spreading his arms as if embracing the entire marina. "America's new frontier!"

His press secretary, a woman named Kelsey who had been grinding her teeth so aggressively she'd cracked a molar, leaned into a nearby microphone. "Maritime, Senator. MARE-ih-time."

"That's what I said."

"You said MARE-it-time."

"Kelsey, I've been saying this word for two years."

"I know, sir."

He had been a personal injury attorney in Tallahassee before entering politics—the kind who advertised on park benches and the backs of buses, whose face appeared on so many billboards that local children thought he was a fictional character, like Ronald McDonald but with worse hair. His maritime experience consisted of a booze cruise in Cabo San Lucas that he once described, in a moment of creative autobiography, as "an extended naval operation." He had never clarified this statement. His staff had never asked.

The tour of the marina was choreographed like a state visit to a country that didn't quite exist yet. Lee shook hands with crew captains, examined boats he couldn't name the parts of, and delivered remarks to a crowd of privateers who listened with the expression of soldiers watching a civilian try on their uniform.

"This program," Lee said, standing at a podium that someone had set up near the fuel depot, "represents the very best of American innovation. When I wrote this bill—"

"Co-wrote," Kelsey murmured.

"—I did so with a vision. A vision of American entrepreneurs—hardworking, brave, freedom-loving entrepreneurs—taking the fight to the cartels that threaten our shores." He gripped the podium. "Some people said it couldn't be done. Some people said, 'Richard, you can't privatize the War on Drugs.' And to those people I say: watch me."

He paused for applause. The applause was adequate.

"I have always believed," Lee continued, "that the private sector does everything better than the government. Mail? Private. Healthcare? Getting there. National defense? Let's be honest, Blackwater did some of their best work—"

"Moving on," Kelsey said loudly.

"—and now, marit-time interdiction. The results speak for themselves. Since this program launched, we have seen—" he consulted a card— "a four hundred percent increase in privateer applications. Four hundred percent! That's—" he did math in his head, visibly— "a lot more percent."

In the crowd, Marcus stood between Dana and Frank, watching the senator with the specific disbelief of a person who had spent twenty-two years in the service the senator was claiming to improve.

"He doesn't know what any of this means," Marcus said quietly.

"He doesn't need to," Frank replied. "He needs it to sound good for three minutes and photograph well from the left. That's what senators do. They're not leaders. They're logos."

Dana said nothing. She was watching the senator's security detail—two men who stood with the practiced alertness of professionals assigned to protect someone they privately thought was an idiot. She recognized the body language. She'd had that assignment more times than she could count.

The Senator was now attempting to board a nearby privateer vessel for a photo opportunity. The vessel was the Tax Write-Off—a converted shrimp trawler whose captain, a former used car salesman named Pete, was trying to explain that the deck was wet and the senator might want to watch his step.

Lee stepped aboard in his boat shoes. He slipped immediately.

Not a fall—not quite. A lurching, arms-pinwheeling recovery that his security detail handled with the reflexive efficiency of men who caught this particular human being on a weekly basis. One of them had actually developed a technique—a smooth hip check that redirected the senator's momentum toward the nearest stable surface while appearing, to cameras, like a casual touch.

"I'm fine!" Lee announced, gripping the rail. "The deck is slippery because—that's maritime conditions. That's what real sailors deal with."

"He's never been on a boat," Click said from behind Marcus. "His center of gravity is wrong. He's shifting his weight to his heels instead of his toes. That's a landlocked instinct."

"Thank you, Click."

"Also, his boat shoes are brand new. The soles haven't been scuffed. Nobody who actually wears boat shoes has unscuffed soles. Those were purchased for this visit."

"You can tell that from here?"

"I can tell everything from here." Click paused. "I can also tell that his press secretary is on her fourth antacid in twenty minutes. I've been counting."

Kelsey, across the dock, unwrapped a fifth antacid.

"Five," Click amended.

The photo opportunity lasted twelve minutes. During this time, Senator Lee managed to mispronounce "maritime" three more times, refer to a bow as "the front pointy part," and ask a privateer captain whether his vessel ran on "regular or premium."

The captain, a former Navy SEAL who had once defused an IED with a pocketknife in Helmand Province, stared at the senator for a full four seconds without speaking.

"Diesel, sir," he said finally.

"Right, right. Diesel. The strong gas."

"That's not—"

"Kelsey! Get a picture of me with this hero!"

After the tour, Lee held a press conference in the marina's clubhouse. He stood in front of a flag he had never served, beneath a banner that read AMERICAN COURAGE ON THE HIGH SEAS, and delivered remarks that bore the same relationship to reality that horoscopes bear to astronomy.

"Anchors aweigh!" he concluded, pumping his fist.

"Away," Kelsey said. "Anchors A-WAY."

"That's what I—"

"You said A-WEIGH. Like a scale. It's A-WAY. Like leaving."

"Kelsey, I'm the senator."

"Yes, sir. The anchors are still away."

The motorcade departed. The marina returned to its normal state of organized chaos. And Marcus stood in the parking lot, watching the SUVs disappear, trying to reconcile the fact that the man who had just confused diesel with "the strong gas" had authored the law that governed his entire professional existence.

"You know what the worst part is?" Frank said, appearing beside him with a flask. "He's going to get reelected."

"You don't know that."

"I do know that. Because he's likeable, he's harmless, and nobody votes against likeable and harmless." Frank took a drink. "The smart ones are dangerous. The dumb ones are durable."

The orientation was held in a room that had been designed for corporate retreats and repurposed for something significantly weirder.

A projector displayed a PowerPoint titled "EXCELLENCE IN INTERDICTION: Best Practices for the Modern Privateer." The Privateer Marina logo—a skull wearing aviator sunglasses over crossed anchors—appeared on every slide.

Approximately forty people sat in folding chairs, representing maybe a dozen different crews. The demographics were exactly what Marcus had expected: mostly men, mostly ex-military or law enforcement, mostly wearing the expression of people who had made a series of questionable life choices and were only now beginning to grasp the full scope of those choices.

Dana scanned the room with the systematic thoroughness she brought to everything. "I count three women," she murmured to Marcus. "Two people of color, including me. Forty-seven guns, visible. And one man in the back row who is definitely asleep."

"You counted the guns?"

"I always count the guns. I also count the exits, the cameras, and the people who look like they know what they're doing." She paused. "That last number is two. Us."

A woman in a blazer stood at the front, clicking through slides with the enthusiasm of someone who had given this presentation many times and had stopped believing in it around presentation number three.

"Asset recovery in the modern maritime environment requires a commitment to compliance, documentation, and—" she clicked— "brand consistency."

The slide showed a pie chart. Marcus had no idea what the pie chart represented. He suspected the pie chart didn't know what it represented either.

"Each licensed crew is expected to maintain social media presence across at least two platforms. Engagement metrics are factored into quarterly performance reviews."

Frank leaned over. "Did she just say we need to post on Instagram?"

"I think she said we need to post on Instagram."

"About what? 'Just seized a metric ton of cocaine, hashtag blessed'?"

"Hashtag privateer life," Gator added helpfully.

"Hashtag federal authorization," Click contributed.

"Hashtag I miss when crime was simple," Frank muttered.

The woman continued, oblivious. "Successful crews understand that interdiction is only part of the value proposition. The other part is narrative."

She clicked to a slide showing a crew posing with seized goods, all of them making finger-guns at the camera. One of them was wearing sunglasses indoors. Another was doing what appeared to be a bicep flex while standing next to wrapped bricks of cocaine worth approximately twenty million dollars.

"The Reasonable Doubt," she said. "Seventeen thousand followers. Sponsorship deals with three tactical gear companies. They understand synergy."

Dana put her head in her hands.

After the presentation, there was networking.

This was, as far as Marcus could tell, an excuse for privateers to size each other up while eating crab cakes and pretending they weren't mentally calculating who they could take in a fight.

He was on his second crab cake when Trevor Kline found him.

Marcus knew who he was before he introduced himself. Half the Booty, LLC was already legendary—three months of operation, twelve seizures, an estimated forty million in recovered assets. Their social media presence was impeccable. Their boats were immaculate. Their crew looked like they'd been recruited from a modeling agency that specialized in "menacing but approachable."

Trevor himself was exactly what Marcus had expected: late thirties, handsome in a way that suggested expensive skincare and regular workouts, wearing a polo shirt that probably cost more than Gator's truck.

"Captain Hale," Trevor said, extending a hand. "Trevor Kline. Half the Booty."

"I know who you are."

"And I know who you are. Coast Guard, right? Twenty-two years. Honorable discharge." Trevor's smile didn't waver. "You're the one who actually believes in this."

"Believes in what?"

"The system. The process. The idea that if you do everything right, it'll all work out." Trevor took a sip of his drink—something clear with ice, probably expensive. "It's charming. Naive, but charming."

"You don't believe in it?"

Trevor laughed. It was a pleasant laugh, the laugh of a man who found genuine amusement in watching people misunderstand how the world worked.

"Captain, I believe in efficiency. I believe in optimization. I believe in extracting maximum value from every opportunity." He gestured around the room. "This—all of this—is a system. Systems have rules. But systems also have tolerances. Margins. Space between what's written and what's enforced."

"You're talking about skimming."

Trevor's smile sharpened. "I'm talking about asset management."

"There's a legal distinction?"

"There's a legal distinction between everything, Captain. That's the whole point." Trevor raised his glass in a mock toast. "The law is just a language. We're fluent. You're still using a phrasebook."

"So you skim."

"I optimize. You seize a thousand kilos, report nine hundred. Ten percent loss to 'rough seas.' Nobody questions it because everybody does it. The rest gets redistributed to competing market participants who aren't the ones you took it from. It stabilizes prices. If you think about it."

"I'm trying not to think about it."

"Your loss." Trevor shrugged. "Literally."

"And when you get caught?"

"Caught by who?" Trevor spread his hands. "The DEA is overwhelmed. The IRS is auditing bigger fish. The Coast Guard is applying for privateer licenses." He leaned back. "We're not breaking the system, Captain. We are the system now." Marcus said nothing.

"Look," Trevor continued, his voice softening into something that might have been genuine advice, "I'm not saying you have to do what we do. I'm saying you can't do what you're doing. Perfect numbers. Full reporting. Complete transparency." He shook his head. "It makes you look like a narc. Or an idiot. Neither is good for business."

"Maybe I'm not here for business."

"Then what are you here for?"

"Something else," Marcus said.

Trevor studied him for a long moment.

"You know," Trevor said finally, "I almost believe you. And that's the saddest thing I've heard all week."

Meanwhile, Marcus spotted Gator at the fuel dock, talking with Eddie Reyes—the same man from the Rusty Anchor, the one who'd been watching them with eyes that didn't match his casual pose.

Frank noticed too. He appeared beside Marcus, holding a crab cake in one hand and his flask in the other, watching the conversation from thirty yards away.

"Your boy's chatty," Frank said.

"He's always chatty."

"Yeah, but look at the other guy. Eddie." Frank studied the interaction with the focused attention of a man who'd spent thirty years reading body language in interrogation rooms. "His feet are angled toward Gator but his shoulders are square to the dock. That's interview position. He's gathering information while projecting casual. His hand movements are mirroring Gator's—classic rapport-building technique."

"You can tell all that from here?"

"Hale, I once identified a killer at a barbecue from the way he held a corn cob. Human behavior is my only remaining skill." Frank took a drink. "That guy is working your friend. Professionally. Whether it's for himself or someone else, I don't know yet. But that's not a conversation between friends. That's an extraction."

Marcus filed this away. Two sources now—Frank's reading and the feeling in his own gut.

Two people now. Two separate warnings about the same man.

He should tell Gator.

He should warn him about Eddie, about the danger of talking too freely, about the cost of being liked by the wrong people.

But Marcus thought about the conversation they'd had when he recruited Gator. "I'm a friendly guy. I talk to people. That's how I know what I know."

He'd accepted the risk.

Now he just had to hope the calculation was correct.

The crew regrouped at the taco truck.

"So," Gator said through a mouthful of carnitas, "we're the weird ones."

"We're the honest ones," Marcus corrected.

"Same thing here, apparently." Gator took another bite. "I met a guy from the Tax Write-Off. You know what they do? They seize boats, report 'em as destroyed, then flip 'em through shell companies in the Bahamas. Dude was bragging about it like it was a life hack."

"I talked to someone from the Reasonable Doubt," Dana said. "They're all disbarred lawyers. They use legal technicalities to seize boats that aren't even involved in drug trafficking. Just... boats they want. One of them tried to recruit me."

"For what?"

"For my 'operational aesthetics.' His words." She looked disgusted. "I think he was hitting on me."

Click was unusually quiet.

"What about you?" Marcus asked.

Click looked up from his taco. "I found the armory. They have things I've only read about. Military surplus. Experimental ordnance. Stuff that's technically decommissioned but mysteriously still functional." His eyes had a faraway look. "I may have made some friends."

"Click, please tell me you didn't—"

"I didn't buy anything illegal." Click paused. "I did trade some schematics for access to their testing range, but that's just professional networking."

Luis had been silent throughout, eating methodically, watching the crowd.

"You notice Black Flag isn't here," Luis said.

Marcus frowned. "What?"

"Black Flag Group. The ones everyone whispers about. They're not at this orientation. They're not in the marina. They're not anywhere visible." Luis set down his food. "Which means they don't play by these rules. Not even the fake ones."

"Who are they?"

"I've heard stories. From the old days." Luis's voice was flat. "They're not privateers. They're not even criminals in the traditional sense. They're... what happens when you give legal authority to people who wanted violence anyway."

Frank whistled low. "Sounds like my kind of party."

"It's not." Luis looked at him. "They kill witnesses. They torture for fun. They run operations that make cartels look like the Rotary Club."

"And they're licensed?"

"Same as us."

The taco suddenly tasted like nothing.

"So," Gator said slowly, "to summarize: we're surrounded by thieves, con artists, psychopaths, and influencers. Did I miss anything?"

"The IRS," Click added. "I heard they're sending auditors."

"Oh good," Frank said. "Something worse than psychopaths."

CHAPTER SEVEN

THE AUDIT

Agent Denise Rourke arrived at 0742 hours with a rolling briefcase and the expression of a woman who had never once been surprised by human awfulness.

She was forty-six years old, according to records Click had pulled within thirty seconds of hearing her name. IRS Criminal Investigations for eighteen years. Forensic accounting specialty. Conviction rate of ninety-three percent, which was the kind of number that made defense attorneys wake up screaming.

She also, according to Click's deeper dive, had once made a hedge fund manager cry during a deposition. Actual tears. On the record.

Marcus decided to be very careful.

"Captain Hale." Rourke stepped aboard without waiting for permission, heels clicking on the deck like a countdown. "Your seizure reports are clean."

"Thank you?"

"That wasn't a compliment." She set her briefcase on the deck and opened it, revealing files organized with a precision that suggested either a brilliant mind or a terrifying one. Possibly both. "Clean reports are suspicious. Perfect numbers are lies waiting to be discovered. Honest people don't exist in systems like this."

"Maybe we're the exception."

"There are no exceptions. There are only people who haven't been caught yet."

She pulled out a tablet and began swiping through documents.

"Three hundred seventy-two kilos. Exactly as reported. Exactly as weighed at processing. Exactly as verified by three separate chain-of-custody checkpoints." She looked up. "Do you know how unusual that is?"

"We're thorough."

"You're suspicious." Rourke set down the tablet. "The average privateer crew reports weights that are fifteen to twenty percent below verified recovery. Some of that is legitimate loss—rough handling, water damage, evidentiary requirements. Most of it is theft dressed up as logistics."

"We don't steal."

"Everyone steals."

"We don't."

Rourke stared at him with the particular intensity of someone trying to determine whether they were talking to a liar or a lunatic.

"I'm going to audit your crew," she said. "Individually. I'm going to examine your finances, your backgrounds, your associations. I'm going to find whatever you're hiding."

"And if we're not hiding anything?"

Rourke almost smiled. Almost.

"Then I'll find out what you're stupid enough to believe instead."

She started with Gator.

"Mr. Wilkes," Rourke began, sitting across from him in the galley with her tablet ready. "You have no documented income for the past three years."

"Cash economy, ma'am. Very Florida."

"You also have two arrests involving—" she checked her tablet— "'reckless discharge of novelty ordnance' and what witnesses described as 'aggressive manatee behavior.'"

Gator leaned forward earnestly. "Ma'am, with respect, those manatees were up to something. I could feel it."

"You could feel it."

"In my bones. And I know how that sounds, I do. But here's the thing." Gator reached under the table and produced a folder that was significantly thicker than anything Rourke had brought with her. "I've been documenting their patterns for three years."

Rourke looked at the folder. Then at Gator. Then at the folder again.

"You have a file on manatees."

"I have a file on SUSPICIOUS manatees. There's a difference." He opened it. Inside were hand-drawn maps, printed satellite images with circles drawn in marker, and what appeared to be a timeline written on the back of a Waffle

House placemat. "See, most people think manatees are just fat water cows floating around eating seagrass. And maybe most of them are. But there's a pod—a GROUP, I don't know the word—"

"The word is an aggregation."

"There's an AGGREGATION near Crystal River that has been consistently present at the same coordinates where drug shipments enter Florida waters. Consistently. I got dates." He jabbed a finger at the Waffle House placemat. "March fourteenth. April second. April nineteenth. May eighth. Every time there's a major shipment through that corridor, the manatees are there first. You explain that."

"Migration patterns."

"That's what THEY want you to think."

"Who is 'they'?"

Gator paused. "I haven't figured that part out yet."

Rourke closed her eyes for a count of three. When she opened them, she had the expression of a woman who had devoted eighteen years of her life to criminal investigations and was now watching a man in a tank top present a conspiracy theory about manatees using a Waffle House placemat as evidence.

"Mr. Wilkes. I am going to ask you a question, and I need you to answer honestly. Not creatively. Not entertainingly. Honestly."

"Yes, ma'am."

"Are you involved in drug trafficking in any capacity?"

"No, ma'am."

"Have you ever been involved in drug trafficking?"

"Not the drug part. I ran a boat for a guy one time who turned out to be moving stuff, but I didn't know that 'til later. I thought we were hauling lobster traps. Turns out lobster traps don't usually have a street value."

"And the manatees?"

Gator gathered his folder protectively. "The manatee investigation is ongoing and I'd appreciate it if you didn't share my findings with competing researchers."

"I assure you," Rourke said, "there are no competing researchers."

"That's what concerns me."

Rourke stared at him for a very long time.

"Mr. Wilkes, are you aware that obstruction of a federal investigation is a felony?"

"Oh, I ain't obstructing." Gator grinned. "I'm just weird. There's a legal distinction."

"Paperwork?"

"Now you're gettin' it."

Click was next.

"Mr. Harrow. You've been raided by ATF three times."

"Visited. They visited." Click smiled serenely. "All items returned. No charges filed. Turns out I was ahead of regulatory interpretation."

"The second visit involved something called a 'kinetic acoustic deterrent device' that shattered windows in a three-block radius."

"Unintended secondary effects. The primary function worked perfectly."

"Which was?"

"Deterrence." Click shrugged. "Nothing entered that three-block radius. Mission accomplished."

Rourke rubbed her temples. "I've audited pharmaceutical companies. I've taken down Ponzi schemes. None of those people confused me as much as you do."

"Thank you?"

"That wasn't a compliment."

Luis was calm. Rourke was, for the first time, equally calm.

They sat across from each other like chess players in the opening moves of a very long game.

"Mr. Calderón. Nine years federal incarceration. Distribution, conspiracy, money laundering."

"Correct."

"You moved over ten thousand kilos of cocaine during your career."

"According to the prosecution. I believe the actual number was higher."

Rourke raised an eyebrow. "You're admitting to more than you were charged with?"

"I'm being accurate. There's a difference." Luis met her gaze evenly. "I spent nine years thinking about what I did. I'm not interested in lying about it now."

"And yet you're working on a privateer crew. Stopping the very trade you built." Rourke leaned forward. "Why?"

"My daughter died while I was inside. Overdose. The same product I spent years moving." His voice didn't waver. "I'm not looking for redemption. I'm looking to do damage."

Rourke studied him.

"You know," she said finally, "most people in your position lie. They claim rehabilitation. Personal growth. They make themselves sound like victims of circumstance."

"I was never a victim. I made choices. I'm making different choices now."

"That's... surprisingly honest."

"I find honesty saves time." Frank was drunk.

Not visibly drunk—he was a professional—but drunk enough that Rourke noticed the careful way he was forming words, the deliberate precision of someone compensating.

"Detective Mulligan. Forced retirement. Multiple IA complaints."

"None sustained."

"You were investigated for excessive force on four separate occasions."

"And cleared on four separate occasions. Funny how that works."

"There was also an incident involving a domestic disturbance call at your own residence."

Frank's jaw tightened. "My ex-wife called during an argument. We were both drunk. Nothing happened."

"The responding officers noted—"

"The responding officers noted that two people who used to love each other were having a loud conversation about how they didn't anymore." Frank's voice was flat. "Welcome to Florida, agent. We specialize in failed relationships and bad decisions."

Rourke made a note.

"Why are you here, Detective?"

Frank was quiet for a moment. Then something shifted in his face—the mask of belligerence slipping, just briefly, to reveal the raw exhaustion underneath.

"Because I woke up six months ago in a hospital after my third blackout in a week. And the nurse—kid, maybe twenty-five—she looked at my chart and said, 'You're a detective?' Not rude. Just surprised. Like she couldn't reconcile what I was with what I am." He turned his glass in his hands. "That's when I knew. Not that I needed to stop drinking—I've known that for years. But that I needed a reason to stop. The badge wasn't a reason anymore. The marriage wasn't a reason. My kids stopped being a reason when they stopped being my kids."

He looked up at Rourke with eyes that were, for just a moment, completely clear.

"This stupid pirate shit might be a reason. I don't know yet. But it's the first thing in three years that made me want to find out."

Rourke didn't respond immediately. She wrote something on her tablet. Then she wrote something else, crossed it out, and wrote a third thing.

"That wasn't an answer to my question," she said finally.

"It wasn't?" Frank blinked. "What was the question?"

"Why are you here?"

"Oh." He thought about it. "Yeah, that was the answer. I just told it to you wrong." Dana was professional.

"Sergeant Kessler. Exemplary service record. Three tours in classified locations. Honorable discharge." Rourke looked up. "You're the only person on this crew I can't find anything wrong with."

"Thank you."

"It's suspicious."

"Everything's suspicious to you."

"That's my job." Rourke leaned forward. "Why are you here?"

"Because I was tired of protecting people who didn't deserve protection." Dana met Rourke's gaze. "I spent six years keeping executives safe while they did things that hurt everyone else. I watched them break laws, destroy lives, and walk away clean because they had money and connections."

"And this is different?"

"This is messy. This is weird. This is a bunch of broken people trying to do something that might matter." Dana smiled faintly. "It's probably going to end badly. But at least we're choosing our own ending."

Marcus was last.

Rourke sat across from him with her tablet closed, her briefcase shut, her expression unreadable.

"You're not like the others," she said.

"I'm their captain."

"That's not what I mean." She leaned back. "The others are damaged. Broken in visible ways. They're here because they have nowhere else to go. But you—you had options. You had a pension. You had a career you could have quietly ended."

"I had a system that didn't work."

"Systems never work. Not completely. That's not news."

"Maybe I wanted to try something different."

Rourke was quiet for a moment. "Or maybe you're running from something. The question is whether you're running toward something better, or just running."

Marcus didn't answer.

"Your crew is a liability," Rourke continued. "An ex-con, a drunk, a weapons designer who probably should be in prison, and a man who thinks manatees have hidden agendas. You're leading them into waters where nobody stays clean for long."

"I know."

"And yet your numbers are clean. Your reports are accurate. Your documentation is better than agencies with ten times your resources." She tilted her head. "Either you're the most ethical privateer in existence, or you're hiding something so well I haven't found it yet."

"Which do you think it is?"

Rourke stood.

"I think you're going to fail," she said. "I think this system is going to eat you alive. I think your honesty is going to become a weapon used against you by people who profit from dishonesty."

She picked up her briefcase.

"But I also think you're going to try anyway. And that might be the most interesting thing happening in this entire corrupt mess."

She walked toward the ladder, then paused.

"I'll be watching, Captain. Try not to disappoint me."

She climbed out into the sunlight.

Marcus sat alone in the galley, thinking about all the ways this could go wrong.

The list was getting longer.

CHAPTER EIGHT

THE WEDDING

Marcus almost didn't go.

Not because he didn't want to. He wanted to go in the abstract, desperate way of a man who understood that his daughter's wedding was a thing he should attend and should want to attend and should have feelings about attending, but who had spent so many years treating family events as scheduling conflicts that the muscles required for showing up had atrophied.

His suit didn't fit. He'd lost weight—the ocean diet of stress and sporadic meals had carved away the mass that desk work and Denny's parking lots had added. The jacket hung on his shoulders. The pants needed a belt he didn't have.

"You look like a kid wearing his dad's clothes," Frank observed, watching Marcus try to tie a tie in the galley mirror. "Except you ARE the dad, which makes it sadder."

"Thank you, Frank."

"Just being honest. You want me to lie? I can lie. You look fantastic. GQ cover material. The tie is perfect."

"The tie is crooked."

"The tie is a metaphor for your life. Leave it."

Marcus drove to Boca Raton in the crew's shared vehicle—a 2009 Toyota Tacoma that Gator had acquired through means he described as "a trade" and Dana described as "probably not stolen but I'm not asking." He arrived forty minutes early because the alternative was arriving on time and having to interact with people immediately.

He sat in the parking lot of the venue—a waterfront restaurant that Sarah had chosen because, she'd told him on one of their brief calls, "it has an ocean view and Matt's mother can't complain about the food because the food is expensive." This was, Marcus recognized, Laura's strategic thinking expressed through Sarah's more diplomatic delivery.

The wedding was small. Sixty people. Marcus knew almost none of them—Sarah's friends, Matt's family, the collected social infrastructure of a life that had been built in his absence.

Laura was there.

He saw her across the room during the cocktail hour. She was wearing blue—the same shade she'd always worn to things that mattered, a detail Marcus hadn't realized he'd remembered until he saw it. She looked good. She looked like a woman who had spent three years building a life without him and had succeeded at it, which was exactly what he'd expected and exactly what hurt.

They didn't speak until the reception.

Marcus was standing near the bar—not drinking, just standing, performing the awkward role of a father at his daughter's wedding when the father hasn't earned the right to be center stage—when Laura appeared beside him.

"You came," she said.

"I said I would."

"You've said that before."

"I know."

They stood together, watching Sarah dance with Matt. The song was something Marcus didn't recognize—something current, something from a world he hadn't been paying attention to while he was paying attention to other things.

"She looks happy," Marcus said.

"She is happy." Laura's voice was careful. The voice of a woman speaking to a man she'd loved and left and wasn't sure how to categorize anymore. "Matt is good for her. He shows up."

The knife was gentle but precise. Laura had always been precise.

"I deserved that," Marcus said.

"You did." Laura was quiet for a moment. "But you're here. That's—that's something."

"Is it enough?"

"It's a start." She looked at him. The same eyes. The eyes that had seen through every excuse and every justification and every performance of duty that he'd offered in place of presence. "She wants you in her life, Marcus. She won't say it because she's spent too many years being disappointed. But she wants it."

"I want it too."

"Then don't leave." Laura's voice was simple. Final. "Don't leave early. Don't check your phone. Don't find an excuse. Stay for the whole thing. The boring parts. The awkward parts. The part where Matt's uncle makes a toast that goes on too long and everyone pretends it was charming."

"How long does the toast go?"

"Fourteen minutes last rehearsal. He cries twice."

"Jesus."

"Stay for both cries, Marcus. That's the job."

He stayed.

He stayed for the toasts (Matt's uncle cried three times, a personal record). He stayed for the dancing, even though he didn't dance, even though standing at the edge of a dance floor watching your daughter spin in a white dress was its own specific form of joyful agony. He stayed for the cake cutting and the bouquet toss and the moment, near the end, when Sarah found him by the bar and hugged him without saying anything.

She smelled like champagne and flowers and the particular soap she'd used since she was a teenager, a detail that hit Marcus in the chest like a physical thing.

"Thank you for coming," she said.

"Thank you for inviting me."

"I almost didn't." She pulled back. Her eyes were wet but her voice was steady. "But Mom said I should. She said people can change. She said she didn't believe it anymore, but she thought I should give you the chance to prove her wrong."

"I'm going to try."

"I know." She squeezed his hand. "That's why I'm giving you the chance."

He drove back to the marina at midnight. The Tacoma smelled like the reception—food and flowers and the accumulated warmth of sixty people celebrating something good.

Gator was awake on deck. Of course Gator was awake.

"How was it?" Gator asked.

"Good. She's happy."

"Good. Happy's good." Gator handed him a beer. "You okay?"

Marcus took the beer. Sat down. Looked at the water.

"My ex-wife told me to stay for the boring parts," he said. "So I stayed for the boring parts."

"Were they boring?"

"They were the best parts."

Gator grinned. "That's the secret, Cap. The good stuff is always in the boring parts. The boring parts are where the people are."

The thing about Click was that he understood machines better than people. This wasn't a metaphor. Machines had inputs and outputs. They followed logic. People lied about what they needed.

Gator, of course, did not get the memo. The man materialized without warning. One moment Click would be alone calibrating frequencies. The next, Gator would be there—covered in grease, holding two beers.

"Hey, Click."

"How did you—I have motion sensors."

"I know. I crawled under 'em."

Before Click could object, Gator pulled a crumpled napkin from his pocket. On it, in handwriting that looked like it had been produced during an earthquake, was a diagram. Click stared.

"This is a fuel injection optimization for a marine diesel," Click said slowly. "Using variable timing advance to compensate for saltwater humidity effects on combustion efficiency."

"Yeah. I drew it in the head. Best ideas happen in the head."

"Where did you learn thermodynamics?"

"I didn't learn it. I just know engines. You listen to an engine long enough, you start to understand how it thinks."

"Engines don't think."

"Sure they do. They just think in RPMs instead of words."

Gator wasn't stupid. Gator was a different kind of smart.

He pinned Gator's napkin to the wall above his console. It stayed there for the rest of the voyage.

CHAPTER NINE

THE PERFECT RUN

The fourth seizure was the one where everything worked.

They would remember this later, after the fire and the blood and the hearings and the funerals, and they would wonder if that was the problem—that perfection was the thing that made them visible, that drew the attention of people who couldn't afford to let perfection exist.

Day eighty-seven.

On the morning of April 14th, cutting through a three-foot chop eighteen miles south of Key West, they didn't know any of that yet.

They were just good.

The dawn came in layers—black to gray to the color of a bruise to a sudden, vicious orange that turned the Gulf into hammered copper. Marcus stood at the helm and felt the boat move under him the way you feel a horse move when it knows the trail—the slight lean into a swell, the engine note dropping half a register as the bow lifted, the way the Second Chance found her rhythm in rough water and held it like a heartbeat.

He was learning her. After three months aboard, he was finally learning her.

The hull talked. Every boat does, if you listen. The Second Chance creaked when she took a swell on the starboard quarter—a specific, repeating groan from somewhere near the waterline that Gator said was a hull plate settling and Dana said was the boat complaining and Click said was "structurally irrelevant but acoustically fascinating." She hummed at fourteen knots—not the engines, the hull itself, a low vibration you felt in your feet and your teeth. She went quiet above twenty-two knots, and that silence was more unsettling than the noise, because it meant she was working too hard to talk.

Marcus had started to love that silence. It meant they were hunting.

"Contact," Click said from the communications station. His voice was the measured monotone he adopted when the data was interesting and the seasickness was manageable—roughly a six on his personal scale of "fine" to "the ocean is a war crime." He'd taken two Dramamine, eaten nothing, and positioned a bucket within arm's reach. The bucket was labeled, in his own handwriting, OPERATIONAL CONTINGENCY RECEPTACLE.

"Where?"

"Bearing two-one-five, eighteen nautical miles, speed twenty-six knots. Running south-southeast on a heading that intersects with the Yucatán corridor." Click's fingers moved across his screens. "Radar profile suggests a forty-five to fifty-foot vessel. Possibly modified sportfisher."

"Luis."

Luis appeared from below deck with the unhurried precision of a man who had been awake for hours and wanted you to know it without saying so. He studied the radar display the way a sommelier studies a wine list—not reading, exactly. Tasting.

"Fast boat, heavy load," Luis said. "Twenty-six knots in this chop means they've got power to spare but they're not pushing it. Confident. Experienced. Not their first run." He traced the heading with his finger. "This route runs parallel to the main corridor—two miles east of where the Coast Guard concentrates patrols. Someone told them where the gaps are."

"Size of the load?"

"At that speed, with that draft?" Luis did the math in his head—a calculation that combined hull dynamics, engine capacity, and twenty years of watching boats carry things they shouldn't. "Eight hundred kilos. Maybe more."

Frank whistled from the deck. "That's a career."

"That's a target," Marcus corrected. "Dana?"

Dana was already at the weapons locker, moving with the economy of motion that came from doing the same preparation so many times it had become meditation. Shotgun. Rifle. Sidearm. Vest. Comms. Each item checked, each action performed in an order she could execute blindfolded, had executed blindfolded, in places she couldn't legally describe.

"Ready," she said.

"Gator?"

Gator's voice came from the engine room, where he had been since 4 AM doing things to the fuel injection system that he described as "encouragement" and Dana described as "mechanical assault."

"She's ready, Cap. I got her purring like a kitten who's been to finishing school."

"What did you do?"

"Adjusted the fuel-air mixture on the port engine. She was running a little lean—you could hear it in the exhaust note, sort of a flat sound, like she was holding her breath. Now she's breathing full and deep." Gator's head appeared through the hatch, streaked with grease. "Also I may have bypassed a thing."

"What thing?"

"A thing that was limiting a thing."

"Gator."

"The governor. I bypassed the governor. She can do twenty-eight knots now instead of twenty-four."

"That's—is that safe?"

"Define safe."

"Not exploding."

"Then yeah, probably."

"Probably."

"Almost certainly." Gator grinned. "Engines want to run, Cap. It's what they're built for. Keeping 'em throttled back is like putting a leash on a dolphin. Cruel and pointless."

"Dolphins don't explode when you take the leash off."

"See, that's where you and me disagree about dolphins."

Marcus chose not to pursue this.

They closed on the target from the northeast, using the morning sun as cover—an old Coast Guard tactic that Marcus had used a hundred times and that worked because staring into a sunrise made everything behind it invisible. The Gulf was alive around them—pelicans diving in the distance, their prehistoric silhouettes punching into the water like feathered missiles. A pod of dolphins paced them for half a mile, riding the bow wave, oblivious to the violence being planned above them.

The salt was everywhere. In the air, on the deck, crusted on the rail where the spray dried in the wind. It got in your eyes, your clothes, the cracks in your skin. After a few weeks on the water, you stopped noticing it the way you stop noticing gravity—it was just the medium you existed in. Gator said salt was the ocean's way of marking you. "She wants you to know you been here," he'd said once, scraping crystals off his forearm. "Even after you leave."

"Target is maintaining course," Click reported. "No deviation. No evasive behavior. They haven't seen us."

"They will," Luis said. "Closing to five nautical miles. At this speed, we're four minutes from visual range."

Marcus felt the familiar pre-engagement tightness—the sharpening, the narrowing, the way the world reduced to vectors and decisions. Twenty-two years of this, and it never got routine. The day it got routine was the day you got killed.

"Frank," Marcus said. "What do you see?"

Frank was at the bow with binoculars, sober and sharp in the way he could only manage when the work was more compelling than the whiskey. The morning light caught the silver in his stubble and the particular intensity in his eyes—the detective's gaze, the one that read situations the way other people read menus.

"Three visible on deck," Frank said. "One at the helm, two amidships. The helm is focused—not checking flanks, not scanning horizon. He trusts the route. The two amidships are relaxed. One's smoking. The other's..." He adjusted the binoculars. "Eating a sandwich."

"A sandwich."

"What appears to be a sandwich. Could be a burrito. Hard to tell at this distance." Frank lowered the binoculars. "Point is, they're not expecting company. Body language says 'Tuesday commute,' not 'smuggling operation.' These guys have done this run so many times it's boring."

"Good," Marcus said. "Bored is slow."

"Bored is also unpredictable," Dana countered from the bow. "Bored people do stupid things when they panic."

"Then let's not let them panic." Marcus picked up the loudspeaker. "Standard approach. By the book. Click, you recording?"

"Recording started seven minutes ago. I also have thermal imaging, two fixed cameras, and a directional microphone that may or may not be legal in territorial waters."

"Is it legal?"

"It's legal-adjacent."

"Click."

"The precedent is ambiguous and I choose to interpret ambiguity as permission."

Marcus decided, not for the first time, that plausible deniability was a management strategy.

They hit visual range at 0647.

The target was a converted sportfisher—maybe forty-eight feet, white hull, twin outboards that had been upgraded well past factory spec. She was riding low in the stern, heavy, the waterline telling the story that the crew's casual posture was trying to hide.

Marcus keyed the loudspeaker.

"ATTENTION VESSEL. THIS IS PRIVATEER LLC, OPERATING UNDER FEDERAL AUTHORIZATION. YOU ARE ORDERED TO REDUCE SPEED AND PREPARE FOR BOARDING."

A pause.

Then the sportfisher's engines screamed.

"Here we go," Gator said, and hit the throttle.

The Second Chance surged forward, the bypassed governor letting the Caterpillars open up with a roar that Marcus felt in his sternum. The bow lifted, spray exploding over the rail, and for a moment the world was nothing but speed and noise and the raw ecstasy of a boat running flat out.

Gator was in his element. His hands on the wheel moved with instinct rather than thought—adjusting for swells, reading the water's surface for the flat spots between waves, finding the path of least resistance the way a river finds a valley. He wasn't steering the boat. He was negotiating with the ocean, and the ocean, for once, was saying yes.

"Closing," Luis reported. "Two nautical miles. They're running at thirty-one knots."

"We're at twenty-eight," Click said, then paused. "Twenty-nine. Thirty." He looked at Gator. "How are we at thirty?"

"Encouragement," Gator said.

"We're gaining," Dana observed from the bow, where she was braced against the rail with her rifle ready, her body absorbing the motion the way a surfer absorbs a wave—flexing with it rather than fighting it. "They can't outrun us with that load."

The chase lasted nine minutes.

Nine minutes of spray and sun and the closing distance between what was right and what was profitable. Nine minutes of Click recording everything, Luis tracking the target with a predator's patience, Frank watching the crew's body language for the moment panic replaced boredom.

"They're slowing," Frank called. "Helm is checking something—phone, maybe. He's getting instructions."

"From who?"

"Someone who isn't on that boat. Someone who's watching this happen and deciding whether to cut losses."

The sportfisher's engines dropped from a scream to a growl. She settled in the water, her wake collapsing behind her, and Marcus could see the crew moving—not dumping cargo, not reaching for weapons. Just standing. Hands visible. Waiting.

"They're surrendering," Dana said.

"They're smart," Luis corrected. "Their handler told them to cooperate. Dump the loss, cooperate with the privateers, live to run another day. It's standard protocol for expendable crews."

They pulled alongside. Marcus delivered the boarding announcement—authorization number, legal basis, the whole script that was starting to feel less like law and more like theater.

The boarding was clean.

Dana went first, weapon ready, covering angles. Marcus followed. Frank positioned himself where he could watch the crew's faces—reading micro-expressions, cataloging lies before they were told.

The cocaine was in the fish hold, beneath ice that was melting in the morning heat. Black plastic, yellow tape. Mendoza stamps, exactly as Luis predicted.

Eight hundred and forty-one kilos.

Luis counted twice. Marcus counted once. Click's scale confirmed.

"Eight hundred forty-one," Luis announced. His voice was perfectly neutral, but his hands—his hands rested on the black plastic for just a moment longer than necessary, and Marcus saw something pass across his face that had nothing to do with the operation and everything to do with a girl in Tampa who had wanted to be a veterinarian.

Luis pulled his hands away and wrote the number down.

The crew cooperated. Frank questioned them with the quiet efficiency of a man who'd been doing this since before the smugglers were born—no threats, no posturing, just the patient unpacking of truth from lies that came so naturally to Frank it was almost gentle.

"Mid-level crew," Frank reported afterward. "Contract runners. Third trip on this route. They'll give us the route coordinator's name if we recommend leniency."

"We'll recommend based on cooperation, not on trade," Marcus said.

"That's not how this works anywhere else."

"That's how it works here."

Frank shrugged. "Your call, Captain."

The handoff happened at the Coast Guard station in Key West. Marcus had called ahead—proper channels, proper documentation, proper chain of custody. Lieutenant Commander Sarah Vasquez met them at the dock with two petty officers and a look of professional curiosity.

"Captain Hale." She accepted the evidence manifest—eight pages of documentation that Click had prepared with the obsessive thoroughness of a man who believed that paper was more powerful than bullets. "Eight hundred forty-one kilograms."

"Eight hundred forty-one."

"Your numbers always match."

"That's the point."

Vasquez studied the manifest for a moment. "You know most crews report losses of twenty percent."

"I've heard that."

"You know what happens to this after I sign for it? It goes into evidence processing. Then federal storage. Then, eventually, a courtroom." She paused. "At every stage, people touch it. Count it. Move it. And at every stage, the number gets a little smaller."

"Is that a warning?"

"It's a fact." Vasquez signed the form and handed it back. "I'm just wondering why you bother being precise when nobody else in the chain is."

Marcus looked at her.

"Because someone has to go first," he said.

Vasquez held his gaze for a moment. Then she almost smiled.

"Good luck with that, Captain."

They sailed back to the marina in late afternoon light that turned the Gulf into a sheet of liquid gold. The kind of light that made you forget, for a few minutes, that the water beneath you was full of things people wanted to hide.

Gator had the helm. Click was asleep in the communications chair, his head resting on a keyboard that would almost certainly have consequences when he woke up. Frank sat on the stern with a beer—his first of the day, which for Frank was practically sobriety.

Luis stood alone at the port rail, watching the water. He'd been quiet since the seizure. Quieter than usual, which for Luis was essentially silent.

Dana found him there.

She didn't say anything. She just stood beside him and watched the same water, the same light, the same horizon where the sky and the sea were having an argument about who got to be blue.

After a while, Luis spoke.

"Eight hundred forty-one kilos," he said. "Street value, roughly twenty-five million. Enough to destroy—" he did a calculation that was automatic and merciless— "roughly thirty thousand lives, if you measure by individual doses."

"That's a lot of lives."

"It's a lot of product that won't reach them." Luis's voice was flat, careful, the voice of a man holding something fragile. "I used to count the other way. How many kilos moved, how much revenue generated, how many distribution points supplied. The math was the same. The units were different."

He looked at his hands.

"My daughter would have been twenty-six this week," he said. "I don't know what she would have looked like. I don't know if she would have become a veterinarian. I don't know if she would have forgiven me." He paused. "I just know that eight hundred forty-one kilos won't reach whoever's twenty-three-year-old daughter is hurting somewhere tonight. And that's not enough. It's never enough."

Dana stood with him until the light faded.

She didn't offer comfort. Comfort wasn't what Luis needed. What he needed was someone to stand beside him while he carried something too heavy to put down.

She could do that.

Back at the marina, Marcus filed the report. Eight hundred forty-one kilos, documented to the gram, chain of custody complete, crew names and cooperation status noted. He submitted it at 7:47 PM and received an automated confirmation email that said YOUR REPORT HAS BEEN RECEIVED and nothing else.

No acknowledgment. No feedback. No indication that anyone would ever read it.

He sat at his desk—a card table wedged into the cabin, covered in forms and coffee rings—and felt something he hadn't felt since his last good day in the Coast Guard.

Satisfaction.

Not happiness. Not redemption. Just the plain, solid feeling of having done something correctly in a world that rewarded doing things wrong.

"Cap." Gator appeared in the doorway, holding two beers. "The crew wants to celebrate."

"Celebrate what?"

"Not dying. Making money. Being pirates." He handed Marcus a beer. "Come on. Even you gotta admit today was a good one."

Marcus took the beer.

"Yeah," he said. "Today was a good one."

On deck, the crew had assembled in what Gator called "debriefing formation," which meant they were sitting in a loose circle with drinks and the general air of people who had survived something together and were still surprised by it.

Click had woken up and was examining the keyboard marks on his face with scientific interest. Frank was telling Dana a story about a case that was almost certainly classified. Gator was microwaving something that would almost certainly catch fire.

Luis sat slightly apart, watching. Not participating, exactly, but present. Close enough to feel the warmth without needing to touch it.

Marcus sat down among them and drank his beer and listened to his crew talk about nothing important.

The stars came out.

The harbor water was flat and black and full of reflections—dock lights, boat lights, the distant glow of Key West making the horizon look like it was on fire.

Somewhere out there, boats were moving. Product was being loaded. Routes were being planned. The machine was grinding on, as it always did, as it always would.

But tonight, eight hundred forty-one kilos wouldn't reach their destination.

Tonight, the numbers were clean.

And for the crew of the Second Chance, floating together in a harbor that smelled like salt and diesel and the fragile optimism of people who hadn't yet learned what the world did to optimism—

Tonight was enough.

Marcus's phone buzzed. Not Sarah. Not anyone from the crew.

Laura.

The text said: *Sarah told me about your work. Be careful. Not for your sake. For hers.*

Three sentences. No greeting. No sign-off. Classic Laura—precision communication, zero waste.

Marcus typed four different replies. Deleted all of them.

He settled on: *I will.*

The typing indicator appeared on her end. Three dots, pulsing. He watched those dots for thirty seconds.

The dots disappeared. No message came.

Marcus put the phone away and went back to the celebration. But something had shifted—the way a room shifts when someone opens a window. Air from somewhere else. A reminder that the world outside this boat was still there.

CHAPTER TEN

BLACK FLAG

They met Black Flag on a night so dark the ocean looked like a hole in the world.

The Second Chance was running a standard patrol—Click's radar sweeping, Dana on watch, everyone else getting what sleep they could. Three weeks since the first seizure. Two more successful operations. Numbers still clean. Reputation still weird.

Gator was the first to notice something was wrong.

"Cap," he said, voice unusually serious. "We got a ghost."

Marcus was on deck in thirty seconds.

"Show me."

Click pulled up the radar. There was their blip, bright and normal. And behind them—far enough back to be invisible, close enough to be intentional—a second blip that flickered in and out of existence like it couldn't decide whether to be there.

"That's signal masking," Click said. "Military-grade. Someone's spending real money to not be seen."

"Cartel?"

"Cartels don't have this tech." Click's face was pale in the screen's glow. "This is… this is us. This is privateer."

Luis appeared from below deck, already armed.

"Black Flag," he said. Not a question.

Then the radio crackled.

"Second Chance." The voice was calm, almost pleasant. "Please reduce speed and prepare for boarding."

Marcus grabbed the mic. "This is Captain Marcus Hale. We're a federally licensed privateer vessel. Identify yourself."

A laugh. Soft, amused.

"Captain Hale. I know who you are. The honest pirate. The one who files accurate reports." A pause. "You're making things complicated."

"Complicated for who?"

"For everyone who understands how this actually works."

The ghost blip was visible now—a matte-black hull sliding out of the darkness like something that had been waiting there all along. No lights. No markings. Just shape and menace.

They boarded without permission.

Marcus could have resisted. Probably should have resisted. But the numbers were wrong—eight heavily armed men flowing onto his deck with professional efficiency, taking positions that covered every angle while leaving their own captain a clear line of retreat.

These weren't amateurs playing pirate. These were operators.

Anton Voss stepped aboard last.

He was maybe fifty, gray at the temples, with a face that looked like it had been carved from something harder than bone. There was a scar across his cheek—old, faded, a wound that should have killed him but hadn't. His eyes were the worst part. Not crazy. Not angry. Just... empty. Like whatever had once made them human had been carefully removed and replaced with something more efficient.

"Captain Hale," Voss said, as if they were meeting at a cocktail party. "Permission to come aboard."

"You're already aboard."

"I like to observe formalities. They remind us of the distance between civilization and everything else." Voss looked around the Second Chance. "Interesting crew. An ex-con, a drunk, a weapons enthusiast, and..." He looked at Gator. "I'm actually not sure what you are."

"I'm a Florida man," Gator said proudly. "Born and raised."

"Ah." Voss nodded. "That explains the energy."

He turned back to Marcus.

"You're disrupting the market."

"I'm doing my job."

"Your job is supposed to include a certain amount of... flexibility. Unreported losses. Creative documentation. The understanding that everyone takes their share." Voss shook his head. "You're not taking your share."

"I report what we seize. Accurately."

"Yes. That's the problem." Voss stepped closer. "Do you know what happens when one crew reports accurate numbers? It makes everyone else look corrupt. It invites scrutiny. It creates complications."

"Maybe everyone else is corrupt."

Voss smiled. It wasn't pleasant.

"Everyone is corrupt, Captain. The question is merely the form corruption takes."

Frank, who had been leaning against the cabin wall with his arms crossed, studying Voss the way he'd once studied suspects across an interrogation table, chose this moment to speak.

"You're ex-military," Frank said conversationally. "European. Scandinavian, maybe—the vowels are wrong for German. You've been out of uniform for at least fifteen years based on the haircut, but you still stand like you're at parade rest. The scar is from a blade, not a bullet, which means close-quarters work, which means you were either special forces or you were hunting them." He took a drink from his flask. "And your men are too disciplined to be mercenaries but too well-equipped to be government. Private military contractor who went independent?"

The silence that followed was so complete Marcus could hear the ocean breathing.

Voss looked at Frank with an expression that might have been surprise or might have been the first stirring of genuine respect.

"Detective Mulligan," Voss said slowly. "I've read your file. Thirty years MDPD. A man who was once very good at his job."

"Still am. Just need a drink first."

"I like you," Voss said. "I'm probably going to kill you someday, but I'll enjoy the conversation first."

He turned back to Marcus.

"Here's what's going to happen, Captain. You're going to start operating like everyone else. A little skim. A little loss. Numbers that are believable instead of accurate. In return, you'll have my protection. My guidance. My market access."

"And if I refuse?"

Voss tilted his head, considering.

"Then I'll wait. I'll watch. And when you make the mistake that everyone eventually makes—and you will make a mistake, Captain, because no one is as clean as they pretend to be—I'll be there to document it. Share it. Ensure that your perfect reputation becomes your perfect destruction."

He signaled his men. They began moving back toward their boat.

One of Voss's men produced a sealed evidence bag and tossed it onto the deck. Inside: a brick of cocaine stamped with the Second Chance's seizure marker.

"A reminder," Voss said pleasantly, "that distance is an illusion. I can reach anything you think is safe."

The black hull slid back into darkness.

Within minutes, the radar showed nothing.

As if they'd never been there at all.

No one spoke for a long time.

Finally, Gator broke the silence.

"So that guy was fuckin' terrifying."

"Yeah," Dana said. "He was."

"Like, I've met some scary people. Gator hunters. Meth cookers. This one lady in Palatka who had seventeen cats and definitely killed her husband. But that guy…"

"Was different," Luis finished. "Yes."

Marcus picked up the evidence bag Voss had left behind.

"We keep going," Marcus said. "Same as before. Clean numbers. Accurate reports. No skimming."

Frank took a long drink from his flask.

"The point is staying alive," he said.

"Maybe." Marcus looked at the brick in his hands. "But maybe there are things worse than dying."

"Yeah." Frank capped his flask. "Working for people like Voss."

The ocean was quiet.

But somewhere in the darkness, something was watching.

Waiting for the mistake.

CHAPTER ELEVEN

PROFESSIONAL COURTESY

The package arrived at the marina on a Tuesday.

No return address. No postmark. No indication of how it had gotten past dock security, which was either a commentary on the quality of dock security or a demonstration that dock security was irrelevant when the person sending the package wanted it delivered.

Gator found it on the Second Chance's helm console. Brown paper. Twine. Old-fashioned in a way that felt deliberate, like a message from someone who wanted you to know they could have used any method and chose the one that required the most access.

"Cap," Gator called. "You should see this."

Marcus opened it.

Inside was a photograph.

It was a picture of Sarah.

Not a surveillance photo—nothing grainy, nothing taken from a distance with a long lens. It was a casual shot, the kind taken by a friend. Sarah at what appeared to be a coffee shop, laughing at something off-camera, her hand resting on a table next to a cup that had her name written on it in barista handwriting.

A perfectly ordinary photograph.

That was the point.

Beneath the photograph was a folded piece of paper. Expensive stock. No header.

Captain Hale,

Your daughter drinks a flat white, extra hot, every Tuesday and Thursday at the same café in Boca Raton. She arrives between 8:15 and 8:30 AM. She sits at the same table, near the window. She reads on her phone while she waits for her drink.

She's recently married. Her husband's name is Matt. He drives a gray Honda Accord. They live in a house with a blue front door.

I'm not telling you this as a threat. I'm telling you this so you understand the difference between a threat and a demonstration. A threat is what I gave you last time—a brick of cocaine and a warning. A demonstration is showing you that the distance between your world and mine is zero.

I can reach anything. Anyone. At any time.

This is not a threat because I don't need to threaten you. I need you to understand the landscape. You are operating in a space where the rules you believe in don't apply, and the sooner you accept that, the sooner we can have a productive conversation about your future.

The photograph was taken by someone your daughter considers a friend. I won't tell you who. I want you to wonder.

Consider this a professional courtesy.

— V

Marcus read it twice.

Then he sat down.

He didn't call Sarah. Calling would confirm to whoever was watching—and someone was watching, he was now certain—that the message had landed. He didn't tell the crew. Not yet.

He sat very still, holding the photograph, and thought about the woman with the gold cross. The three bodies on the go-fast boat. The captain who walked free.

He'd spent his career believing that following the rules protected people.

The photograph in his hands said otherwise. He called Dana.

"We need to talk," he said. "About security. Not ours. My daughter's."

Dana's voice went flat in the way that meant she was already thinking three moves ahead.

"Tell me everything," she said. He did.

By evening, Dana had arranged private security for Sarah's neighborhood through contacts she'd never explained and Marcus had never asked about. Former operators. Discreet. Capable.

Sarah never knew.

Marcus never told her.

Some protection was better invisible.

Dana found Frank cleaning the interrogation space at 2 AM.

"You're cleaning," Dana said.

"I'm resetting. After a good interview, you reset the room."

"Did you have a good interview?"

"The guy from the last seizure. The one who didn't want to talk." Frank stood up, wincing at his knees. "He talked."

"How?"

"I listened." Frank tossed the rag in a bucket. "Everyone thinks interrogation is about pressure. But the best interviews are about listening. You shut up. You wait. And eventually the silence becomes heavier than the secret."

Dana leaned against the doorframe. "That's how I was trained. You learn to hear the thing that isn't being said."

"You're good at it."

"I'm good at a lot of things." Dana paused. "You're good at this specific thing. The reading. The waiting. I've watched you with witnesses and you see things nobody else sees."

"I see things because I'm too old and too tired to pretend they're not there."

They were quiet for a moment.

"Can I ask you something?" Dana said.

"You're going to anyway."

"The drinking. When you're sober—when you're really sober—you're the best operator on this crew. Better than me, in some ways. Why do you make it so hard for yourself?"

Frank was quiet for a long time.

"Because being good at this means being open. Seeing everything. Feeling everything. And everything includes the stuff I don't want to feel." He looked at his hands. "The booze doesn't make me dumber. It makes me thinner. Filters some of the input."

"That's the saddest thing I've ever heard."

"Yeah, well. I'm a sad guy. It's on brand."

"Frank. For what it's worth—you're the person on this crew I'd want covering me in a fight. Not Marcus. Not Luis. You."

Frank blinked. "Why?"

"Because you see everything. And you care about what you see. Most people who see everything stop caring. You didn't. You just started drinking instead."

"That's either a compliment or a diagnosis."

"It's both." She walked away.

Frank sat in the interrogation chair for a while, in the clean room, in the silence. Then he went to bed sober.

CHAPTER TWELVE

CIVILIAN

The storm arrived without the courtesy of a warning.

Florida weather had two settings: beautiful and catastrophic. There was no transition period. No gradual darkening. No polite meteorological buildup that gave you time to reconsider your decisions. One moment the Gulf was flat and blue and sparkling like God's screensaver. The next, the sky looked like someone had thrown a tarp over the sun and the water was trying to climb into the boat.

Click's radar had shown the squall line twenty minutes ago. Twenty minutes should have been enough. Twenty minutes was enough to alter course, run for shelter, do the sensible thing.

But twenty minutes ago, they'd been forty seconds from intercepting a cigarette boat that Luis had tracked for three days through a network of contacts he refused to name, running product on a route that connected to a distribution hub that connected to a processing facility that connected to the upper levels of the Mendoza cartel's Florida operation.

"This boat matters," Luis had said, in the tone he used when something was non-negotiable. "Not the product. The data. The phones, the GPS, the navigation logs. This crew knows things that other crews don't. If we take them, we take their intelligence."

So Marcus had made a call.

The wrong call, as it turned out.

The squall hit them broadside at 0947 hours. Forty-knot winds. Rain that fell sideways and hit exposed skin like gravel. Visibility dropped to approximately nothing—the world becoming a gray wall of water in every direction, no horizon, no sky, just the furious, immediate reality of an ocean that had remembered it was bigger than everything on it.

The Second Chance handled rough water the way she handled everything—with stubborn, graceless endurance. She didn't cut through waves so much as shoulder them aside, her hull groaning with each impact, the engines maintaining their roar against water that was trying to crawl down the exhaust pipes.

"I've lost the contact!" Click shouted over the wind. His screens were useless—the rain creating so much radar clutter that every direction looked like a threat and no direction looked clear. "They could be anywhere!"

"They're running!" Luis was at the bow, gripping the rail, squinting into the gray. The man did not appear to experience weather the way normal humans did. Rain hit him and failed to register. Wind pushed him and he leaned into it as if it were an inconvenience rather than a natural force. "In this weather, they'll run for shallow water. Find me the nearest shoal."

"I CAN'T FIND ANYTHING!" Click's voice cracked. "My radar is showing me what appears to be the entire ocean! There's a contact at every bearing! Some of them might be boats! Some of them might be WAVES! I cannot, at this juncture, tell the DIFFERENCE!"

"Calm down," Dana said from somewhere behind Marcus, which was impressive because Marcus could barely see two feet in front of him.

"I AM CALM! This is what calm sounds like when the OCEAN IS TRYING TO MURDER ME!"

Marcus wiped rain from his eyes and tried to think. The cigarette boat was faster than them in good conditions. In this weather, with a load, the advantage shifted—the Second Chance was heavier, more stable, better able to take punishment. But "better able to take punishment" was a relative term when the punishment was forty-knot winds and eight-foot swells.

"Gator! Can you hold this heading?"

"I can hold any heading!" Gator shouted from the helm, both hands white-knuckled on the wheel. "Whether the ocean agrees is a different conversation!"

A wave hit the starboard side and the Second Chance rolled hard enough to send unsecured equipment sliding across the deck. Frank, who had been standing near the weapons locker, grabbed a stanchion and held on with the stubborn intensity of a man who had survived thirty years of police work and was not about to be killed by water.

"Permission to state for the record," Frank called out, "that this is a TERRIBLE IDEA!"

"Noted!" Marcus shouted back.

"I would also like to state that I am SOBER for this terrible idea and I would prefer to be DRUNK!"

"Also noted!"

The cigarette boat appeared without warning—a dark shape materializing from the gray wall approximately two hundred yards ahead, close enough that Marcus could see the spray coming off its hull, close enough that the two boats were on a collision course that neither captain had intended.

Both vessels swerved.

What neither captain saw—because neither captain could see anything in the wall of rain and spray—was the third vessel.

A sailboat.

A thirty-six-foot sloop with a white hull and blue trim, carrying what Marcus would later learn was a retired couple from Sarasota named Don and Peggy Hartwell, who had been on a leisurely crossing to the Dry Tortugas and had gotten caught in the same squall that was ruining everyone's morning.

The sailboat was directly between them.

"CONTACT!" Click screamed. "CONTACT DEAD AHEAD! CIVILIAN! CIVILIAN!"

Gator saw it at the same time the radar did—his eyes processing the shape faster than Click's equipment processed the blip. He wrenched the wheel hard to port. The Second Chance heeled over, the starboard rail dipping toward the water, the engines howling in protest.

They missed the sailboat by approximately fifteen feet.

Fifteen feet is a comfortable margin in a parking lot. On open water, in a storm, at speed, it's the distance between a near-miss and a funeral.

The cigarette boat was not as lucky.

Or rather, it was lucky in a different way—it missed the sailboat too, but the evasive maneuver pushed it into a trough between swells. The overloaded hull caught the next wave wrong and the boat broached—spinning sideways, tipping, not quite capsizing but close enough that product began sliding across the deck and one of the crew went over the rail and into water that was not interested in giving him back.

"MAN OVERBOARD!" Dana was already moving, already calculating angles and drift and the casual cruelty of Gulf currents in a storm. "Bearing one-seven-zero, approximately fifty yards!"

Marcus looked at the cigarette boat—disabled, drifting, crew in chaos. The prize Luis had spent three days tracking was right there. The intelligence, the phones, the navigation logs. Everything they needed.

And fifty yards away, a man was drowning.

"Leave the target," Marcus said. "Get the man."

"Captain—" Luis started.

"GET THE MAN."

Gator didn't hesitate. He swung the Second Chance around, engines fighting the swells, the boat shuddering with each wave impact. Dana was at the rail with a life ring, scanning the surface for the dark shape of a human body in water that was the same color as everything else.

"There!" Frank pointed. He could barely see through the rain, but thirty years of looking for things that didn't want to be found had given him an eye that worked in conditions that defeated equipment. "Ten yards, two o'clock, he's not moving!"

Gator brought them alongside. Dana threw the ring. The man—young, terrified, already half-drowned—grabbed it with the desperate strength of someone who had just learned, definitively, that he wanted to live.

They hauled him aboard. Click wrapped him in a thermal blanket. He vomited seawater for two minutes straight, then lay on the deck shaking and staring at the sky with the wide eyes of someone who had just renegotiated his relationship with mortality.

The cigarette boat was gone.

In the minutes it had taken to rescue the drowning man, the cigarette boat's crew had gotten their vessel under control, dumped whatever product they could reach, and disappeared into the storm. When the squall cleared twenty minutes later, the ocean was empty. No boat. No product. No intelligence.

Luis stood at the bow and stared at the place where the target had been with an expression that Marcus couldn't read and didn't want to.

"We lost them," Luis said.

"We saved a man."

"We saved a cartel runner. He'll be back on the water in a week. Running the same route. Carrying the same product." Luis's voice was flat. "The intelligence on that boat could have disrupted operations for months. Could have led to the processing hub. Could have—"

"Could have." Marcus stood beside him. "But didn't. Because a man was in the water."

"We could have done both."

"Could we?"

Luis didn't answer. Because the honest answer was: maybe. And maybe was the distance between the people they wanted to be and the people the job required them to be, and that distance was not always crossable.

The sailboat found them an hour later.

Don and Peggy Hartwell pulled alongside the Second Chance in their sloop—the Blue Heaven, out of Sarasota, registration current, insurance paid, everything about them legitimate and normal and wholesome in a way that made Marcus feel like an alien visiting the planet of people who made good decisions.

Peggy was sixty-three years old, wore a sun visor that said LIFE'S A BEACH, and had the tan of someone who had spent retirement doing exactly what retirement was designed for. She stood at the rail of the Blue Heaven and looked at the Second Chance and its crew—armed, wet, surrounding a shivering cartel runner wrapped in a blanket—with a studied calm of a woman who had raised four children and was no longer capable of being surprised.

"Is everyone all right?" she asked.

"Everyone's fine, ma'am," Marcus said. "Sorry about the close call."

"Close call?" Peggy waved a hand. "Don almost hit a whale last Tuesday. This was nothing." She peered at their vessel. "Are you Navy?"

"Privateers, ma'am."

"Oh! Like the pirate thing? We saw that on the news." She turned to Don. "Don, they're pirates!"

"Privateers," Marcus, Dana, Click, and Gator said simultaneously.

Don Hartwell appeared at the rail. He was sunburned, wearing cargo shorts, and holding a beer at ten in the morning with the unapologetic confidence of a retired man who had earned every sip.

"Need anything?" Don asked. "We've got sandwiches. Peggy made tuna salad."

Marcus looked at his crew. Wet, frustrated, adrenaline-crashed, and hungry.

"We could use some sandwiches," he admitted.

They tied up alongside the Blue Heaven and ate tuna salad on the deck of a sailboat while their rescued cartel runner sat in the corner eating a sandwich of his own, still wrapped in the thermal blanket, looking like the most confused person in the Gulf of Mexico.

"So you catch drug dealers?" Peggy asked, passing out napkins.

"We interdict suspected narcotics trafficking," Dana said.

"With guns?"

"Sometimes."

"How exciting!" Peggy beamed. "We mostly just sail and listen to Jimmy Buffett. Don has all the albums."

"All of them," Don confirmed. "Even the weird one from '83 where he tried to be a country singer."

"Don has opinions about that record."

"It's not about having opinions. It's about having *standards*."

Frank, eating his third sandwich, leaned over to Marcus.

"This is the most surreal thing that has ever happened to me," Frank whispered. "And I once interrogated a man who insisted he was being framed by his own reflection."

"Just eat your sandwich."

"I'm eating my sandwich. I'm just noting that we are having lunch with retirees while a cartel runner eats tuna salad twelve feet away. This is not in any training manual."

"We don't have a training manual."

"We should write one. Chapter one: tuna salad protocol."

They parted ways with the Hartwells after an hour. Peggy waved goodbye with her LIFE'S A BEACH visor. Don saluted with his beer. The Blue Heaven sailed off toward the Dry Tortugas at three knots, carrying two people who had almost been killed by a privateer chase and didn't seem to mind.

The rescued cartel runner was processed and handed over to the Coast Guard at Key West with a full report. No seizure—the product had been dumped. No intelligence—the phones and GPS were on the boat that got away. Just one life saved and one operation lost.

In the report, Marcus wrote: *Target vessel escaped during storm conditions. One crew member recovered from the water. No casualties. No seizure.*

It was the first report he'd filed that felt like a failure.

Luis read it over his shoulder.

"You made the right call," Luis said.

Marcus looked at him. "You didn't think so an hour ago."

"An hour ago I was angry. Now I'm not." Luis paused. "The intelligence would have been valuable. But the man in the water was a person. And the day we stop pulling people out of the water is the day we become the thing we're fighting."

"That's very philosophical."

"I've had a lot of time to think. Nine years of it."

They sailed home in late afternoon light. The storm was gone, replaced by the golden clarity that Florida produced after violence—the air washed clean, the water impossibly blue, the sky so clear it hurt to look at.

Click was reviewing the radar data, looking for patterns in the cigarette boat's escape route that might predict future runs. Gator was in the engine room, sweet-talking the Caterpillars through their post-storm complaints. Frank was asleep in a deck chair with his SEIZED MY COFFEE mug balanced on his chest, rising and falling with his breathing.

Dana sat at the bow and watched the pelicans fishing in the calm after the storm. She didn't flinch. She didn't reach for a weapon. She just watched them—dive, surface, swallow—and for the first time, Marcus noticed that she wasn't tracking them as threats. She was just watching. The way anyone would watch birds after a storm.

In her hand was a small leather notebook. She was writing in it. She didn't see him see her. He didn't stay to look. But he caught enough—neat column of entries, today's date, a tally mark next to something—to know he'd stumbled into the edge of a private life he was not meant to witness.

He didn't mention it. Some victories were too small and too important to name.

Dana watched the horizon with the tired patience of someone who was learning, very slowly, to coexist with things she couldn't control.

Marcus filed the report.

No seizure. No intelligence. No glory.

One life.

He wasn't sure it was enough.

But it was honest.

CHAPTER THIRTEEN

INFLUENCERS

The next morning brought something worse than Black Flag.

It brought content creators.

Marcus was on his second cup of coffee—the good stuff, French press, his one luxury—when Dana appeared in the galley doorway with the expression of someone who had just witnessed a war crime.

"You need to see this."

On deck, riding at anchor like a hallucination, was a vessel that made the Second Chance look like a museum piece.

It was a sleek sixty-footer, all chrome and carbon fiber, with LED strips that pulsed in patterns that probably meant something to someone. The hull was decorated with what appeared to be stylized flames and a logo: SENT IT MARITIME. Beneath the logo, in the particular sans-serif font used by people who had not yet met a font they didn't like, was the tagline: *Seize the Day. Seize the Drugs. Seize the Moment.*™

A drone circled overhead.

On deck, a young man with frosted tips and a tactical vest worn over a bare chest was doing what appeared to be some kind of victory dance while a woman with a selfie stick filmed him.

"What the fuck," Gator said reverently, "am I looking at?"

"That," Click said, checking his phone, "is Chad Bryson. One point two million followers on TikTok. Six hundred thousand on Instagram. He started as a fitness influencer, pivoted to 'extreme lifestyle content,' briefly hosted a podcast about cryptocurrency that he deleted after legal action, and six months ago became a licensed privateer. His Instagram bio says 'father, founder, frequency.'"

"A fitness influencer is hunting cartels."

"A fitness influencer is hunting engagement metrics. The cartels are just the hook."

As they watched, Chad completed his dance, pointed at the camera, and shouted something that might have been "SENT IT!" before disappearing below deck.

The drone continued circling.

"This is the worst thing I've ever seen," Dana said. "And I've been to war."

Chad boarded the Second Chance an hour later, uninvited.

"CAPTAIN HALE!" He bounded onto the deck like an overly caffeinated golden retriever. "Bro, I have been wanting to meet you forever! You're like, the original, right? The real deal? The OG honest privateer?"

"I'm... the captain of this vessel."

"So humble!" Chad turned to the woman filming him. "Megan, are you getting this? He's so humble! This is totally going in the doc."

"The doc?"

"Documentary, my guy. Netflix is interested. Maybe Hulu. Definitely YouTube Premium if the others fall through." Chad struck a pose. "'Sent It Maritime: From Fitness to Fighting Crime.' Or maybe 'From Gains to Gains—The Chad Bryson Privateer Story.' We're workshopping titles."

Frank emerged from below deck, saw Chad, and immediately turned around.

"Nope," he called back. "Not doing this."

"DUDE!" Chad started after him. "Is that Frank Mulligan? The drunk detective? Bro, your story is INSANE! We should totally collab!" The door slammed.

Chad turned back to Marcus, undeterred.

"Okay so here's the thing—I've been tracking your numbers, right? And they're super consistent but your engagement is like, zero. No social presence. No brand deals. No merch." Chad shook his head the way a surgeon might shake his head at a preventable death. "You're leaving table stakes on the table."

"We're not here for engagement."

"Everyone's here for engagement, my man. Even if they don't know it." Chad produced a phone from somewhere and started swiping. "Look, I've got a proposal. Sent It Maritime and Privateer LLC—official collab. Joint operations. Shared content. We bring the audience, you bring the credibility."

"The credibility."

"Yeah! Like, when people see you on camera, they know it's real, right? You've got the whole grizzled-veteran thing going on. The authentic vibes. That's worth like, tons in terms of perceived legitimacy."

Marcus closed his eyes.

"Chad. We're not interested in content creation. We're not interested in brand deals. We're interested in interdiction operations conducted in accordance with federal guidelines."

Chad stared at him blankly.

"Chief," he said slowly, "that is literally the most boring thing anyone has ever said to me. And I've done sponsored content for fiber supplements."

Gator, of course, loved him.

"So you just... film everything?" Gator asked, watching Megan adjust lighting equipment.

"Especially the violent parts. Violence is huge right now. Not like, graphic violence—that gets demonetized—but like, implied violence. Tension. The moment before something pops off." Chad made an explosion gesture with his hands. "My agency calls it 'confrontainment.' It's in the deck."

"That ain't a word."

"The trademark filed last quarter. Megan handles IP."

Luis, who had been watching Chad with the quiet fascination of a zoologist observing a new species, finally spoke.

"Mr. Bryson. In my previous career, I worked with many organizations that valued publicity. All of them are now either in prison or dead. The ones who survived longest were the ones who valued silence." He paused, his unshakeable calm fully intact. "I would encourage you to consider the relationship between visibility and vulnerability."

Chad processed this for approximately two seconds.

"Bro, that's super deep. Can I quote you? Like, for my merch? 'Visibility is vulnerability' would look sick on a hat."

Luis blinked. For the first time in three months aboard, he appeared to have encountered a human he could not categorize.

"Permission to throw him overboard," Dana muttered.

"Denied. Barely."

The joint operation was the marina coordinator's idea. Marcus agreed only because the alternative was a formal compliance review, and because Click had pointed out that having Chad's footage could actually be useful—"if something goes wrong, we'll have video evidence from someone with professional equipment and no shame."

They set out at dawn: the Second Chance following the Sent It Maritime toward coordinates that Luis had identified as a probable transit corridor.

Chad's boat was faster. Louder. And apparently had a built-in Bluetooth speaker system that he insisted on using.

"WHAT THE FUCK IS THAT MUSIC?" Frank shouted over the bass.

"It's my pump-up playlist!" Chad's voice came through the radio. "Gets me in the zone!"

"I WANT YOU TO SWITCH IT OFF!"

"Dude, negative energy isn't good for content. Maybe try some deep breaths?"

Frank looked at Marcus.

"If I shoot him," Frank said, "would that be murder or community service?"

The contact appeared at 0943 hours. A mid-sized fishing vessel, running low in the water, course consistent with cartel transit patterns.

"Target acquired," Luis said.

"YOOO!" Chad's voice exploded from the radio. "Is this it? Is this the thing? Megan, tell me you're rolling!"

Marcus grabbed the mic. "Chad, we need to approach carefully—"

The Sent It Maritime surged forward, engines screaming, LED strips flashing, Chad's playlist now apparently set to something with a lot of horns.

"SENT IT!" Chad screamed.

"God fucking dammit," Dana breathed.

The chase lasted forty-seven minutes. During this time, Chad managed to: broadcast their entire tactical communication on an open channel, nearly collide with a pleasure yacht that had wandered into the area, and accidentally deploy a drone that immediately crashed into the Second Chance's radar array.

"MY BAD!" Chad called over the radio. "THAT'S GOING IN THE BLOOPER REEL!"

Click was, for the first time Marcus had ever seen, genuinely furious.

"He destroyed my equipment," Click said, voice shaking. "My calibrated, customized, meticulously optimized equipment. For CONTENT."

"Permission to build something educational for Mr. Bryson's boat."

"Define educational."

"Something that teaches him about the relationship between cause and effect."

"No."

"It would only be mildly catastrophic."

"Still no."

They caught the fishing vessel anyway. The boarding was a catastrophe. Chad insisted on leading it. For content.

Megan had been setting up a second camera angle before Chad finished his pose. She had done this before. She did it in silence, with the efficiency of someone who had learned that her job was not to participate in the circus but to document it in broadcast resolution.

"FREEZE, CARTEL SCUM!" Chad screamed, striking a pose on the fishing vessel's deck.

The three men on the deck stared at him.

One of them started laughing.

The laughing man raised a weapon. Dana shot him.

The second man dove for cover. Luis shot him.

The third man threw up his hands immediately. "Don't shoot! I surrender!"

Chad, who had been frozen in his pose throughout the entire engagement, slowly lowered his arms. "Tell me you got that."

"Got it," Megan confirmed. She had, in fact, gotten all of it, from three angles, with audio—a fact Marcus would only understand later, when the footage hit the internet with an editorial precision no drunk influencer could have achieved.

"THAT WAS INCREDIBLE!"

Marcus climbed aboard the fishing vessel and looked at Chad, who was already reviewing footage on his phone.

"Mr. Bryson. You nearly got yourself killed. You compromised our approach. You destroyed our radar. And you're treating an armed engagement like a fucking TikTok video."

Chad looked up, confused.

"But we got them," he said. "We got the drugs. We won."

"Winning isn't just about the result. It's about how you get there."

Chad stared at him for a long moment.

"Bro," he said finally, "that is literally the most boomer thing anyone has ever said to me. And my dad manages a Chili's."

Chad posted the footage that night. By morning, it had four million views.

"We're going viral," Click reported. "Not the good viral. The 'internet is arguing about whether we're heroes or war criminals' kind of viral."

Someone had already made a meme out of Dana's shooting stance. The most-liked version captioned it *when he says he'll text you back*. Another had her Photoshopped into a Renaissance Annunciation scene. Dana did not use Instagram. Dana did not want to know what any of this meant.

"This is a nightmare," Dana said.

"This is the future," Luis corrected, his calm restored. "Violence as entertainment. Crime as content. Everything becomes a performance eventually."

Gator was watching the video on his own phone, grinning. "Hey, I'm in the background! You can see me for like, two seconds!" He looked up. "Think I should start an OnlyFans?"

"Absolutely not," everyone said in unison.

The next morning, Marcus found Trevor Kline waiting on the dock.

"Captain Hale." Trevor offered a coffee. "I thought we should talk."

Marcus didn't take the coffee. "About what?"

"About your future." Trevor sipped from his own cup. "I watched the footage three times. Not live—we don't consume live. We consume recaps. It's better." He smiled. "Clean shooting. Professional takedown. Forty-seven seconds from approach to cuffs. If you were operating under my banner, that clip would be in a recruiting video by Thursday."

He offered a job. A partnership. Equity in Half the Booty.

Marcus tore the business card in half.

"I've seen what your version of dignity looks like," Marcus said. "I'll take poverty."

Trevor's smile didn't waver.

"Your choice. But remember this conversation, Captain. When your crew starts falling apart. When the money runs out." He raised his coffee cup in a mock toast. "I'll still be here. I'll still be winning."

He walked off the dock without looking back.

Marcus stood there for a long moment, watching him go.

The card fragments drifted in the harbor water.

And somewhere in the back of his mind, a voice he didn't want to hear whispered: what if he's right?

CHAPTER FOURTEEN

HOME

The night they played poker was the night Marcus realized he would die for every person on this boat, and that this was either the most noble or the most stupid thing that had ever happened to him.

It started because Gator found a deck of cards—so old the faces were faded and the edges were soft as cloth. The queen of hearts was missing. Someone had replaced her with a business card for a bait shop in Key Largo. The bait shop's slogan was "WE GOT WORMS."

They settled on dried beans as chips. Lima beans were ones. Black beans were fives. A single chickpea, found in a jar so old the label had faded to an abstract concept, was the hundred.

Gator was terrible at poker and magnificent at not caring.

"All in," Gator said on the second hand, pushing his entire pile of beans to the center.

"You haven't looked at your cards," Frank observed.

"Don't need to. I'm a vibe player."

"'Vibe player' is not a recognized poker strategy."

"It's recognized by ME."

He had a pair of threes. He won. Because Click folded a straight after calculating that the odds of Gator bluffing were "mathematically insignificant, which paradoxically makes it the perfect bluff, which means I can't trust my own analysis, which means I fold."

Luis played the way he did everything—quietly, patiently, and with a competence that suggested decades of practice in rooms where losing had consequences beyond beans. He won three hands in a row without changing his expression.

"You're cheating," Frank said.

"I'm observing. You scratched your left ear before folding. Click's typing speed increases when he has a strong hand. Gator breathes through his mouth when he's excited. And the captain —" he looked at Marcus—"touches his coffee cup when he's bluffing."

Everyone looked at Marcus's hand, which was resting on his coffee cup.

"I have a straight," Marcus said.

"No you don't," Luis said.

Marcus turned over his cards. Pair of sevens.

Dana didn't play at first. She sat on a supply crate slightly outside the circle, cleaning a weapon she'd already cleaned.

Frank noticed. "Get in here, Kessler."

"I don't gamble."

"We're gambling with beans. The financial risk is approximately zero."

Dana sat down. She won the next six hands consecutively.

"HOW?" Gator screamed.

"I spent six years playing poker with Navy SEALs in locations I can't disclose." Dana organized her beans into a precise formation. "They were better than you."

Frank poured himself a drink—water, Marcus noted, not whiskey—and leaned back.

"You know what this is?" Frank said. "This right here? This is the thing. The actual thing. Everything else—the seizures, the paperwork, the clean numbers—that's the job. This is the thing." He gestured at the circle. "Six idiots on a boat playing cards with beans."

He raised his water glass.

"To idiots," he said.

"To idiots," they said.

Mr. Whiskers descended from a storage locker, walked through the center of the poker game, scattered the bean pots with his tail, and sat on the deck of cards.

"The cat folded for all of us," Dana said.

They sat on deck for another hour, talking about nothing—that kind of nothing that happens between people who have stopped performing for each other and started just existing together.

Gator told a story about an alligator that was almost certainly fabricated. Click described a conspiracy theory about the postal service that was almost certainly true. Luis said nothing for twenty minutes and then observed that the stars looked different from prison, and nobody asked him to elaborate.

Dana fell asleep against the rail. Nobody woke her. Gator quietly moved a coil of rope so her head had something soft to rest against, and he did it with the careful tenderness of a man who was learning that the most important things he could do for the people he loved were small, invisible, and never mentioned.

Marcus sat among them and felt something he hadn't felt since before Laura left.

Home.

Not a place. Not a structure. A deck. A sky. People who showed up.

Marcus's phone rang at 7 AM on a Tuesday. He was on deck, coffee in hand, watching the marina wake up.

"Dad?"

He almost dropped the coffee. Sarah hadn't called him in four months.

"Sarah. Hi."

A pause. The particular pause of an adult child calibrating how much of themselves to offer a parent who'd historically failed to notice what was offered.

"I saw something on the news. About privateers. Some crew got shot at?"

"That wasn't us."

"I know. I looked it up." Another pause. "I just wanted to make sure."

Marcus sat down on the deck. A heron was standing on the neighboring boat's bow, perfectly still, waiting for something only it could see.

"I'm okay," he said. "We're careful."

"You've never been careful. You've been competent. There's a difference."

She sounded so much like Laura that Marcus's throat closed.

"Dad? Matt and I got some news. I'm—I'm pregnant. Due in February."

The marina was loud around him. Engines starting. Lines being cast.

Marcus heard none of it.

"That's wonderful," he said. His voice sounded wrong—too thick, too much. "Sarah, that's wonderful."

"Yeah." Her voice softened. "It is."

"I'm going to be a grandfather."

"If you want to be."

The "if" was a door. Not open, exactly. Unlocked. Waiting to see if he'd reach for the handle.

"I want to be," he said. "I want to be there. For everything. The boring parts especially."

"The boring parts?"

"The boring parts are the ones I missed. The ordinary Tuesdays. That's where life actually happens."

Sarah was quiet for a long time.

"Okay," she said. "We'll figure it out."

"Dad? Call me back this time."

"I will." He did.

The second phone call was harder than the first.

Sarah called on a Saturday morning, three weeks after telling him about the pregnancy.

"I need to tell you something," Sarah said, "and I need you to listen without fixing it."

"Okay."

"I'm scared. Not about the baby. About being a parent. About doing to this kid what you did to me."

Marcus opened his mouth.

"Listening," Sarah reminded him.

"I catch myself already," she continued. "Matt will be talking and I'll be thinking about work. I'll make a plan and cancel it because something felt more urgent." She paused. "Sound familiar?"

"Can I talk now?"

"If you're going to tell me I'll be fine, don't bother. Mom already said that."

"I'm not going to tell you you'll be fine. I'm going to tell you that the fact you're scared means you're already better at this than I was. I wasn't scared. I was confident. Confidence is what let me ignore the evidence that I was failing."

"That's not encouraging."

"It's honest. And here's the other honest thing: you're not doing this alone. You have Matt. You have your mom. And you have me—imperfect, late, still learning—but here." Sarah was quiet.

"I'm going to screw up," she said.

"Definitely."

"You're supposed to say I won't."

"You will. Every parent does. The question isn't whether you screw up. It's whether you notice. Whether you stop and come back and say 'I was absent,

I'm here now.'" He paused. "I didn't do that for twenty years. But I'm doing it now."

"That's the most useful thing you've ever said to me."

"Fifty-three years of doing it wrong is excellent preparation for doing it slightly less wrong."

Sarah laughed—not the careful laugh of an adult child managing expectations, but a real one.

"Dad? I'm glad you answered the phone."

"Me too, kid."

Dana found Chad at the marina dock at 3 AM, sitting on a piling with his phone dark and his knees pulled to his chest.

No camera. No Megan. No "bro."

She almost walked past. But something about Chad without the performance was disorienting enough to be interesting.

She sat down on the next piling over.

"You don't have to do this," she said. "The privateer thing. You have money. You have followers."

"Nobody's died because of me."

"Yet."

Chad was quiet. The water lapped against the dock.

"My dad was career Navy," Chad said. "Twenty-six years. Submariner."

Dana tilted her head. "Before, you told Marcus your dad managed a Chili's."

"Yeah. That's the bit."

"Why?"

"Because nobody follows a guy whose dad's a submariner. They follow a guy whose dad's a Chili's manager who made something of himself." Chad looked at his hands. "He never talked about his work. Not once. I used to think he was a coward. For not showing us what it was really like." Chad's voice cracked, just slightly, in a way that no audience would ever hear. "Then I started doing this and I realized—he wasn't being a coward. He was protecting us. From knowing."

"So why don't you stop?"

"Because the content matters. Not the engagement. The actual documentation. What Marcus is doing—nobody would know about it without the footage. Trevor Kline would lie to Congress and nobody would have evidence." He paused. "I'm not brave enough to do what you do. But I can make sure someone's watching. That has to count for something."

"It counts," she said.

They sat in silence for another minute. Then Chad pulled out his phone and the transformation happened—shoulders straightening, energy returning.

But Dana had seen the other version. She filed it away in the folder she kept for things that changed her opinion of people. It was a small folder. It was getting bigger.

CHAPTER FIFTEEN

FRACTURES

Day one-forty-one.

The argument started, as most arguments do, with money.

They were sitting in the galley two days after the Chad Bryson incident, dividing up the proceeds from their latest seizure. Four hundred and sixteen kilos. Their cut: just over a million dollars each.

Clean money. Reported accurately. Documented completely.

And it wasn't enough.

The galley of the Second Chance was not designed for crew meetings. It was designed for heating canned soup and regretting your life choices. The table seated four if nobody breathed. Six people arranged around it created the atmosphere of a subway car at rush hour, if the subway car also smelled like diesel and Gator's personal interpretation of hygiene.

Frank slapped a printout on the table. The table wobbled. Click's laptop slid three inches. Luis caught it without looking.

"Half the Booty made twelve million last week," Frank said. "Each. Because they skim, they flip, they work the system like it's designed to be worked."

"Their system is crime," Marcus said.

"Our system is poverty." Frank tapped the printout. "Twelve. Million. Each. You know what we made? After fuel, after repairs, after the docking fees and the insurance and the fourteen thousand dollars Click needs for a frequency modulator that I'm pretty sure he just made up—"

"I did not make up the frequency modulator. The frequency modulator is essential for—"

"We made one-point-one million. Split six ways. Before taxes." Frank leaned back. "One hundred eighty-three thousand dollars. For risking our lives against people with automatic weapons. My dental hygienist makes more than that."

"Your dental hygienist doesn't get shot at," Dana said.

"You haven't met my dental hygienist."

Marcus pressed his palms flat on the table—a gesture the crew had learned meant *I'm holding the line and you're going to hear about it.*

"We are not skimming. We are not 'optimizing.' We are not doing whatever corporate euphemism Half the Booty uses for theft. Our numbers are clean. That's the mission. That's the whole point."

"The point is also surviving, Marcus." Frank's voice dropped to something quieter and more dangerous than shouting. "Honor doesn't fix the radar. Honor doesn't buy ammunition. You know what honor gets you at a boat supply store? A confused look and a request for a valid credit card."

"I agree with Frank," Click said.

Everyone looked at him.

"Not about the skimming," Click added quickly. "About the radar. MY radar. The radar that Chad Bryson's DRONE destroyed. The radar I spent four months calibrating. The radar that is currently held together with marine epoxy and prayers." His fingers drummed the table—the involuntary rhythm that meant his brain was running faster than his mouth. "I need fourteen thousand dollars to replace the frequency modulator alone, and our operating budget is six hundred dollars and a gas station gift card that Gator won in a raffle. Chad's management emailed me last week. They'll pay for the repairs. They'll pay for all of it. Exclusive rights to film our next three operations."

"No," Marcus said.

"I said no. I'm just noting that the option exists."

"It was a good raffle," Gator said defensively.

"It was a twenty-dollar gift card to a Shell station."

"Twenty-two dollars. There was a bonus."

Dana held up her hand. "Can we focus? The issue isn't whether we maintain our reporting standards. The issue is revenue."

"Thank you," Marcus said. "That's exactly—"

"I have a proposal," Dana continued. "Private security contracts during downtime. Executive protection, asset escort. Legal supplemental income."

"We're privateers, not bodyguards."

"We're privateers who can't afford fuel." Dana let that land. "The Second Chance burned through four hundred gallons last week. At current diesel prices, that's over two thousand dollars. Our fuel budget is twelve hundred. The math doesn't work, Marcus. It hasn't worked for six weeks. I've been covering the shortfall from my personal savings, and my personal savings are not infinite."

Marcus stared at her. "You've been paying for fuel?"

"Someone had to." Dana's expression didn't change. "I didn't mention it because I knew you'd feel guilty, and guilty Marcus is less functional than regular Marcus, and I need you functional."

The silence in the galley was the kind that has weight.

"I have a different proposal," Gator announced, apparently unbothered by the emotional gravity of the moment. "Charter service. Off-days. Fishing tours. Bachelor parties. I already talked to some guys at the marina—"

"You did WHAT?" Dana's voice went flat in the specific way that preceded violence.

"Just chatted. Just casual. Just mentioned we might be open to—"

"You told STRANGERS at the MARINA that we have DOWNTIME? That we have GAPS in our OPERATIONAL SCHEDULE?"

"I said we might take some tourists fishing!"

"To anyone listening, you just told them when we're NOT on the water. Which means they know when our patrol sectors are EMPTY." Dana turned to Marcus. "This is what I've been warning about. He talks to everyone. He physically cannot stop himself. He's a GOLDEN RETRIEVER in human form and he is going to get us all killed."

"That's unfair," Gator said. "Golden retrievers are loyal and intelligent."

"Golden retrievers eat shoes."

"Different skill set."

"ENOUGH," Marcus said, and his voice had the hard edge that meant the commander was overriding the man. "Nobody is starting a charter service. And nobody is hiring us out as bodyguards. We are going to continue operating within the framework of the Lee Bill, filing accurate reports, and maintaining our standards."

"With what money?" Frank asked.

"With whatever money the next seizure brings."

"And if it doesn't bring enough?"

"Then we figure it out."

"That's not a plan, Marcus. That's a prayer."

"Well, Frank, sometimes prayer is all you've got."

"Great. GREAT. The captain's financial strategy is divine intervention. That's going in my resignation letter."

"You're not resigning."

"I'm THINKING about resigning."

"You're not thinking about resigning. You're thinking about a drink."

The entire table went silent.

The words hung in the air like something dropped from a height—still falling, not yet shattered.

Frank stared at Marcus. His jaw worked. Something ugly moved behind his eyes—not anger, exactly. Something older and sadder and more familiar. The look of a man who'd had his worst quality named out loud by someone he respected.

"That," Frank said quietly, "was a shitty thing to say."

Marcus closed his eyes. The commander retreated. The man was left standing in the wreckage.

"Yeah," he said. "It was. I'm sorry."

The silence held for ten seconds. Ten seconds is a long time when six people are sitting in a space designed for canned soup and regret.

"I need some air," Frank said, and left.

Nobody followed him. There was an unspoken agreement among the crew—when Frank needed space, you gave it, because the alternative was watching a man decide in real time whether today was the day he fell apart.

Luis, who had not spoken during the entire argument, watched Frank go. Then he looked at Marcus.

"You're losing them," Luis said.

"I know."

"Not because you're wrong. Because being right isn't enough when people are hungry."

Click quietly closed his laptop. Dana studied the table with the intensity of someone memorizing a crime scene. Gator looked at his Shell gift card like it contained answers to questions nobody was asking.

The meeting ended without resolution.

Which was, in itself, a resolution. Just not the kind anyone wanted.

Gator didn't sleep that night.

He lay in his bunk—the narrow coffin of foam and sweat-stained sheets that passed for crew quarters on a fifty-four-foot boat—and listened to the Second

Chance breathe. The hull ticking. The bilge pump sighing. The water moving against the hull in patterns that meant nothing and everything.

He thought about the money.

Not the abstract concept of money—the specific, physical, this-is-what-we-need money. Fourteen thousand for Click's radar. Two thousand for fuel. Ammunition. Dock fees. The hundred small expenses that kept an operation alive and that Marcus seemed to believe would materialize through the sheer force of moral clarity.

Gator loved Marcus. He did. The man had purpose, and purpose was something Gator had spent forty-one years looking for the way some people look for God—with occasional desperate sincerity and long stretches of not really trying.

But love didn't fix radars.

He got up at 3 AM.

The marina was quiet. Dock lights reflected off water that looked like spilled oil—black and thick and holding secrets. The air smelled like bait and salt and the low-grade rot that lived in every marina on the Gulf, the smell of things the ocean had chewed on and spit back.

Gator walked to berth 23.

Eddie Reyes was waiting.

Eddie was one of those people who existed in the spaces between legitimacy—a dockworker, a fisherman, a man who knew people and moved things and never asked questions that would require him to know answers. Gator had known him for fifteen years. They'd fished together. Drunk together. Shared the easy, uncomplicated friendship of men who operated in gray areas and didn't judge each other for it.

"You sure about this?" Eddie asked.

"No," Gator said. "But I'm sure about the alternative. We can't operate without that radar. And Marcus ain't gonna bend."

"How much?"

"Four kilos. From the last seizure. I marked it as handling loss."

Eddie studied him. The dock light caught his face—weathered, patient, the face of a man who'd been having this exact conversation with different people for decades.

"Eighty thousand," Eddie said. "Cash. I can have it by morning."

Eighty thousand dollars. Enough for the radar. Enough for fuel. Enough to keep them operational while Marcus polished his halo and the rest of the crew pretended that virtue was a renewable resource.

"Do it," Gator said. They shook hands.

Gator walked back to the Second Chance with a heaviness of a man who had just crossed a line he couldn't uncross and was already constructing the story he'd tell himself about why it was okay.

It's not stealing. It's management. Four kilos out of four hundred and sixteen. Less than one percent. A rounding error. Nobody gets hurt.

He climbed back into his bunk.

The Second Chance breathed around him.

He didn't sleep.

Luis noticed the discrepancy in fourteen hours.

This should not have surprised anyone. Luis Calderón had spent twenty years counting product for organizations that killed people over miscounts. He had once identified a two-kilo discrepancy in a five-thousand-kilo shipment—not because the numbers were off by a percentage that mattered, but because his brain simply did not allow numbers to be wrong. It was a compulsion. A sickness. The same sickness that had made him excellent at his former career and now made him indispensable to his current one.

He found Gator on the foredeck at sunset, pretending to check mooring lines with the studied casualness of a man who was extremely aware of being watched.

"We need to talk," Luis said.

Gator didn't turn around. "About what?"

"About the four kilos you sold to Eddie."

The line went still in Gator's hands.

"How'd you know?"

"Because the inventory reads four-twelve and I counted four-sixteen." Luis moved to the rail and stood beside him. "And because I spent twenty years doing what you just did."

Gator stared at the water. The sunset was doing something absurd—painting the Gulf in shades of orange and pink and purple that looked like God was showing off. Beautiful. Indifferent.

"It was for the radar," Gator said. "And fuel. And ammunition. And all the shit we need to keep running that Marcus thinks is gonna fall out of the sky."

"I know why you did it."

"Then you know I didn't have a choice."

"There's always a choice." Luis's voice was quiet—not angry, not judging. Something worse than either. Patient. "I told myself the same thing. For twenty years. There's no choice. It's business. It's supply and demand. It's just how the system works."

"This ain't the same."

"It's exactly the same. The scale is different. The justification is different. But the act—taking product that doesn't belong to you and selling it to someone who shouldn't have it—is the same act I performed a thousand times." Luis paused. "And every single time, I told myself it was management."

Gator's hands tightened on the rail.

"My daughter's name was Maria," Luis said.

He said it the way you'd say it if you'd practiced—not to make it sound natural, but because saying it at all required rehearsal. Saying the name of someone you'd killed, not with a weapon but with a career choice, was not something the human voice was designed to do easily.

"She wanted to be a veterinarian," Luis continued. "She wrote me letters in prison. Every week. For two years. Then the letters stopped and I thought she'd given up on me. She hadn't given up. She was dead. Three months dead before anyone told me. Needle in her arm. My name in her wallet."

The sunset continued, oblivious.

"I moved ten thousand kilos. Maybe more. Every kilo went somewhere. To someone. To someone's daughter or son or brother or friend. And I told myself it was business. Just like you're telling yourself four kilos is management."

"It IS four kilos," Gator said. His voice was rough. "Not ten thousand."

"It starts with four." Luis looked at him directly. "That's how it always starts. A small amount. For a good reason. And the next time it's a little more. And the reason is a little less good. And eventually you're standing in a federal courtroom and the prosecutor is saying 'ten thousand kilograms' and you're thinking, *how did I get here from four?*"

Gator's eyes were wet. The sunset light caught it and he turned away.

"What do I do?" he asked.

"You tell Marcus. And you return the money."

"He'll kick me out."

"Maybe."

"I can't—" Gator's voice broke. "This is the only thing I ever— This crew is the only—"

He stopped. He couldn't finish the sentence, but Luis heard it anyway. *The only thing I've ever belonged to. The only people who ever needed me for something that mattered.*

"I know," Luis said. "That's why it has to be you who tells him. Because if I tell him, or Click finds it in the numbers, it's a betrayal. If you tell him, it's a mistake you're trying to fix. There's a difference."

"Is there?"

"I spent nine years in prison learning the difference." Luis put his hand on Gator's shoulder—briefly, firmly, the touch of a man who didn't touch people often and meant it when he did. "You're not me, Gator. You don't have to become me. But this is the moment you decide who you're going to be."

They stood at the rail while the sunset burned itself out and the Gulf went dark.

"Tomorrow," Gator said finally. "I'll tell him tomorrow."

"Tonight," Luis said.

"Tonight."

"Tonight."

Gator found Marcus in the wheelhouse at 9 PM.

Marcus was doing what Marcus always did when he couldn't sleep—studying charts, reviewing routes, planning operations that might never happen. The wheelhouse was lit by the amber glow of instrument panels and the blue light of the radar screen, which was currently displaying the Portuguese weather forecast because Click hadn't finished the repairs.

"Cap," Gator said from the doorway. "I gotta tell you something."

Marcus looked up. He saw Gator's face and set down the chart.

"Sit down," Marcus said.

"I'd rather stand."

"Sit down, Gator."

Gator sat.

He told him everything. The four kilos. Eddie. The eighty thousand. The radar parts already ordered, the fuel already paid for, the ammunition already purchased. He told it without excuse, without justification, without the story he'd been constructing about management and necessity and the pragmatism of imperfect choices.

He just told the truth.

It was the hardest thing he'd ever done.

Marcus listened without interrupting. His face went through a sequence that Gator watched the way you watch a storm approach—first the stillness, then the darkening, then the pressure drop that meant something was about to break.

"How much," Marcus said when Gator finished.

"Four kilos. I reported it as handling loss."

"Handling loss." Marcus's voice was flat. "Four kilos of cocaine reported as handling loss. Sold to a man at the marina for eighty thousand dollars. With our seizure stamps on it."

"Yes, sir."

"You understand what you've done."

"Yes, sir."

"Not the theft. The theft I can deal with. You understand that you've given someone our seizure stamps on product we reported as lost. Which means that product can be traced back to us. Which means that anyone who wants to frame us—anyone who wants to prove that we're not as clean as we claim—now has physical evidence that our numbers don't match."

Gator hadn't thought about that.

The realization hit him like a wave he hadn't seen coming—the kind that catches you broadside and fills your lungs before you can close your mouth.

"Oh god," Gator whispered.

"Yeah." Marcus stood up. He walked to the window and looked out at the dark water. "You didn't just steal from us, Gator. You gave someone the ammunition to destroy us."

"I'll get it back. I'll find Eddie. I'll—"

"Eddie's already sold it. Or passed it along. Or told someone who told someone who told someone." Marcus's hands were flat against the console. "In my experience, product moves faster than regret."

The silence stretched until it was something you could feel—a physical presence in the wheelhouse, sitting between them like a third person.

"Are you going to kick me out?" Gator asked.

Marcus turned from the window.

This was the hardest conversation Marcus Hale had ever had. Harder than his divorce. Harder than his retirement. Harder than looking at three bodies on a go-fast boat and knowing the man who killed them would walk free.

Because Gator wasn't wrong about the money. He wasn't wrong about the radar. He wasn't wrong that Marcus's moral clarity was a luxury funded by other people's sacrifice—Dana's savings, Click's improvised repairs, the whole crew's willingness to be poor because Marcus believed in being honest.

But if he let this slide—if he made an exception because Gator was useful, because Gator was family, because they needed him—then everything he'd said about clean numbers was a speech. Words without weight. The kind of thing that sounded good and meant nothing.

"Return the money," Marcus said. "Eighty thousand. All of it. And never again."

"The radar—"

"We'll find another way. We always find another way." Marcus paused. "And Gator—you're staying. Not because what you did was okay. Because you told me. You could have hidden it. You could have let Luis handle it. You came in here and told me the truth, and that means the thing I need most from you—honesty—still works."

Gator nodded. His face was wet and he didn't wipe it.

"Okay," he said. "I'll figure out the money."

"We'll figure it out together."

"Cap?"

"Yeah?"

"I'm sorry. I'm real sorry."

"I know." Marcus sat back down. "Now go get some sleep. And for God's sake, stop talking to Eddie."

Gator left.

Marcus sat alone in the wheelhouse, listening to the boat breathe, wondering how long it would take for the damage to find them.

Not long, as it turned out.

Not long at all.

CHAPTER SIXTEEN

THE KNIFE

Eddie Reyes had always been a friendly man.

This was his primary professional skill—friendliness as infrastructure. He remembered birthdays. He bought rounds. He asked about your mother, your boat, your bad knee. He existed at the center of a web of small kindnesses that made people feel comfortable, valued, and—critically—willing to share information they wouldn't share with someone who hadn't earned it.

Eddie was not a bad person. He was a practical person who had learned that the difference between survival and failure, in the spaces between legitimacy where he lived, was not intelligence or strength but *proximity*. Being near things. Knowing things. Being the guy who knew the guy.

When Gator sold him four kilos with Privateer LLC seizure stamps, Eddie didn't think: *this is evidence I can weaponize*. He thought: *this is product I can move*. The stamps were irrelevant. The cocaine was currency. And currency, in Eddie's world, moved in one direction—toward whoever was buying.

The buyer, this time, was a man Eddie had never met. The transaction was brokered by a man Eddie had met once, at a bar, six months ago, who had purchased Eddie a drink and remembered his birthday and asked about his mother.

Friendliness as infrastructure.

The four kilos with Privateer LLC seizure stamps reached Anton Voss's people within forty-eight hours.

And Voss smiled.

Not because the cocaine mattered—four kilos was nothing, a rounding error in an empire that moved tonnage. But the stamps mattered. The documentation mattered. The proof that the honest pirates' numbers didn't add up—that their spotless reports contained at least one lie—mattered enormously.

Because you don't destroy honest people by proving they're dishonest. You destroy them by proving they're *human*. One crack in the armor. One deviation from perfection. And then you widen the crack until the whole thing collapses.

Voss picked up a phone.

"Prepare forty-seven kilos from the evidence reserve," he said. "Half the Booty seizure stamps. Pre-2024 dates. I want them placed aboard the Second Chance within seventy-two hours."

A pause on the other end.

"No," Voss said. "Don't kill anyone. I want them alive. I want them discredited. Dead martyrs are dangerous. Living failures are useful." He hung up.

The knife was in motion.

Click's sensors detected the intrusion at 3:17 AM.

This was, in retrospect, both the best and worst thing about Click's paranoia—the security system he'd installed on the Second Chance was designed to detect threats that ranged from "plausible" to "the CIA is personally interested in me," and it worked with a sensitivity that made actual threats indistinguishable from a cormorant landing on the bow rail.

The alarm went off seventeen times a week, on average.

Sixteen of those times, it was birds.

On this particular night, Click was asleep at his console—a state he entered approximately every forty hours, when his body overrode his brain's objections and shut down like a laptop running out of battery. The alarm brought him vertical in 0.8 seconds, a response time he had measured and was privately proud of.

"Perimeter breach," he announced into the crew comms, his voice carrying the urgent certainty of a man who had been right about threats three times and wrong about them approximately nine hundred times and was betting tonight was a right night.

"Click." Dana's voice came through the speaker with the exhausted patience of someone who had been woken by Click's alarms so many times she'd stopped fully dressing for them. "Is it a bird?"

"Negative. Thermal signature is human-sized. Moving port side, aft section, toward the cargo hold."

Silence.

"You're sure," Marcus said.

"I'm sure." They moved.

Dana was first on deck—weapon drawn, barefoot, moving in the shadows with the instinct of someone who had cleared buildings in the dark so many times her body did it while her brain was still waking up. Marcus followed, sidearm ready. Frank emerged from below deck with the specific alertness of a man who had been sober for exactly two hours and was operating on the fumes of professional instinct.

The aft deck was empty.

The cargo hold was not.

The hatch was open—not forced, but picked. Clean work. Professional work. The kind of lock-picking that cost money and training and spoke to resources that exceeded anything a random dock thief would have.

Inside the cargo hold, they found forty-seven kilos of cocaine they had never seized.

The bricks were marked with Half the Booty seizure stamps. The dates predated Privateer LLC's existence. The placement was precise—wedged behind equipment in a way that would look like deliberate concealment rather than recent addition.

Click ran his hands over the bricks without touching them.

"Planted," he said. "Within the last thirty minutes. The thermal signature I caught was the tail end of someone leaving." He pulled up his laptop. "I have partial footage from the dock camera—a figure, approximately six feet, wearing dark clothing, face obscured. Professional. They knew the camera angles."

"Black Flag," Dana said.

"Almost certainly." Click's jaw tightened. "They used our own seizure stamps against us. Gator's four kilos gave them the proof that our documentation has gaps. Now they've filled those gaps with evidence of crimes we didn't commit."

Marcus stared at the bricks.

Forty-seven kilos of cocaine bearing someone else's stamps, sitting in his cargo hold, turning his clean record into a crime scene.

He thought about calling the Coast Guard. Reporting it. Explaining that someone had planted evidence on his vessel. He thought about the conversation that would follow—the skepticism, the investigation, the slow bureaucratic process of proving a negative while the positive sat in his cargo hold looking exactly like guilt.

He picked up the phone anyway.

"Lieutenant Commander Vasquez. This is Captain Hale, Privateer LLC. I need to report a security breach and evidence tampering aboard my vessel."

The response was professional, procedural, and completely inadequate.

"We'll send a team, Captain."

"When?"

"Morning."

"This can't wait until morning. Someone planted—"

"Captain, I understand your concern. The team will be there at 0800. Please do not disturb the scene." She hung up.

Marcus looked at the cocaine. At the stamps that weren't his. At the future that was evaporating in the cargo hold of a boat that smelled like diesel and betrayal.

"Don't disturb the scene," he repeated.

"They're not coming to help," Frank said quietly. He was leaning against the bulkhead, arms crossed, reading the situation the way he'd read a thousand crime scenes—not for what was there, but for what was coming. "They're coming to process. There's a difference."

"Maybe they'll see it's planted."

"Maybe." Frank's voice carried a sadness of a man who had watched evidence be exactly what powerful people needed it to be, regardless of what it actually was, for thirty years. "Or maybe they'll see forty-seven kilos of cocaine on a boat operated by a convicted drug trafficker, a weapons builder investigated by ATF, and a detective who was forced to retire. And they'll see what they're supposed to see. What someone paid them to see."

"Nobody paid—"

"Somebody always pays, Marcus." Frank pushed off the bulkhead. "That's how the system works. You pay with money or you pay with consequences. The only people who don't pay are the ones writing the bills."

The Coast Guard arrived at 7:43 AM. Not a team—a boarding party. Armed. Official. The kind of presence that arrived when someone had already decided what they were going to find.

Lieutenant Commander Vasquez was not among them. The lead officer was someone Marcus had never met—a lieutenant with a clipboard and the expression of a person executing orders she hadn't written and didn't question.

"Captain Hale. We have a warrant to search this vessel."

"I called you. I reported the breach."

"Yes, sir. And the warrant was issued based on your report and additional intelligence received overnight."

"Additional intelligence from who?"

The lieutenant didn't answer.

They searched the Second Chance for four hours.

Marcus stood on the dock and watched.

He watched strangers go through his wheelhouse, his quarters, his charts. He watched them photograph the cargo hold where the planted cocaine sat like a confession written in someone else's handwriting. He watched them catalog the weapons locker, the communications array, Click's modifications that lived in the gray area between innovation and indictment.

Dana stood beside him. Her hands were at her sides, loose, the posture of someone who was controlling the impulse to intervene through sheer force of professional discipline.

"This is wrong," she said.

"I know."

"No. I mean the procedure is wrong. They're not documenting the door lock—the evidence of the pick. They're not taking thermal readings of the cargo hold to establish when the product was placed. They're not questioning dock security about overnight access." Her voice was tight. "They're not investigating a crime. They're building a case."

Gator sat on a piling at the edge of the dock, watching the boarding with the absolute stillness of a man who understood, with devastating clarity, that he had caused this. Not the planting—that was Voss, that was Black Flag, that was a system that punished honesty by weaponizing the smallest deviation from it. But the opening. The crack in the wall. The four kilos that had traveled from his hands to Eddie's to someone who knew exactly how to turn a mistake into a murder weapon.

He didn't speak.

He didn't need to.

The guilt on his face was louder than anything he could have said.

At 11:47 AM, the lieutenant emerged from the Second Chance with a clipboard and an expression that had solidified into bureaucratic finality.

"Captain Hale. We've recovered forty-seven kilograms of cocaine from your cargo hold bearing seizure stamps from operations predating your crew's licensing. Additionally, we've identified discrepancies between your reported seizure weights and processed weights consistent with mishandling or diversion of controlled substances."

The discrepancy. Gator's four kilos. The handling loss that wasn't.

"This vessel is impounded pending investigation. Your privateer licenses are suspended effective immediately. Your crew is ordered to surrender all federal authorization materials and vacate the vessel within two hours."

Marcus reached into his pocket.

His laminated card was there. The same card that the man in the strip mall had handed him with warm ink. CAPTAIN MARCUS HALE. PRIVATEER, LLC. FEDERAL AUTHORIZATION NUMBER 747-BRAVO-12.

He held it for a moment. Felt the weight of it—not physical weight, but the weight of everything it represented. The crew. The mission. The belief that honesty meant something in a system that priced it at zero.

He handed it over.

The lieutenant took it without ceremony. Added it to the clipboard. Moved on.

Two hours later, the Second Chance sat behind yellow tape and federal seals.

It took them forty minutes to process the impounding. Forty minutes to end everything Marcus had built.

They stood on the dock with their personal belongings in duffel bags—six people who had been a crew and were now just people, standing in the Florida heat, watching their home become evidence.

"Day one-fifty-one," Click said quietly. He was the only one who'd been tracking. "Twenty-nine days until our licenses expire."

Twenty-nine days.

The clock was still ticking.

PART THREE

THE FALL

INTERNAL MEMORANDUM—PERSONAL / DESTROY AFTER READING FROM: Trevor Kline

TO: [SELF]

RE: [NONE]

DATE: [REDACTED]

I'm not sending this to anyone. I'm writing it because I need to think, and thinking out loud in this organization gets you a visit from Anton, and visits from Anton are just meetings where one person doesn't know it's a performance review.

Marcus.

Not Captain Hale. Not "the honest privateer." Not "the operational integrity enthusiast" or whatever HR-approved language I'm supposed to use. Marcus.

I met him once, at the marina awards. I expected a zealot. What I found was worse—a tired man who knew exactly what he was doing and why, and wasn't angry about the opposition but sad about its existence. That's harder to fight than anger. Anger makes mistakes. Sadness just endures.

His numbers are still clean. After everything—the frame, the impounding, the suspension—his crew is still out there, on a shrimp trawler, filing reports that nobody reads because the system I built is designed to make accurate reports invisible.

Here's what keeps me up:

I'm not afraid of Marcus because he's honest. I'm afraid of him because he makes me remember that I used to be.

Not like him. Not heroic, not principled, not any of that Boy Scout bullshit. But honest—in the basic sense of knowing the difference between what I was doing and what I was pretending to do, and caring about the gap.

I stopped caring about the gap seven years ago. Maybe eight. There wasn't a moment. There was just a gradual loosening, like a bolt backing out of a thread one turn at a time, so slowly you don't notice until the whole thing comes apart in your hand.

Marcus's numbers are a mirror. I said that to his face. I told him people don't destroy mirrors because they're afraid of what they'll see. They destroy them because the reflection is inconvenient.

What I didn't tell him—what I'm writing here, in a memo I'll delete in five minutes—is that some reflections aren't inconvenient.

They're unbearable.

The operation continues. Anton is handling the tactical response. I'm handling the narrative. We're professionals. This is what we do.

But I'm going to delete this memo, and tomorrow I'm going to wake up and put on the suit and smile at the cameras and be Trevor Kline, CEO, Half the Booty, Global.

And somewhere, on a shrimp trawler that smells like bait, Marcus is going to wake up and be himself.

I don't know which of us has it harder.

Yes I do.

—TK

[MEMO DELETED]

CHAPTER SEVENTEEN

THE LUCKY LADY

They regrouped at Gator's cousin's place in the Keys.

Dale Wilkes was the kind of man the Keys produced in abundance—sun-cured, unquestioning, and possessed of the philosophical calm that comes from living on a spit of coral between two bodies of water that could erase you without effort. He ran a charter fishing operation out of a dock that was connected to a house that was connected to another dock that was connected to what might have been a second house or might have been an ambitious shed. The property lines were drawn to confuse tax assessors and discourage visitors, which Dale considered features, not bugs.

"Stay long as you need," Dale said when they arrived in a rented van at midnight, looking like refugees from a war that nobody else knew was happening. "Don't touch the bait freezer. Don't ask about the shed. And if a man named Cornelius shows up, tell him I'm in Guatemala."

"Are you in Guatemala?" Gator asked.

"I'm standing right here."

"Right. But if Cornelius asks."

"Guatemala. Three weeks minimum."

Dale's charter boat was docked at the end of the pier—a fifty-two-foot shrimp trawler named the Lucky Lady that smelled like diesel, bait, and the accumulated regret of every fish that had ever been caught within a hundred yards of her hull.

"She ain't pretty," Gator said, running his hand along the rail with the tenderness of a man greeting an ugly but beloved relative.

"She's hideous," Dana said.

"She floats. She moves. She don't show up on nobody's watch list." Gator patted the hull. "Right now that makes her the prettiest boat in Florida."

They scattered across the dock like debris from an explosion—which, in a way, they were. Each person finding their own piece of ground, their own distance, their own way of processing what had happened.

On the second morning, a man named Cornelius showed up.

Cornelius was eighty-one years old, wore a tank top that read LAW-ABIDING CITIZEN despite strong evidence to the contrary, and was owed money by Dale in an amount that had evolved over the years from "one hundred and twenty dollars" into a philosophical abstraction. He arrived on a scooter. The scooter had a sidecar. The sidecar had a chicken in it. The chicken was not in a carrier. The chicken was simply present, eyeing the marina with the specific contempt that chickens reserve for places below sea level.

"Where's Dale," Cornelius said.

"Guatemala," Gator said.

"Since when."

"Three weeks minimum."

Cornelius considered this with the slow gravity of a man who had been lied to about Dale's whereabouts since approximately 1987. He looked at the Lucky Lady. He looked at Gator. He looked at the chicken, which looked back.

"Tell Dale," Cornelius said, "that when he gets back from 'Guatemala,' he owes me one hundred and twenty dollars and a new carburetor. Tell him I know where he lives, which is here."

"Yes, sir."

"Also that chicken is Dale's."

"I thought you brought her."

"I am *returning* her." Cornelius stepped off the scooter with the effort of a man whose joints had opinions. "She has been in my yard for six weeks. Dale knows what she did."

Gator looked at the chicken. The chicken looked at Gator. The chicken was now apparently his.

"I don't know what she did," Gator said carefully.

"Dale knows." Cornelius remounted the scooter. "Also there's a man in your bait freezer. I didn't ask."

He drove away.

Gator stood very still.

"There is no man," he said, to no one in particular, "in the bait freezer."

There was no man in the bait freezer. There was, however, a large plywood crate labeled DO NOT OPEN—DALE, which everyone agreed to respect with the unanimous energy of people who had already broken enough rules this week.

The chicken, whom Frank named Patricia without consulting anyone, took up residence on the bow rail of the Lucky Lady and refused to be relocated. Click theorized that she had decided the shrimp trawler was her territory and was now running a hostile takeover against the pelicans who had previously held that position. Dana, who knew more about pelicans than the situation required, confirmed that brown pelicans would not contest a full-grown chicken and then declined to explain how she knew this.

By the third day, Patricia had laid an egg on top of the radar housing. Click photographed it for documentation. Nobody ate it. It sat there.

The Lucky Lady's shower, they discovered on day one, produced water at exactly two temperatures: scalding and theoretical. Click spent an afternoon attempting to fix the mixing valve and emerged with second-degree burns on his left hand and a new theory about plumbing as "a field dominated by sadists."

"The valve is designed to fail," Click explained, wrapping his hand in gauze. "Not gradually. Instantionally."

"That's not a word," Dana said.

"It is now. The existing words are insufficient to describe the malice of this shower."

Click set up his laptop on an overturned crate and began doing what Click always did when the world stopped making sense—looking for patterns in data, searching for the signal in the noise, building walls of information around himself like a digital fort.

Mr. Whiskers, who had been smuggled off the Second Chance in a duffel bag that Click had packed before his own belongings, curled up on the crate beside him and watched the dock with the practiced surveillance of a cat who had detected ATF operations three times. He also, within twelve hours of arrival, had arrived at an uneasy détente with Patricia the chicken, the terms of which neither of them would disclose but which involved an apparent mutual agreement about the bow rail being Patricia's and the crate being Mr. Whiskers's, with the middle of the deck as contested neutral territory that both parties crossed with visible reluctance.

Frank sat at the end of the pier with his feet hanging over the water and a bottle he'd bought at a gas station on the way down. He was drinking steadily, not quickly—the pace of a man who had lost the only thing keeping him from this and was now rediscovering its familiar weight.

Dana did a perimeter check of the property. Twice. Then she cleaned the weapons she'd managed to grab during the evacuation. Then she cleaned them again. On the third pass, Marcus gently took the rifle from her hands.

"It's clean," he said.

"I know."

"Then stop."

Dana looked at the rifle. At her hands. At the dock and the water and the sky full of stars that didn't care.

"What else am I supposed to do?" she asked.

It wasn't rhetorical. She was actually asking.

"I don't know," Marcus said. "I've never been here before."

Luis made calls. He'd been making calls since the van ride—quiet conversations in Spanish, in English, in the careful tone of a man activating a network he'd spent years building and never expected to need. Each call was brief. Each call ended with Luis's face slightly more composed, slightly more resolved, as if he were assembling something in his mind that the rest of them couldn't see yet.

Marcus found him at the bow of the Lucky Lady at 2 AM, staring at the water with the patience of a man who knew that the water always had the last word.

"What are you planning?" Marcus asked.

"A response."

"What kind of response?"

Luis looked at him. In the dock light, his face was all planes and shadow—a face built for difficult decisions in dark places.

"The kind that requires information we don't have yet." He paused. "I've been calling people. Old contacts. People who owe me things that can't be repaid with money. The planted evidence—the forty-seven kilos—those stamps are traceable. Half the Booty seizure stamps from specific operations on specific dates. If I can identify which operations, I can identify who handled the product after seizure, and that gives us the chain from Voss to our cargo hold."

"That's a lot of ifs."

"That's how investigations work. One if at a time until the ifs become facts." Luis almost smiled. "Frank taught me that. He doesn't know he taught me that, but he did. He talks about detective work the way I used to talk about logistics—like it's a puzzle with a solution, and the solution is patience."

Marcus looked back toward the pier, where Frank was silhouetted against the dock light, bottle in hand, staring at nothing.

"He's drinking again," Marcus said.

"Yes."

"He'd stopped. He was doing better."

"He was doing better because he had something to be better for." Luis's voice was gentle. "Take that away and the default is all that's left."

"Can we get it back?"

"The sobriety or the purpose?"

"Both."

Luis was quiet for a moment.

"Give him something to investigate," Luis said finally. "That's what he needs. Not support. Not encouragement. A problem. A mystery. Something that requires the thing he's best at." He looked at Marcus. "Frank Mulligan is the best investigator I've ever met. And I've met investigators who work for organizations that make the FBI look like mall security. Give him the puzzle. Let him solve it. The sobriety will follow the purpose."

Marcus nodded.

He walked back down the pier to where Frank sat with his bottle and his silence and his view of water that reflected nothing.

"Frank."

"Captain."

"I need a detective."

Frank looked at him. His eyes were bloodshot and bright—a combination of drunk and alert that was Frank's factory setting.

"I need someone to trace forty-seven kilos of cocaine from a Half the Booty evidence locker to our cargo hold. I need to know who handled it. Who transported it. Who planted it. And I need to know before our licenses expire in twenty-eight days."

Frank set down the bottle.

Not dramatically. Not symbolically. He just set it down, the way you set down something you were done holding for the moment.

"Twenty-eight days," Frank said.

"Twenty-eight days."

"That's not a lot of time."

"That's why I need the best."

Frank studied him. Searching for pity, for charity, for the condescension of a man offering a drunk a lifeline and calling it a job. He didn't find it. He found a captain who needed a detective.

"I'm going to need Click's data," Frank said. "All of it. The surveillance footage, the dock records, the radar logs. Everything he's been hoarding."

"Done."

"And I'm going to need to talk to people. Dockworkers. Coast Guard personnel. The people who handle evidence at processing. People who might not want to talk."

"Also done."

"And I'm going to need—" Frank paused. Looked at the bottle. Looked at the water. Looked at the bottle again.

"Coffee," he said. "I'm going to need a lot of coffee." He stood up.

He left the bottle on the pier.

The tide took it eventually. Carried it out into the dark water, spinning slowly, catching the dock light until it was too far away to see.

Marcus watched it go.

Then he went back to the Lucky Lady and started planning.

They were going to fight back. Not because they were confident. Not because they had a strategy. Because they were angry, and anger—properly directed—was the only fuel they had left.

Twenty-eight days.

The clock was ticking.

The Lucky Lady's head was broken in a way that defied explanation and plumbing.

"It flushes sideways," Gator reported on day two. "Full perpendicular. The bowl drains LEFT."

"How is that possible?" Click asked.

"I'm not sure it is possible. I think the toilet has achieved something that physics doesn't currently support." Gator paused. "I'm a little impressed, honestly."

He fixed it in three hours. It then flushed diagonally. "Compromise," Gator said.

Click installed a security system that was, by any reasonable standard, excessive for a shrimp trawler. When Dana asked why the acoustic monitors were calibrated to detect manatees, Click said: "Gator asked."

"The folder has TABS now," Click told Dana. "He's organized them by subspecies."

From below deck: "I HEARD THAT AND THE MANATEES HEARD IT TOO."

And for the first time since the Coast Guard had boarded his boat, Marcus Hale felt something he recognized.

Not hope, exactly.

Purpose.

The call came on a burner phone at 11 PM.

"Is this Captain Hale?" The voice was controlled, precise. Familiar.

"Agent Rourke."

"I'm calling from a payphone. I didn't know payphones still existed, but here we are." A pause. "I've been reassigned. My investigation into privateer financial irregularities has been transferred to another agent. The transfer came from two levels above my supervisor."

Marcus gripped the phone. "They're shutting you down."

"They're redirecting me. To an office in Omaha that handles agricultural subsidy fraud." Rourke's voice was flat. "I have a PhD from Johns Hopkins. I didn't get it to count corn."

"What do you want from me?" A long silence.

"I want you to know that someone inside the system saw what you were doing and thought it mattered. And I want you to know that the documentation exists. I've secured copies in locations that my supervisors haven't thought to check, because my supervisors underestimate women who are angry and thorough."

"Be careful, Captain. The people protecting these numbers have more resources than you do." She hung up.

Marcus sat in the Lucky Lady's wheelhouse, holding the burner phone. Somewhere in Omaha, a woman who had made hedge fund managers cry was packing her desk for a corn subsidy office because she'd committed the sin of doing her job.

The system wasn't broken. The system was working perfectly. That was the problem.

Marcus checked on Javier three times.

The first time: charged with conspiracy to distribute. His public defender filed a motion to separate his case. Denied.

The second time: Javier had taken a plea. Two years. Marcus's notation in the seizure report had been dismissed as "the arresting crew's subjective assessment."

The third time, from the Lucky Lady: Marcus wrote a letter to the judge. Three pages. Everything Frank had observed about Javier's hands, his terror.

"Cap," Gator said afterward. "You wrote three pages for a kid you met for twenty minutes."

"His name is Javier."

"I know his name. You wrote three pages. When everything's falling apart."

"Writing things down matters."

"Does it?"

"I don't know. But Frank thought it did."

CHAPTER EIGHTEEN

THE HEARING

Congress, as it turned out, had opinions.

The House Subcommittee on Maritime Affairs and Fisheries—a body that normally concerned itself with salmon quotas and shipping lane regulations—had suddenly discovered that its jurisdiction included the rapidly expanding world of legal privateering.

They were not pleased.

The hearing room was wood paneling, uncomfortable chairs, and a raised platform where elected officials could look down at witnesses with various degrees of theatrical disappointment. Cameras lined the walls. The C-SPAN operator, a woman whose expression suggested she had filmed enough congressional hearings to have lost faith in democracy but not in her camera equipment, positioned her lens on Marcus with professional disinterest. Someone had brought a sketch artist, presumably in case the cameras failed to capture the full scope of the humiliation.

Marcus sat at the witness table.

His crew was in the gallery, surrounded by federal marshals. Chad Bryson was also in the gallery, filming everything with a phone he'd hidden inside what appeared to be a potted plant. Megan had a camera disguised as a water bottle. The security team had checked them both and found nothing, which said more about Chad's commitment to content than it did about congressional security.

The committee chair, Representative Patricia Holbrook (D-California), gaveled the session to order.

"This hearing will examine recent incidents in the federal privateer program."

The ranking member, Congressman Bill Harmon (R-Texas), leaned into his microphone before the chairwoman had finished her opening statement.

"Madam Chair, before we begin, I want to note for the record that the privateer program has been an unqualified success in disrupting cartel operations, and I resent the implication that our brave maritime entrepreneurs—"

"Representative Harmon, this is my opening statement."

"I just want to get ahead of any partisan—"

"You will get ahead of nothing. This is my gavel." She held it up. "When you have the gavel, you can interrupt. Until then, sit down."

Harmon sat down, but his face achieved a shade of red that suggested medical intervention might be necessary.

"Captain Hale," Holbrook began. "Can you explain how forty-seven kilograms of cocaine ended up on your vessel?"

"Someone planted it, ma'am."

"Planted it." Holbrook's tone suggested she found this explanation somewhere between implausible and insulting. "And do you have evidence of this planting?"

"The cocaine bore seizure stamps from another privateer crew's documented operations. That evidence was in custody before my crew was even formed."

Harmon jumped back in. "Captain Hale, isn't it true that your crew includes a convicted drug trafficker?"

"Luis Calderón served his sentence and completed his supervised release. His participation is fully legal."

"Legal, maybe. But you have to admit it looks bad. A drug dealer catching drug dealers?" Harmon chuckled at his own joke. "That's like hiring a fox to guard the henhouse."

"With respect, Congressman, the fox analogy doesn't hold. Mr. Calderón's expertise in cartel logistics has been invaluable to—"

"Well now, I wouldn't know about that. I don't have experience with cartel logistics." Harmon mugged for the cameras. "I'm just a simple country lawyer from east Texas."

"You're a graduate of Harvard Law School," Representative Angela Morrison (D-New York) observed without looking up from her notes. "You own three houses. Your campaign received two hundred thousand dollars from defense contractors last quarter. Let's not do the folksy thing."

The gallery laughed. Harmon's red deepened to maroon.

Morrison leaned into her microphone. "Captain Hale, your seizure reports have been consistently accurate. Unusually accurate. Can you explain why?"

"Because we report what we seize. Accurately."

"Other crews report losses of fifteen to twenty percent."

"Because they're stealing."

The room went quiet.

"I mean—" Marcus caught himself. "They report losses that are inconsistent with standard handling protocols. Our numbers are what they are because we don't lose product."

Morrison nodded. "And this accuracy—this commitment to doing things correctly—is that why other crews might want to discredit you?"

Before Marcus could answer, a new voice entered the proceedings.

"Madam Chair!" A congressman Marcus didn't recognize—young, energetic, wearing a tie that appeared to feature tiny anchors—stood up. "Madam Chair, I'd like to raise a point of order regarding the terminology being used in these proceedings."

Holbrook sighed. "What terminology, Representative Dawkins?"

"The word 'pirate.' I've heard it used multiple times. These are privateers. The legal distinction—"

"Paperwork," the entire gallery said in unison.

Even the sketch artist laughed.

Holbrook gaveled the room to order. "Representative Dawkins, thank you for that contribution. Moving on."

The next hour was a masterclass in congressional theater.

Holbrook called witnesses from three other privateer crews, each one more damaging than the last. A captain from the Tax Write-Off who couldn't explain why his reported seizure weights had declined by exactly twenty percent on every single operation for eighteen months. A logistics coordinator from the Reasonable Doubt who, when asked to define "maritime interdiction," accidentally described money laundering. A compliance officer from a crew called Manifest Destiny who burst into tears when Morrison asked about the Cayman Islands accounts and had to be escorted from the room by a marshal who looked like he'd rather be literally anywhere else.

Then they called Darren Holcomb.

Marcus recognized him from the news coverage—the former captain of the Coastal Compliance, the man whose burning yacht had started this whole insane experiment. The man who, according to his post-incident media tour, had been "forged in the fires of maritime combat" and was now "America's most experienced privateer safety consultant."

He had written a book. It was called Privateer Grit: Lessons in Leadership from the Front Lines of Freedom. It had sold four hundred copies, three hundred of which had been purchased by his ex-wife's new boyfriend as a tax write-off.

"Mr. Holcomb," Morrison began, "you are here as an expert witness on privateer operational safety. Is that correct?"

"Yes, ma'am." Holcomb straightened in his chair with the practiced confidence of a man who had convinced himself his own lies were true. "I've been in this space since day one. Boots on the deck. Or—shoes, I guess. We didn't have boots. Budget was tight."

"Mr. Holcomb, your vessel, the Coastal Compliance, was attacked during your first and only operation. Your first mate was shot. Your boat caught fire. A cartel leader gave you back your radio out of pity." Morrison paused. "Can you tell us what lessons you drew from that experience?"

"Absolutely. The key takeaway was the importance of adequate preparation and risk assessment—"

"Your preparation consisted of one afternoon of paintball."

"Tactical paintball."

"At a facility run by a man who had previously managed a Cinnabon."

Holcomb's mouth opened and closed several times. In the gallery, Marcus could hear someone—possibly Gator—trying very hard not to laugh and failing.

"The paintball background of our training facilitator is irrelevant to the broader—"

"Mr. Holcomb, your crew's total maritime experience at the time of your operation was seventeen hours. Seventeen. A shift at Denny's is longer than that." Morrison looked at him over her glasses. "And yet you were granted a federal authorization to intercept armed drug traffickers. How is that possible?"

Holcomb glanced toward the committee members, looking for an ally. Harmon was studying his notes with sudden fascination. Dawkins was adjusting his anchor tie. Nobody met his eyes.

"The licensing standards were... flexible," Holcomb admitted.

"Flexible." Morrison wrote something down. "Thank you, Mr. Holcomb. That may be the most honest thing anyone has said in this room today."

Senator Lee, who was not on the committee but had been invited to observe, chose this moment to lean into a nearby microphone.

"If I may, Madam Chair—I want to emphasize that the program's licensing framework was designed with appropriate safeguards that—"

"Senator Lee, you are not a member of this committee."

"I understand that, but as the author of the legislation—"

"The author of the legislation," Morrison said coolly, "is welcome to testify under oath at a future hearing. Until then, he is a guest in this room and guests do not speak."

Lee's face went through a remarkable sequence of emotions—offense, calculation, and ultimately the tactical retreat of a man who realized that arguing would only draw more attention to his involvement.

He sat back. He adjusted his boat shoes. He did not speak again.

The real disaster came when they called Trevor Kline.

He walked to the witness table like a man approaching a stage he'd been waiting for his whole life. Calm. Confident. Every hair in place.

"Mr. Kline, you run Half the Booty, Global. Can you describe your relationship with Captain Hale's crew?"

"Of course." Trevor smiled warmly. "We've had minimal direct contact, but I've always been concerned about their approach. Their crew composition is unusual. An ex-con. A disgraced detective. Someone investigated by ATF multiple times." He paused for effect. "And Captain Hale himself retired under circumstances that were never fully explained."

"I tried to mentor them," Trevor continued, voice dripping with practiced concern. "I reached out. Offered guidance. But Captain Hale was resistant. Paranoid, honestly."

"Those stamps are not forgeries," Marcus said before he could stop himself. "They're authentic. And Mr. Kline knows it because—"

"Captain Hale!" Holbrook's gavel came down. "You will not interrupt testimony."

Trevor turned to look at him with an expression of wounded surprise that belonged in an Oscar reel.

The hearing ended four hours later with nothing resolved.

Trevor Kline gave three interviews in the hallway about the importance of "accountability in maritime operations."

But outside the building, Chad was waiting. He'd gotten it all. Every frame. Every lie Trevor told, every uncomfortable expression the committee members tried to hide, every moment where the truth was visible to anyone paying attention.

"Bro," Chad said, showing Marcus the footage on his phone. "This is CONTENT. This is the best content I've ever filmed. Trevor Kline lied to Congress ON CAMERA. We have like twelve angles."

"When are you posting it?"

"Already did." Chad grinned. "Live-streamed the whole thing. Fourteen million views and counting."

Marcus looked at the view count climbing in real time.

Maybe—just maybe—the influencer was going to be useful after all.

CHAPTER NINETEEN

THE PARTY

The yacht was called Regrettable Decision, which either showed remarkable self-awareness or none at all.

Two hundred and forty feet of floating excess, lit up like a casino, anchored twelve miles offshore in water deep enough to hide anything. The intel said it belonged to a shell company that belonged to another shell company that eventually traced back to a Panamanian law firm that specialized in not answering questions.

The intel also said that tonight, the yacht was hosting what was euphemistically called a "networking event" for the privateer industry's most successful operators.

Translation: Trevor Kline and Anton Voss were throwing a party, and everyone who mattered in the corruption economy was invited.

Luis had gotten them the intel. Luis always got the intel. He had contacts inside contacts, relationships that stretched back twenty years, people who owed him favors they'd never fully repay.

"Voss will be there," Luis said, spreading photos across the Lucky Lady's cramped galley table. "Trevor will be there. Half a dozen other privateer captains, all of them dirty. Cartel liaisons pretending to be businessmen. Businessmen pretending to be legitimate. Politicians pretending to be human."

"And we're crashing this party because...?" Gator squinted at the photos.

"Because they think we're dead." Marcus studied the yacht's layout. "Because they think they destroyed us when they burned the Second Chance. Because arrogant people in safe spaces say things they shouldn't."

"We're gathering intel," Dana clarified. "Not starting a war."

"Yet," Click added cheerfully.

Marcus ignored him. "Luis, you said you could get inside."

Luis nodded slowly. "Voss knows me. From before. We have… history. If I approach under a flag of truce, request a meeting, he might honor it. Old traditions."

"Or he might kill you," Dana said.

"That's possible."

"More than possible. Probable."

Luis shrugged with the ease of a man who had made peace with his own expendability. "I've been living on borrowed time since Maria died. Every day I hurt these people is a day I didn't expect to have."

The galley went quiet.

"There's another option," Luis continued. "Voss is hosting this party because he's consolidating power. Bringing the other crews into line. Making sure everyone understands who runs the ocean now that Black Flag has won." He tapped one of the photos—a man in an expensive suit with the dead eyes of a shark. "This is Carlos Medina. He handles Voss's cartel connections. Logistics, distribution, the business side. He's also the man who approved the hit on our boat."

"You want revenge," Frank said.

"I want access." Luis looked at Marcus. "Medina keeps records. Not on computers—he doesn't trust digital. Physical files. Contracts, account numbers, distribution networks. Everything Black Flag does flows through his office on that yacht."

"So we steal his files?"

"We copy them. Photograph them. Take what we need and leave without anyone knowing we were there." Luis paused. "If we can get that information out, we have leverage. Real leverage. The kind that can bring down the whole operation."

Marcus thought about it.

They were a crew without a ship, without resources, without official standing. They had a shrimp trawler, six people, and a lot of anger.

This was either brilliant or suicidal.

He thought about Sarah, suddenly. Unbidden. Unwelcome.

She'd called last week to tell him she was pregnant. Just into the second trimester. Due in the spring. She'd sounded nervous, like she wasn't sure how he'd react, like she was bracing for disappointment because that's what he'd taught her to expect.

He'd said congratulations. He'd said he was happy for her. He'd said they should talk more, soon, when things settled down.

Things never settled down. That was the point. That was the excuse.

If he died tonight—on this stupid, reckless mission that was either brilliant or suicidal—his grandchild would grow up with no memory of him at all. Just stories, maybe. Just the absence where a grandfather should have been.

Just like Sarah had grown up with the absence where a father should have been.

"Walk me through it," Marcus said.

Because stopping wasn't an option. Because the mission was the mission. Because he still didn't know how to choose the people who needed him over the purpose that defined him.

But maybe—maybe after this was over—he'd figure it out.

If he survived.

The plan was simple, which meant it would definitely go wrong.

Phase one: Luis approaches the Regrettable Decision in a small boat, alone, unarmed, requesting an audience with Voss. He plays the role of a former associate seeking to make peace—or at least seeking to negotiate terms of surrender.

Phase two: While Luis occupies Voss's attention, the rest of the crew approaches from the yacht's blind side. Click's jamming equipment keeps their signature off the radar. Dana leads the infiltration team through a service entrance on the lower deck.

Phase three: They find Medina's office, copy everything they can, and exfiltrate before anyone notices.

Phase four: Luis excuses himself from the meeting, rejoins the crew, and they disappear into the night.

Simple.

"There are approximately seventeen ways this goes wrong," Click announced, having apparently run the numbers.

"Only seventeen?" Dana asked.

"Those are the ones I could model. There are probably more."

"Encouraging."

"I prefer to think of it as realistic."

"How likely is each one?" Gator asked.

Click considered this with the seriousness of a man who had genuinely done the math. "Catastrophic failure scenarios cluster around two probability spikes. The first is during Luis's initial approach—Voss could simply have him shot on the water. I rate that at fourteen percent."

"Manageable," Luis said.

"The second is during exfiltration. If they realize what we've taken before we're clear, the yacht's onboard security plus the patrol boats give them maybe a six-minute response window. We need to be off the water before that closes."

"And the other scenarios?"

"A grab bag. Equipment failure. Civilian casualties. The Coast Guard arriving for unrelated reasons and getting confused. One scenario where a guest panics and shoots the wrong person, which then causes everyone to shoot everyone." Click paused. "That last one is more likely than you'd think. Cocaine and firearms are not stable companions."

Frank, who had been listening with the quiet attention of a man who'd been to enough crime scenes to know what cocaine and firearms looked like together, nodded slowly.

"He's right. Mass-casualty events at parties are almost always triggered by one person making a bad choice. The trick is making sure none of us is that person."

"Encouraging speech, Frank."

"I'm a homicide detective. Everything I say is encouraging in the same way that gravity is encouraging."

Marcus looked at Luis. "You're sure about this?"

Luis was checking the small pistol he'd be leaving behind—appearing unarmed was part of the plan, even if being actually unarmed was suicide. He'd switched to a pair of ceramic rounds that Click had built into the lining of his jacket, indistinguishable from fabric reinforcement. Two shots. That was all he'd have if things went wrong.

Two shots had ended empires before. He'd just never been the one holding the gun.

"I've been sure since Maria died," Luis said. "This is just the first time I've been able to do something about it."

"If it goes sideways—"

"Then you leave me and take the information." Luis's voice was flat. "The mission matters more than any one person. Even me. Especially me."

Marcus wanted to argue. Wanted to say that no one was expendable, that they didn't leave people behind, that the mission wasn't worth dying for.

But he looked at Luis's eyes and saw something that didn't leave room for argument.

This was what Luis had been building toward. His whole second life.

Whether it ended tonight or in fifty years, this was the purpose he'd chosen.

"Don't die," Marcus said finally. "That's an order."

Something shifted in Luis's expression—not warmth, exactly, but the memory of warmth.

"I'll try to fit it into the schedule."

At 10:58 PM, Luis Calderón lowered a small inflatable dinghy into the water.

He was dressed simply—clean clothes, nothing threatening, nothing that screamed former drug trafficker here to settle scores. He looked like what he was pretending to be: a man who had been beaten, who was looking for a way out, who wanted to negotiate terms.

"Radio check," he said quietly.

"Reading you clear," Click's voice came back. "Good luck."

"Luck is for people who haven't prepared." Luis started the dinghy's small motor. "I'll be in touch."

He motored away from the Lucky Lady, toward the blazing lights of the Regrettable Decision, toward Anton Voss and whatever was waiting for him there.

Marcus watched him go.

"He knows the risks," Dana said beside him.

"He's been waiting for this his whole life."

"That's what worries me." She was quiet for a moment. "People who don't care if they live are dangerous. Usually to themselves."

"Luis isn't suicidal."

"No. He's patient." Dana checked her weapon one more time. "But patience ends eventually. And when it does, people like Luis either find peace or they find martyrdom."

Marcus didn't have an answer for that.

He just watched the small boat get smaller and smaller, until it was swallowed by the glow of the yacht and there was nothing to do but wait.

Luis approached the Regrettable Decision like a supplicant approaching a throne.

He cut his motor fifty yards out and let momentum carry him forward, hands visible, posture submissive. A spotlight swung toward him immediately—they were expecting visitors, just not this kind.

"IDENTIFY YOURSELF," the voice boomed through a loudspeaker.

"Luis Calderón," he called back. "I'm here to speak with Anton Voss. Tell him an old friend from Medellín wants to discuss terms."

A pause. Murmured conversation on the deck.

"HOLD YOUR POSITION." Luis held.

Three minutes passed. Four. Five.

Then a voice—different, calmer, somehow more dangerous—spoke from the yacht's rail.

"Luis. I didn't expect to see you again." Luis looked up.

Anton Voss stood at the rail, drink in hand, studying him with the mild curiosity of a collector examining an interesting specimen. He was dressed casually—linen shirt, expensive watch, understated wealth that whispered louder than any designer suit could shout.

"Anton." Luis kept his voice neutral. "I thought we should talk."

"Talk about what? You're a dead man working with other dead men. What could we possibly have to discuss?"

"Survival. Specifically, mine." Luis let desperation seep into his voice—not hard, given the circumstances. "The crew I was working with is finished. The captain's a fool. I'm looking for opportunities."

Voss was quiet for a moment.

"You're lying," he said finally. "You were always a terrible liar, Luis. Even in Medellín. You'd show your cards with your eyes."

"I'm not lying. I'm negotiating."

"With what leverage?"

"Information." Luis raised his hands slightly. "I know things about Marcus Hale's operation. His contacts. His methods. His vulnerabilities. Information that might be valuable to someone in your position." Voss smiled.

It was not a friendly expression.

"Come aboard," he said. "Let's discuss this like civilized people."

A ladder dropped over the rail. Luis climbed.

The trap was set.

Now they just needed to spring it.

The party was exactly what Luis expected.

Beautiful people doing ugly things in expensive clothes. Champagne flowing like water. Cocaine flowing like champagne. Conversation that sounded civilized but smelled like blood money.

Voss led him through the main deck without stopping, past guests who didn't look twice at them, past security personnel who looked very carefully.

The party was everything Luis expected. Champagne flowing. Cocaine flowing faster. A woman in a designer dress casually snorting a line off a silver tray held by a server who seemed to find this completely normal. At one point, Luis was almost certain he saw a sitting United States senator demonstrating something to a young woman with a cocktail shrimp. He chose not to look directly at it. Some things, once seen, could never be unseen, and Luis was already carrying enough.

Near the bar, a woman in tactical boots and a cocktail dress was holding court with three cartel liaisons who looked like they were simultaneously terrified of her and hoping she'd notice them. Luis recognized her from the dossier Click had compiled: Captain Rachel Okafor, formerly of Nigerian Naval Intelligence, now running a privateer crew called Sovereign Remedy out of Key West. Her seizure numbers were second only to Half the Booty's, and unlike Trevor's, hers were rumored to be accurate—because Rachel Okafor took things other than drugs from the boats she intercepted. Things that didn't appear on federal reports. Things that people paid very well to have quietly returned.

She was, according to Click's assessment, "the most dangerous person in the privateer program who isn't actively psychotic."

She caught Luis looking and raised her glass with a half-smile that said she knew exactly who he was and found his presence entertaining.

Luis did not return the smile. He had enough complications.

"Business has been good," Luis observed.

"Business is always good when you're not burdened by scruples." Voss gestured toward a doorway. "This way."

They entered a private study—wood-paneled, leather-chaired, a room that belonged on a British estate, not a yacht. Trevor Kline was already there, lounging on a sofa with a drink in his hand.

"Luis!" Trevor's smile was bright and empty. "I heard you were dead."

"Reports of my death were exaggerated."

"Clearly." Trevor's eyes were calculating even as his mouth performed friendliness. "You're here to negotiate, Anton said. What exactly do you have to offer?"

"Information about Hale's operation. Their contacts, their methods, their plans."

"Their plans?" Trevor laughed. "What plans could they possibly have? We destroyed their boat. Killed their reputation. They're finished."

"They're rebuilding." The laughter stopped.

"What do you mean, rebuilding?" Voss asked quietly.

Luis kept his expression neutral. This was the part where he needed to be careful—give enough to seem valuable, hold back enough to stay alive.

"Hale has resources you don't know about. Contacts. A new vessel." Luis paused. "And a plan to expose your entire operation."

Silence.

Voss and Trevor exchanged a look.

"That's... concerning," Trevor said slowly. "If true."

"It's true." Luis met Voss's gaze. "I'm here because I don't want to go down with that ship. I've done the prison thing. I don't recommend it."

Voss studied him for a long moment.

"Why should we trust you?"

"You shouldn't. But you should use me." Luis sat down uninvited in one of the leather chairs. "I know how Hale thinks. I know his weaknesses. I know where he'll strike and when. That information has value."

"And in exchange?"

"I want out. Clean. New identity, seed money, guarantee of protection." Luis shrugged. "I'm not greedy. I just want to survive."

Trevor was nodding slowly. "It's not unreasonable."

Voss said nothing. The silence stretched.

"We'll discuss it," Voss finally said. "In the meantime, enjoy the party. Have a drink. Don't leave the yacht."

"Am I a guest or a prisoner?"

"You're an opportunity being evaluated." Voss smiled his cold smile. "Those are the only options I offer."

He left the room.

Trevor lingered, studying Luis with an expression that was harder to read than Voss's open menace.

"You're playing a dangerous game," Trevor said softly.

"I'm surviving. Same as you."

"No." Trevor shook his head. "You're planning something. I can tell. I've seen that look on too many faces right before they did something stupid."

"Maybe you're projecting."

"Maybe." Trevor finished his drink. "But just in case—I'd be very careful about what you do next. Voss isn't forgiving. And neither am I." He walked out.

Luis was alone.

He checked his watch.

11:47 PM.

The crew should be approaching now. Dana and Marcus, moving through the shadows, looking for Medina's office.

All Luis had to do was keep Voss and Trevor distracted for another hour.

Should be easy.

Famous last words.

CHAPTER TWENTY

THE CHAOS

The infiltration started so smoothly that Marcus should have known it was about to fall apart.

Dana led them through the service entrance on the lower deck like she'd designed the floor plan herself. Click had hacked the yacht's manifest the day before and identified which catering company had been hired—a regional outfit called Coastal Cuisine that, in the manner of all third-tier service providers, had no rigorous vetting process and would happily accept day-of additions to their staff if the paperwork looked official enough. The paperwork had looked very official, because Click had made it.

So Marcus and Dana boarded as catering staff, dressed in white shirts and black pants, carrying trays. The trays held actual hors d'oeuvres on top—Click had insisted on this for verisimilitude—and tactical gear underneath.

A pelican had nested on the service entrance platform.

Dana froze for half a second, then stepped around it with the deliberate calm of a bomb disposal technician navigating a live minefield. The pelican watched her with the vacant malevolence that only seabirds can achieve. It did not move. It did not threaten. It simply existed, three feet away, in a way that violated every principle of Dana's mental tactical map.

"Don't say anything," she murmured to Marcus.

"I wasn't going to."

"Your face was going to."

They moved past the bird. Dana exhaled in a controlled four-count.

Marcus had spent twenty-two years in the Coast Guard. He had personally rescued seventeen people from active drowning situations. He had once boarded a vessel that turned out to be carrying live ordnance left over from a 1970s smuggling operation. He had stared down a hurricane at category four strength.

He had never, in any of those situations, seen Dana Kessler look as rattled as she did walking past a bird that weighed less than her sidearm.

He filed this away in the mental folder labeled THINGS WE WILL NEVER, EVER DISCUSS.

The corridor opened into the main service hallway. Two crew members passed them in the opposite direction, carrying ice. Nobody looked twice. The catering uniforms did exactly what catering uniforms were designed to do, which was render the wearer functionally invisible to people who had been raised to consider service workers part of the architecture.

"Stairwell at the end," Dana whispered. "Two flights up to the upper deck. Medina's office is the third door on the right."

"How do you know?"

"Click pulled the yacht's blueprints off a shipping registry six months ago. The original owner sold her to the shell company, but the structural plans are public record."

"Click is terrifying."

"Click is useful. There's a difference." They climbed.

Above them, the party was at full volume. Music. Laughter. The particular sound of expensive people pretending they weren't doing something deeply illegal.

A guard appeared at the top of the stairwell. Heavy set, body armor under a sport coat, the unmistakable bulge of a sidearm at the hip. He saw them, registered the trays, and immediately lost interest.

"Service stays in the lower decks," he said, not unkindly.

"Mr. Voss requested fresh shrimp for the upper salon," Dana said. Her voice had shifted into something Marcus didn't recognize—softer, slightly accented, the kind of voice that performed deference. "His guest specifically asked."

The guard frowned. "What guest?"

"The new one. The Hispanic gentleman. He arrived twenty minutes ago."

The guard processed this. Then he nodded.

"Make it fast. Don't loiter."

"Yes, sir."

They moved past him.

Marcus waited until they were down the corridor before speaking.

"How did you know about Luis arriving?"

"I didn't. I made it up. People will believe almost anything if you say it with the right combination of confidence and subordination." Dana paused at a junction, checked both directions. "I learned that doing protection work for executives. They lie constantly. They lie about everything. But they always assume the help is telling the truth, because the help isn't important enough to bother lying."

"That's depressing."

"That's useful."

They reached the upper deck. The corridor here was carpeted in something thick enough to swallow footsteps. Original art on the walls. Lighting that cost more than most people's cars.

Two guards were posted outside the third door on the right. Standing at parade rest, eyes scanning, weapons holstered but accessible. Professional.

"Trays down," Dana whispered. "Vests on. Sixty seconds."

They ducked into a service alcove. Off came the catering uniforms. On went the tactical gear that had been pressed flat under the trays. Marcus checked his sidearm, felt the comfortable weight of it, the muscle memory of two decades.

"Approach plan?" Marcus asked.

"I take the left. You take the right. Non-lethal if possible. If they get a hand on a radio, lethal. Either way, fast."

"Copy."

They emerged from the alcove walking with purpose, dressed now like security personnel, carrying themselves like they belonged. The guards saw them and registered the uniforms before they registered the unfamiliar faces—exactly the four-second hesitation Dana had bet on.

Dana hit her guard with a precise strike to the throat that didn't quite crush the windpipe but did completely shut down his ability to vocalize. She followed with a chokehold that put him on the floor in three seconds.

Marcus's guard was younger, faster, and already turning with his hand moving toward his weapon. Marcus grabbed the man's wrist, pivoted, and used the guard's own momentum to drive him face-first into the wall. The guard slumped.

Four seconds. No shots fired.

Dana was already zip-tying her guard's wrists with the practiced efficiency of someone who had done this many times in places that did not officially exist. Then she paused.

The unconscious guard's sleeve had ridden up. On his forearm was a tattoo—a stylized poppy, dark ink, faded with age.

Dana's hands stopped moving.

She knew that tattoo. She had memorized it from her brother's autopsy file.

Stylized poppy. Mendoza cartel. The same organization that had supplied the heroin that put David Kessler in a bathtub in Tallahassee with a needle in his arm.

She was alone in a corridor with an unconscious member of the organization that had killed her brother. No witnesses. No oversight. She could tighten the zip-ties past the point of circulation. She could use the pressure points she'd been trained on in places she couldn't legally talk about. She could cause damage that wouldn't kill him but would mean he never worked again, never walked right again, never forgot her face.

She could make it personal.

For about two seconds, she wanted that more than she had wanted anything in three years.

She looked at the kid. Twenty-two, maybe twenty-three. The age David had been when he came back from his first tour. The age David had been when the prescriptions started.

Hurting this kid wouldn't bring David back.

It would just mean she had become the kind of person who hurt unconscious people because it made her feel better.

She finished the zip-ties at regulation tightness.

"Dana?" Marcus whispered. He'd seen her freeze.

"Fine. Let's move."

The office door was locked. Dana pulled a small charge from her vest—Click's design, compact and precisely controlled—and fixed it to the door frame.

"Step back."

The charge popped with a sound less like an explosion and more like a heavy book being dropped. The doorframe disengaged from the wall. The door swung inward.

The office was empty.

No Medina. No guards. Just a heavy oak desk, leather chairs, walls of bookshelves, and a single server rack humming quietly in the corner.

"Where is he?" Marcus murmured.

"Probably at the party. Some men collect art. Some men collect young people. Medina collects functioning relationships with violent organizations.

He's not going to skip the networking opportunity." Dana was already moving to the server. "Plug in. Let's grab what we came for."

Click's device was the size of a deck of cards. Marcus pulled it from his vest, found the appropriate port on the server, and connected.

The device's small LED blinked yellow as it began the handshake.

Then green.

Downloading.

"How long?" Marcus asked.

"Click said three to five minutes for everything. We've got time to look around."

While the device worked, Marcus opened the desk drawers. Standard executive trash—pens, business cards, expensive stationery. The middle drawer was locked. He picked it with the multitool from his vest in about thirty seconds.

Inside: a leather-bound ledger. Hand-written. Names, dates, dollar amounts.

"Dana."

She came over. Read for ten seconds. Looked up.

"Take it."

"The whole book?"

"The whole book. If the digital copy fails, this is the backup. And if the digital copy works, this confirms it." She was already photographing pages with her phone. "Voss kept everything digital. Medina kept everything paper. They both thought they were being clever."

"They both were."

The device on the server blinked from green to a slow pulse.

Marcus looked. The pulse was a different shade—more amber than green.

"Dana."

"What?"

"What does amber mean on Click's device?"

Dana looked. Her face changed.

"That's not a download status. That's an alert. We've been detected."

The alarm went off three seconds later.

Not a quiet alarm. Not a discreet security notification. A full-volume klaxon that shook the walls and immediately killed the music in the main salon below. Strobe lights began flashing in the corridor.

Above them, on the deck, came the sound of dozens of guests realizing simultaneously that the party was over and the running portion of the evening had begun.

"Time to leave," Dana said.

Marcus grabbed the device from the server. Still amber. Still pulsing. He didn't know if the download had completed or not. He shoved it in his vest along with the ledger.

"Service stairs are compromised," Dana said, listening at the door. "I can hear boots on the lower decks. They're sealing the lower exits."

"Then we go up."

"Up takes us to the main party. With armed guards looking specifically for us."

"It also takes us to the railing. Which Gator is currently pulling alongside." Dana paused.

"Three flights up?"

"Three flights up."

"Captain?"

"Yes?"

"This is going to be loud." She was correct.

The next four minutes were the loudest of Marcus's life.

The yacht's interior had become a maze of panic. Guests flooding toward the exits, pushing past each other in designer clothes, their carefully curated facades crumbling into pure animal fear. Security was trying to establish control, but there were too many people, too much chaos, too little information about what was actually happening.

Marcus and Dana used it.

They moved against the flow, pushing upward while everyone else pushed down. The tactical gear bought them hesitation—guards saw uniforms first, asked questions second. By the time anyone thought to challenge them, they were already past.

A guard at a stairwell landing was not so easily fooled. He raised his weapon. Dana fired before he could complete the motion. He went down.

"Civilian witnesses?" Marcus asked.

"Three. All of them too high to remember anything coherent." They kept moving.

On the second-floor corridor, they ran into more resistance. Two guards in tactical positioning, weapons raised, calling commands they couldn't hear over the alarm.

Dana dropped one. Marcus dropped the other.

The civilians who saw it scattered like quail.

"Marcus?" Dana said as they reloaded.

"Yes?"

"How are we feeling about Luis?"

"Worried."

"Same."

The radio in Marcus's ear crackled.

"Marcus, this is Click. Whatever you did, the entire yacht has gone hot. Voss's security is consolidating on the upper decks. They're forming up to defend something."

"Defend what?"

"Probably whatever Luis is currently in the middle of."

"Where's Luis?"

"Last known location was the private study on the upper deck. He's been there for an hour and twelve minutes. He's not responding to comms."

Dana looked at Marcus. "We need to go get him."

"I know."

"That wasn't the plan."

"The plan changed."

The radio crackled again, this time with Frank's voice. "Captain. I'm on the yacht."

"What?"

"Don't argue. I came over with the second wave. I've been moving through the lower deck looking for an exfil route. I can hear gunfire on the upper deck. Luis isn't going to make it out without backup."

"Frank, I told you to stay on the Lucky Lady."

"I know what you told me. But I've been listening to the radio for the last hour, and it sounded like things were going sideways, and I don't know if you've noticed but I have a tendency to make bad decisions when alcohol and other people's danger are both involved." Frank's voice was steady—steadier than Marcus had heard it in months. "I'm not going to be much use in a firefight. But I can hold a position. I can cover a retreat. I can make sure Luis gets out."

"Frank—"

"Captain, with respect. Tell me where to set up."

Marcus closed his eyes for one second.

Then he opened them.

"Service corridor on the upper deck. Junction with the main hallway. Position there and cover our exit."

"Copy."

"Frank?"

"Yeah?"

"Don't die."

"That's the second time someone's said that to me tonight. I'm starting to feel like a project."

The line went dead.

Marcus and Dana reached the upper deck. The corridor outside Medina's office—which they had so carefully cleared four minutes ago—now contained six new guards plus the silver-haired man himself, Carlos Medina, holding a phone to his ear and gesturing emphatically at the closed door of the private study at the end of the hall.

The door behind which, presumably, Luis Calderón was currently in significant trouble.

"Plan?" Dana asked.

"Get to Luis. Get to Frank. Get off the yacht."

"Not a great plan."

"Best one I've got." They moved.

The private study was a frozen tableau of violence by the time Marcus and Dana blew through the door.

Luis stood in the center, one arm twisted behind his back by a guard, a gun pressed to his temple. Two other guards had weapons trained on the doorway. Behind the desk, the silver-haired man—Medina, who had apparently come in through a side entrance Marcus hadn't accounted for—watched the proceedings with the calm of someone who had seen worse.

"Well," the silver-haired man said pleasantly. "More visitors. This is quite the evening."

"Release him," Marcus said. His weapon was up, sighted on the guard holding Luis. "Release him and this doesn't have to escalate."

"I think it already has." The man's smile didn't waver. "You've broken into my yacht, assaulted my staff, and apparently stolen data from my personal server. I'm curious what you think 'de-escalation' looks like from here."

"Like you letting us walk away."

"And why would I do that?"

"Because the alternative is a bloodbath that draws Coast Guard, DEA, and every law enforcement agency within a hundred miles." Marcus kept his voice steady. "You're hosting a party full of people who can't afford to be questioned. Politicians. Businessmen. Celebrities. How many of them will flip the moment they're in custody?"

The man's expression flickered. Just slightly.

"You're bluffing."

"I'm observing. You've built your empire on discretion. On the appearance of legitimacy. All of that ends the moment this becomes a crime scene." Marcus took a step forward. "Let us go. We'll take what we came for. You'll spin this as a security drill or a false alarm or whatever story keeps your guests from panicking. Everyone wins."

"Except me. I lose the data."

"The data is already gone." Marcus nodded toward the server. "That device has been transmitting since it connected. Whatever was on your system is now on ours. Killing us doesn't change that."

The man stared at him. Calculating.

Then he laughed.

"You know," he said, "I almost believe you. The confidence. The righteousness. The absolute certainty that you're in control." He shook his head. "But you're not in control, Captain. You're in my world. And in my world, problems don't negotiate their way out."

He nodded at his guards.

"Kill them."

Three weapons came up at once—the guard behind Luis shifting his grip, the two at the door pivoting toward Marcus and Dana. Marcus did the math in the half-second he had left. Two of them. Three guns. Luis pinned. Nothing he could do in time.

They were going to die here.

The first shot came from the doorway.

Not Marcus. Not Dana.

Frank.

He shouldn't have been there—not in this room, not in this fight. He was supposed to be holding the corridor. But Frank had heard Marcus's voice and Medina's response, and Frank had spent thirty years walking into rooms where people were about to die, and apparently the muscle memory was stronger than the orders.

"Captain needs backup," Frank had said earlier. "That's what crew is for."

His shot took the guard holding Luis in the shoulder. Not fatal—Frank's hands were shaking too much for precision—but enough to break the grip, enough to create an opening. Luis moved.

Twenty years of cartel work had taught him how to survive moments like this. He dropped, twisted, grabbed the falling guard's weapon, and came up firing. One guard down. Then the other.

Dana was already engaging the silver-haired man's personal security—more guards flooding in from the corridor, drawn by the gunfire. She moved with terrifying efficiency, putting herself between the door and Marcus, creating space.

"Get the device," she shouted. "I've got this."

Marcus crossed to the server, grabbed Click's device, and shoved it deeper in his vest beside the ledger.

Medina had vanished. Through a side door, presumably. Marcus didn't have time to pursue.

"Luis. Frank. Move." They moved.

The yacht had become a war zone. Gunfire echoed through the corridors. Guests screamed. Somewhere, a fire had started—whether from a muzzle flash or something else, it didn't matter. Smoke was filling the upper deck.

"Gator, we need extraction. Now."

"Already on my way, Cap. Coming to the stern. Look for the ugliest boat in the water."

They fought their way down through the chaos. Frank was lagging—the adrenaline that had carried him this far was fading, and Marcus could see his hands trembling, could see the cost of the effort in his face.

"Keep moving," Marcus said. "We're almost there."

"I'm fine," Frank gasped. "I'm functional."

He wasn't fine. He wasn't functional. But there was no time to argue.

They reached the main deck. The party had dissolved into pure panic—guests in the water, lifeboats being fought over, the beautiful people tearing at each other to escape. Security was overwhelmed, split between the threat above and the chaos below.

Dana led them to the stern, where the Lucky Lady was approaching with all the grace of a drunk elephant.

"Jump," Gator called from the deck. "I'll catch you."

"You'll catch us?"

"Figure of speech. Just jump."

Dana jumped first. Then Luis. Then Frank, who didn't so much jump as fall and was caught—barely—by Luis and Gator working together.

Marcus was last.

He paused at the rail, looking back at the burning yacht, the screaming guests, the security personnel still scanning for targets.

The silver-haired man was at an upper window, watching.

Their eyes met.

The man smiled.

And Marcus knew, with absolute certainty, that this wasn't over. He jumped.

They were a mile away when the Coast Guard arrived.

The Regrettable Decision was burning now—not completely, but enough. The fire suppression systems had kicked in, but the damage was done. The party was over. The guests would spend the next several hours being questioned, detained, processed.

And somewhere in the digital ether, Click's program was already doing its work.

"The device," Luis said, still breathing hard. "Did it complete?"

Marcus pulled it from his vest. The screen showed green.

"It completed."

Luis closed his eyes. For a moment, he looked almost peaceful.

"Then it was worth it."

"Was it?" Marcus looked at him. At Frank, who was slumped against the rail, pale and shaking. At Dana, who was checking everyone for wounds. At Gator, who was pushing the Lucky Lady's engines as hard as they could go. "We almost died. All of us. For data."

"For leverage," Luis corrected. "For evidence. For a weapon we can use against everyone who profits from this."

Frank coughed from his position against the rail.

"Great motivational speech," he said weakly. "Very inspiring. Can we maybe focus on the part where I'm having some kind of cardiac event?"

Dana was there immediately, checking his pulse, his pupils, his breathing.

"You're not having a cardiac event. You're experiencing the consequences of being a fifty-eight-year-old drunk who just engaged in close-quarters combat." She looked at Marcus. "He needs rest. Fluids. Time."

"I need a drink," Frank muttered.

"You need to shut up and let me help you." Frank shut up.

They sailed into the darkness, leaving the chaos behind, carrying secrets that would change everything.

The data was theirs.

Now they had to figure out what to do with it.

CHAPTER TWENTY-ONE

PSALM

Luis kept the last letter in a Ziploc bag. Not a special bag. A standard quart-sized Ziploc.

He read it at sea, when the crew was sleeping and the space between the water and the stars was big enough to hold everything he couldn't carry in daylight.

Dear Papa,

I got a job at a veterinary clinic in Tampa. I touched a dog's heart yesterday—just a checkup, my hand on his chest—and I felt it beating and I thought: this is what I want to do. I want to keep things alive.

I love you. I know that's hard to hear from the person you think you failed. But you didn't fail me, Papa. You just weren't here. And not being here isn't the same as not loving someone. It's just the same shape, from the outside.

Your daughter, Maria

Luis folded the letter along its creases—worn soft by years of handling—and put it back in the Ziploc bag. He zipped it shut with the care of someone sealing a container that held the last breathable air from a world that no longer existed.

Then he went back to work. Because counting—counting accurately, counting honestly, counting every gram—was the only psalm he knew.

CHAPTER TWENTY-TWO

THE DISCOVERY

They found a cove Luis knew from his previous life—a shallow inlet hidden by mangroves, invisible from the main channels, perfect for disappearing.

The Lucky Lady sat dark and quiet, engines off, crew scattered across the deck like survivors of a shipwreck. Which, in a way, they were.

Frank was propped against the cabin wall, a blanket around his shoulders, color slowly returning to his face. Dana had forced fluids into him and was now keeping watch on the approach channels, weapon ready. Gator was doing something mechanical in the engine room that involved swearing and the sound of metal hitting metal.

Luis sat alone at the bow, staring at the water.

And Click was having what could only be described as a religious experience.

"It's everything," Click whispered, scrolling through screens of data on his laptop. "Everything. Financial records. Communication logs. Shell company structures. Payment schedules. It's—" He looked up at Marcus with undisguised awe. "Do you understand what we have?"

"Tell me."

"We have the architecture." Click turned the laptop so Marcus could see. "This isn't just one cartel's books. This is the interface between the cartel and the legitimate world. Banks. Lawyers. Politicians. Every palm that got greased, every favor that got traded, every relationship that made the whole thing possible."

Marcus studied the screen. Names scrolled past—some he recognized, some he didn't. Dollar amounts that staggered him. Dates that went back years.

"Half the Booty," Click said, zooming in on a section. "They're here. Regular payments from three shell companies that trace back to the Mendoza cartel. Not huge amounts—not enough to attract IRS attention—but consistent. Monthly. For over two years."

"They're on cartel payroll."

"They're on cartel retainer. There's a difference." Click pulled up another screen. "Look at this. Communication logs. Coordination schedules. They're not just skimming product—they're actively protecting cartel shipments. Steering interdiction away from flagged vessels. Sharing intel on Coast Guard movements."

"They're working for them."

"They're working with them. Partnership, not employment." Click's eyes were bright with the particular fever of a conspiracy theorist who had just been proven right. "And it goes higher. Look at this name." He pointed.

Anton Voss.

"Black Flag," Marcus said quietly.

"Black Flag isn't a privateer crew. Black Flag is enforcement." Click pulled up more data. "They're the muscle. When someone doesn't cooperate, when someone threatens the arrangement, when someone needs to disappear—Black Flag handles it. They're not competing with Half the Booty. They're the same organization, operating through different fronts."

Marcus felt the weight of it settle on his shoulders.

He'd known it was bad. He'd suspected it was organized. But this—this was a system. A fully integrated network that had turned the privateer program into a tool for cartel operations.

"Who else knows about this?"

"Based on the communication logs? A lot of people. Congressional staffers. DEA agents. Prosecutors." Click's voice dropped. "People in positions to stop it who chose not to. People who got paid to look away."

"Rourke?"

Click shook his head. "Her name doesn't appear anywhere. Either she's genuinely clean, or she's smart enough not to leave evidence."

"Then she might be an ally."

"Or a trap. There's no way to know." Click closed the laptop. "What I do know is that we have enough here to destroy them. Not just Half the Booty. Not just Black Flag. The whole network. The politicians who enabled it. The lawyers who papered it. The businessmen who profited from it."

"And the people who will fight to keep it hidden."

"Yes." Click met his eyes. "The moment we release this, we become the target. Not just for Voss. For everyone whose name appears in these files. And some of those names have a lot more resources than a cartel."

Marcus looked out at the dark water.

"How many names?"

"In total? Two hundred and seventeen individuals with direct financial connections. Another hundred-plus with documented communication. And those are just the ones who left traces." Click paused. "This isn't a corruption scandal. This is an ecosystem."

Marcus found Luis at the bow, still watching the water.

"You knew," Marcus said. It wasn't a question.

"I suspected." Luis didn't turn. "When I was in the business, there were always rumors about government people. Payments that went somewhere official. Protection that came from badges instead of guns." He shrugged. "I never saw the specifics. I just knew it was too easy."

"Too easy?"

"Moving product. Avoiding interdiction. The way certain routes were always clear while others got hit." Luis finally looked at him. "I told myself it was luck. Or skill. Or the natural incompetence of law enforcement. But some part of me knew. We had help. We'd always had help."

"And you kept going."

"I kept going." Luis's voice was flat. "For twenty years. Knowing, on some level, that the system was rigged in our favor. That the cops who caught us were the exception, not the rule." He paused. "That's the thing about corruption. Once you're inside it, you stop seeing it. It just becomes the way things work."

Marcus sat down beside him.

"My daughter called me this morning," Marcus said. "Sarah. First time in months." Luis waited.

"She wanted to know if I was okay. She'd seen something on the news—some privateer incident, someone getting killed—and she wanted to make sure it wasn't me." Marcus stared at the water. "I didn't call her back. I was busy with the operation. I figured I'd do it later."

"Did you?"

"Not yet."

The silence stretched between them.

"I spent my whole career believing the law meant something," Marcus said finally. "That if you followed the rules, it added up to justice." He shook his head. "It doesn't add up. The math was wrong from the start."

"Does that mean you're going to stop?"

"No." Marcus's voice hardened. "It means I'm going to stop pretending that honesty is a strategy. Honesty is a choice. And sometimes the honest choice is to burn everything down."

Luis let out a breath that might have been a laugh in another life. "That's a dangerous way of thinking."

"It's the only way left."

They gathered in the galley at midnight.

Everyone was there—even Frank, who had insisted on participating despite Dana's objections. He looked terrible, but his eyes were clear. The urgency had burned away the alcohol, at least temporarily.

"We have three options," Marcus said. "First: we release everything now. Upload it to every journalist, every agency, every platform we can find. Maximum chaos. Maximum damage."

"Maximum retaliation," Dana added. "The moment it goes public, every name in those files becomes an enemy. And some of those names have kill teams."

"Second option: we go to Rourke. Hand it over to the IRS investigation. Let the system handle it."

Frank laughed bitterly. "The system that's compromised from top to bottom? The system that's been protecting these people for years? That system?"

"It's still an option."

"It's surrender dressed up as procedure."

Marcus nodded. "Third option: we use it as leverage. Not to release—to threaten. We go to Voss, to Trevor Kline, to whoever's at the top of this, and we make them an offer. Back off. Leave us alone. Or we burn everything."

Gator raised a hand. "How's that work, exactly? 'Hey, evil cartel man, please stop being evil or we'll release evidence that you're evil'? They'll kill us before we finish the sentence."

"Which is why we'd have to make it automatic. A dead man's switch. If anything happens to us, the data releases."

"That only works if they believe we'd really do it," Luis said. "And if they know that killing us triggers the release, they might decide to release it themselves—blame it on us, spin the narrative, get ahead of the story."

"Then we're back to option one."

The room fell silent.

Click was typing furiously, running numbers, building projections.

Frank, who had been listening with the focused attention of a thirty-year detective evaluating a case file, finally spoke.

"There's a fourth option."

Everyone turned.

"You don't release everything. You don't threaten anyone directly. You poison them against each other." Frank leaned forward. His hands weren't shaking. His eyes weren't bloodshot. For the first time in months, he was completely present. "I worked organized crime for twelve years. I watched a dozen criminal organizations destroy themselves from inside without a single law enforcement bullet being fired. You know how?"

"How?" Marcus asked.

"Mistrust. You don't need to prove anyone is betraying anyone. You just need to make the betrayal look possible. Plant the doubt. Let them do the work for you." Frank pulled the laptop toward him. "You leak Trevor's communications to the cartel and make it look like he's been talking to the feds. You leak the cartel's payment schedules to Voss and make it look like he's been cut out of the loop. You leak Voss's enforcement records to Trevor and make it look like Voss has been planning to scapegoat him."

"None of that's true."

"Doesn't have to be true. Has to look true. They'll do the rest." Frank's voice had taken on the rhythm of a detective walking another cop through a case. "Criminal organizations run on trust. Strip the trust and they collapse. The cocaine is still there. The networks are still there. But suddenly everyone's looking sideways at everyone else, nobody's coordinating, nobody's communicating, and the whole machine grinds to a halt."

"That's…" Luis was nodding slowly. "That's how the cartels used to handle internal threats. Make the target's allies suspect them. Let them be killed by their own people."

"Standard counter-intelligence playbook," Frank agreed. "I learned it from a federal agent who'd worked it both directions. He told me criminals are easier to manipulate than legitimate businesses because their entire risk model assumes betrayal."

Click was already typing. "I can fabricate the metadata. Make any communication look like it came from anywhere. The technical part is trivial. The strategic part is what matters."

"How long would it take to plan it right?"

"Forty-eight hours to build the package. Then we leak the first piece and watch what happens."

Marcus looked around the table.

His crew. His family. The broken people who had somehow become the only thing holding him together.

"We do Frank's plan," Marcus said. "Slow and surgical. Build the case, plant the seeds, let them tear each other apart. And we keep a copy—the full package, everything—ready to release if they come for us anyway."

"And if they come anyway?"

Marcus thought about the silver-haired man on the yacht. The smile as they escaped.

"Then we make it expensive," he said. "We make it so expensive that anyone who tries regrets it forever."

Frank raised an imaginary glass. "To expensive regrets."

"To expensive regrets," the others echoed.

It wasn't much of a plan.

But it was the only one they had.

The execution was where things got interesting.

Click set up what he called a "disinformation forge" using three laptops, a satellite modem he'd built from parts that Marcus was legally obligated not to ask about, and a power supply rigged to the Lucky Lady's generator through a series of adapters that Gator called "creative" and Dana called "a fire hazard with ambition."

"I need absolute quiet for the next six hours," Click announced, settling into his workspace with the focused intensity of a surgeon preparing for a seventeen-hour operation. "No talking. No music. No engines. No Gator."

"What'd I do?" Gator asked.

"You exist loudly. It's not a criticism. It's a frequency issue."

"I can be quiet."

"You just said that at seventy-three decibels."

Mr. Whiskers had been brought aboard for what Click described as "operational continuity" and everyone else described as "he wouldn't stop crying when I left." The massive orange tabby had claimed the navigation console as his personal territory and was currently shedding on equipment that had cost more than Gator's truck.

"That cat is destroying my radar," Gator observed.

"That cat has better pattern recognition than half the people I've worked with," Click said. "He once alerted me to an ATF surveillance van forty minutes before they knocked. He can stay."

"How did a cat alert you to—"

"He looked at the window and made a specific sound. Different from his hungry sound, his angry sound, and his 'someone is near my litter box' sound. I have them catalogued." Click didn't look up from his typing. "I know that sounds insane."

"It sounds insane," Dana confirmed.

"It is insane. But I was right and the ATF was surprised, so I'm going to keep listening to my cat."

Marcus had learned not to argue with Click's methods. The results spoke for themselves. The man had been raided three times and convicted zero times. His cat had a better track record than most defense lawyers.

There was a moment, around 2 AM, when Click stopped typing and just sat there, staring at his screens. Marcus found him like that—frozen, hands hovering over the keyboard, eyes unfocused.

"Click?"

"I'm thinking about my mother." Click's voice was different. Smaller. "She's the one who bought me my first electronics kit. RadioShack, 1999. I was seven. I took it apart, rebuilt it, and it picked up police frequencies. She told the neighbors I was a prodigy." He paused. "She stopped calling me that when I got expelled from MIT. Started calling me 'my son who's going through a phase.' The phase is now thirteen years old."

"Does she know what you do?"

"She thinks I'm in IT consulting. Which is technically true in the same way that a bank robber is in asset redistribution." Click resumed typing. "I'd like to tell her someday. Not about the weapons. About this. About being part of something that mattered."

He didn't say anything else.

Marcus didn't push it.

Sometimes the most important conversations were the ones that ended in silence.

The first leak went out at midnight.

Click had designed it like a Russian nesting doll of deception: the outer layer was the communication itself, the middle layer was the fabricated metadata pointing to a federal source, and the inner layer—invisible to anyone without Click's specific tools—was a tracker that would tell them exactly who opened it, when, and what they did next.

"I call it 'The Onion,'" Click said proudly. "Because it has layers. And because it makes people cry."

"That's terrible," Dana said.

"The name or the program?"

"Both. But mostly the name."

By dawn, the first domino had fallen. Three of Trevor's investors pulled their money. By noon, two cartel contacts had gone dark. By evening, Voss was calling Trevor with threats that Click's monitoring picked up in real time.

"He's using the word 'liability' a lot," Click reported, headphones on, transcribing. "Also 'exposure.' Also a word in Norwegian that my translation software says means either 'consequences' or 'elk hunting.' I'm going with consequences."

"Could be elk hunting," Gator said. "I've seen those Scandinavian guys. They're intense about their elk."

"It's consequences, Gator."

"I'm just saying, context matters."

Rourke called on the third day.

Marcus almost didn't answer. But Rourke had been the only federal agent who'd treated them like people instead of problems, and that earned her a conversation.

"Captain Hale. I've been watching the news." Her voice was careful, measuring. "Half the Booty's investors are fleeing. Their cartel contacts are going silent. Someone is dismantling their operation piece by piece using information that looks a lot like what was on that yacht server." Marcus said nothing.

"I'm not going to ask if you're involved," Rourke continued. "Because if you are, I'd have to act on that information, and frankly I'd rather not. What I will tell you is that my own investigation has turned up something interesting."

"What?"

"The evidence that was planted on your boat—the forty-seven kilos? I pulled the seizure stamps. They trace back to a Half the Booty operation from nine months ago. An operation where they reported seizing six hundred kilos."

She paused. "They actually seized seven hundred and twelve. The difference was never accounted for."

"You can prove that?"

"I can prove that their numbers don't add up. I can prove that the stamps on your boat match product that should have been in federal evidence. And I can prove that three people in the chain of custody received payments from shell companies connected to Black Flag." Another pause. "I'm going to include all of this in my next report. That report will be filed Monday morning. I thought you might want to know."

"Why are you telling me this?"

Rourke was quiet for a moment.

"Because you filed clean numbers, Captain. From day one. Every report accurate, every chain of custody documented, every piece of evidence accounted for." Her voice softened, just slightly. "In eighteen years of criminal investigations, I've never seen that. Not once. And I decided that deserved something more than a shrug and a filing cabinet." She hung up.

Marcus stood in the Lucky Lady's galley, holding the phone, feeling something he hadn't felt in a long time.

Hope.

Not the desperate kind. The quiet kind—the one that arrives when you realize you're not entirely alone in a system designed to make you feel like you are.

Later, alone in his cabin, Marcus finally called his daughter.

She answered on the third ring.

"Dad?"

"Hey, sweetheart. Sorry I didn't call back earlier."

"Are you okay? I saw the news—"

"I'm fine. Just busy." He paused. "Actually, that's not true. I'm not fine. But I'm alive, and I wanted you to know that."

Silence on the line.

"I've been thinking about something you said," Marcus continued. "Years ago. About how I was never really there."

"Dad, you don't have to—"

"I do. Because you were right." He closed his eyes. "I've spent my whole life hiding behind the mission. Behind the uniform. Behind being right. And it cost me everything that mattered."

"It's not too late."

"Maybe not." He took a breath. "I'm in the middle of something. Something that might end badly. I can't explain it, and I wouldn't if I could. But I wanted you to know—whatever happens—I'm sorry. For all of it. For not being there. For not seeing you. For choosing the job over the family."

"Dad—"

"I love you, Sarah. I should have said that more. I should have shown it more. I should have been more."

The silence lasted a long moment.

Then his daughter's voice, soft and careful: "I love you too, Dad. Whatever happens... I love you too."

Marcus hung up.

He sat in the darkness, listening to the water lap against the hull, and thought about all the things he couldn't take back.

But maybe—just maybe—he could still do something that mattered.

Outside, the sun was beginning to rise.

They had work to do.

CHAPTER TWENTY-THREE

PRIVATEER VS. PRIVATEER

The war started the next morning.

Not a war of bullets and boats—not yet. A war of lawyers and press releases and regulatory complaints. The kind of war that rich people fight, where the weapons are money and connections and the willingness to bury opponents under mountains of paperwork.

Half the Booty, Global filed injunctions. Cease and desist orders. Defamation claims worth more than Marcus would make in ten lifetimes. Their lawyers were everywhere—on television, in courtrooms, in congressional offices.

The message was clear: Privateer LLC was to be destroyed.

"We're hemorrhaging money," Patricia Reyes reported during an emergency conference call. "Every filing they make requires a response. Every response costs thousands. They're not trying to win—they're trying to bleed you dry."

"We don't have money to bleed," Frank pointed out.

"That's the point."

But in the background, Frank's plan was already working.

Click had spent forty-eight hours building the disinformation package. Not just fabricated communications—a complete ecosystem of evidence, each piece designed to point at someone different, each piece deniable, each piece just credible enough to be trusted by the people most invested in trusting it.

The first leak went out at midnight.

Encrypted communications between Half the Booty and their cartel contacts—re-routed to make it look like Trevor had shared them with federal agents. The cartels would see their own messages, tagged with DEA metadata that Click had fabricated with terrifying precision.

The second leak went out at 2 AM.

Financial records showing cartel money flowing through Half the Booty's accounts—sent to the cartel's competitors with a note suggesting Trevor was playing both sides.

The third leak went out at 4 AM.

Internal Half the Booty communications—edited just enough to suggest Trevor was planning to abandon his partners—sent to those partners directly.

By dawn, Trevor Kline's phone was ringing off the hook.

By noon, three of his investors had pulled out.

By evening, two of his cartel contacts had gone dark.

And somewhere in international waters, a conversation was happening that would change everything.

Anton Voss called Trevor at 11 PM.

They didn't know this because of the tracking program—Voss was too careful for that. They knew because Luis's network included someone on the inside of Black Flag. Someone who owed Luis a debt measured in blood.

The conversation, as relayed, went like this:

"You've become a liability," Voss said.

"This isn't my fault. Someone is sabotaging—"

"Someone is always sabotaging. The question is whether you're worth protecting through the sabotage."

"Anton, we have a partnership—"

"We have an arrangement. Arrangements can be… rearranged." A pause. "I'm going to give you one chance. Find the source of the leak. Eliminate it. Restore confidence."

"And if I can't?"

"Then you become the elimination that restores confidence."

The line went dead.

Trevor figured it out faster than Marcus expected.

The Regrettable Decision was anchored at a marina in Key Largo—neutral territory, away from Privateer Marina's surveillance—when Half the Booty's flagship appeared on the horizon.

Then two more boats. Then three.

"Company," Dana announced, checking her weapon.

Marcus counted the approaching vessels. Five boats. Maybe thirty personnel. All armed.

They had six people and a charter fishing boat with fire damage.

"Options?" Marcus asked.

"We could run," Luis said. "They're faster, but if we hit shallow water—"

"They'll corner us eventually."

"We could surrender," Frank suggested. "Appeal to whatever remains of Trevor's self-preservation instinct."

"He's past self-preservation. He's in survival mode."

Click was doing something on his laptop—typing furiously, muttering equations under his breath.

"I have an idea," Click said.

"Does it involve explosions?"

"It involves the Coast Guard."

Everyone stared at him.

"The Coast Guard that revoked our bail?" Dana asked.

"The Coast Guard that patrols these waters and responds to emergency beacons." Click held up a device. "I may have... acquired... one of their distress frequencies. If I broadcast a Mayday from coordinates about a mile west of here—"

"They'll respond."

"They'll respond in force. And when they arrive, they'll find Half the Booty's armed fleet approaching a civilian fishing charter in what looks very much like an act of piracy."

Gator grinned. "You want to get them arrested for attacking us?"

"I want to get them caught on camera attacking someone. What happens after that is up to the lawyers."

Marcus looked at the approaching boats. Three minutes, maybe less.

"Do it."

Then a different transmission cut through the radio chatter.

"Lucky Lady, this is Sent It Maritime. Boss, I have visual on five hostiles. I am inbound with backup."

Marcus stared at the radio.

"Chad," he said carefully. "Where are you?"

"About six minutes out. I was trailing your signature for content—I know, I know, we'll talk about consent later, but right now please tell me you want backup, because I have backup."

"What kind of backup?"

"My audience." A long silence.

"Chad, what does that mean?"

"I went live thirty minutes ago. I told my followers something was about to happen. I asked anyone with a fast boat in South Florida who wanted to be part of history to come to these coordinates. There are currently—" pause— "twenty-three vessels converging on this location. None of them are armed. All of them are filming."

Dana looked at Marcus. "He's weaponizing influencers."

"He's weaponizing witnesses," Marcus corrected. "Click, hold the Mayday."

"Captain?"

"Hold it. Let's see what Chad brings."

The first boats appeared three minutes later.

Not military. Not law enforcement. A flotilla of fishing boats, pleasure cruisers, jet skis, and one inexplicable houseboat with a hot tub on the upper deck in which three people were actively sitting. Every single vessel had at least one person on board with a phone or camera pointed at the developing situation.

They came in at high speed, peeling off in a circle around the Lucky Lady, forming an impromptu cordon between Privateer LLC and Half the Booty's approaching fleet.

A pontoon boat with "KAREN'S BACHELORETTE VOYAGE" written in streamers across the bow took up a position directly in front of Half the Booty's lead vessel. Seven women in matching pink tank tops that read "ANCHORS AND HANGOVERS" stared down thirty armed men. One of them was holding a bottle of Prosecco like a weapon. Another was livestreaming on three phones simultaneously.

"Oh my God," Dana said.

"Oh my GOD," Chad agreed, but with a completely different inflection.

Chad's voice came over the radio, jubilant and cracking with adrenaline.

"YOU CAN'T MURDER PEOPLE ON LIVE STREAM, BRO. THE FCC HAS RULES."

"I don't think the FCC—"

"DUDE, IT'S CONTENT NOW. WE'RE ALL CONTENT NOW. WE HAVE THIRTY THOUSAND VIEWERS WATCHING THIS LIVE."

The lead boat from Half the Booty slowed.

The men on its deck, who had been preparing to open fire on what they'd assumed was an isolated target, now realized they were surrounded by approximately forty private citizens recording everything they did. Including a bachelorette party. Including three people in a hot tub. Including a man on a jet ski who appeared to be wearing nothing but swim trunks and a GoPro head mount.

The radio chatter from Half the Booty's vessels became chaotic. Marcus could hear arguments over open frequencies. Someone shouting about lawyers. Someone else shouting about livestreams. A third voice—panicked, young—screaming "THERE ARE BACHELORETTES, SIR. WE CANNOT SHOOT THROUGH BACHELORETTES."

Someone—possibly Trevor himself—shouting at everyone to stand down.

But it was too late for stand down.

The lead boat fired anyway.

Whether it was panic, miscommunication, or simply the inertia of men who had committed psychologically to violence and couldn't reverse course in time, three rounds of gunfire cracked across the water. Two missed. One struck the railing of a fishing boat captained by a sixty-five-year-old retiree named Walter who, unbeknownst to everyone including Chad's audience, had served two tours in Vietnam and had been hoping for a quiet day of offshore fishing with his wife, Dolores.

Dolores had not had a quiet day in forty-three years of marriage to Walter.

She was not going to start now.

"WALTER," Dolores screamed. "THEY'RE SHOOTING AT US."

Walter ducked behind his console. He stayed down for approximately two seconds. Then he came up holding a flare gun he kept for emergencies. He was not panicked. He was not scared. He was a sixty-five-year-old Marine who had survived the Tet Offensive, three heart procedures, and Dolores's cooking, and he was not about to let some fraternity reject with a machine gun ruin his Tuesday.

"Walter, don't you DARE," Dolores said, though she was already holding up her phone.

"Dolores, I love you," Walter said. "Film this."

He fired the flare gun directly at the muzzle flash he had just witnessed.

The flare did not explode the attacking vessel. The flare arced across the water in a beautiful parabola of orange phosphorus and landed approximately ten feet short, where it hissed and sputtered on the surface like a very angry birthday candle.

Walter looked at the result.

"Shit," he said.

"LANGUAGE," Dolores said, still filming.

"Dolores, they shot at me."

"And you missed. We'll discuss it later."

On Chad's livestream, which had now reached sixty-two thousand concurrent viewers, the chat was losing its collective mind. Someone had already clipped Walter's shot and set it to the 1812 Overture. Someone else was starting a GoFundMe. The phrase "FLARE GUN GRANDPA" was trending in three countries.

The bachelorette party was chanting "WAL-TER, WAL-TER" in unison.

The man in the hot tub raised a beer in salute.

Then, finally, the Coast Guard arrived.

Three cutters. A helicopter. A full response to what had become, thanks to Chad's livestream, a national news event.

Half the Booty's fleet scattered.

Trevor Kline's flagship was boarded within minutes.

Marcus watched from the deck of the Lucky Lady as his enemy was led away in handcuffs, surrounded by evidence of exactly the kind of violence he'd been pretending not to authorize.

"Holy shit," Frank breathed. "It worked."

"Technically," Click said, "we're also probably going to be arrested."

"But they'll be arrested more."

"That's true."

Gator was watching Walter being interviewed by a local news crew. "I want to be that guy when I grow up."

"You're forty-one."

"Old enough to know what I want. Young enough to start working on it."

Dana put a hand on Marcus's shoulder.

"We won," she said.

Marcus watched Trevor being escorted onto the Coast Guard cutter, his face twisted with rage, his empire crumbling around him.

"We won this," Marcus said. "We haven't won yet." His phone buzzed.

A text from Chad: *bro DID YOU SEE THAT 47K viewers we are TRENDING*

Marcus didn't respond.

But for once, he didn't entirely hate the influencer.

Maybe.

A little.

He'd never admit it.

CHAPTER TWENTY-FOUR

THE RECKONING

Winning, it turned out, was complicated.

Trevor Kline was arrested. Half the Booty's operations were suspended. The evidence of their attack on the Regrettable Decision was clear enough—and famous enough, thanks to Walter the Vietnam veteran and his flare gun—that even compromised prosecutors had to act.

But Privateer LLC's own legal troubles didn't disappear.

They were still fugitives. Still accused of trafficking. Still suspended, impounded, destroyed in every official sense. And Anton Voss was still out there.

They were laying low in Homestead, scattered across safe houses and motels, regrouping after the Second Chance burned. The hearing—the real hearing, the one that would determine whether they went to prison or went free—was scheduled for the following Monday. The charges were serious. The evidence against them, planted or not, was still in federal custody. And the judge assigned to their case had a reputation for being unsympathetic to "creative interpretations of maritime law."

Marcus had called a planning session at a rental house Click had secured through methods no one wanted to examine too closely. They needed leverage. They needed a strategy. They needed everyone present and functional.

Frank was supposed to be there at eight.

By nine-thirty, he still hadn't arrived.

"I'll find him," Gator said, already reaching for his keys.

He found Frank at a bar three miles away—not the Rusty Anchor, but a place even worse, a place that didn't bother with a name because its clientele didn't care. Frank was at the end of the bar, hunched over his fourth or fifth whiskey, talking to no one.

"Frank." Gator sat down beside him. "We got a meeting."

"I know."

"You're late."

"I know that too." Frank took a long drink. His hands weren't shaking, but only because the alcohol had steadied them. "I'll be there."

"When?"

"When I'm ready." Frank turned to look at him. His eyes were bloodshot, unfocused in a way that went beyond the drinks. "You ever think about how none of this matters?"

"What do you mean?"

"I mean we're in a shrimp boat pretending to be pirates. We burned our own ship to fake our deaths. We're living in motels under fake names, planning to take down a criminal empire with duct tape and good intentions." Frank laughed. It was an ugly sound. "And even if we win—even if we somehow pull this off—nothing changes. The system stays the same. The money flows the same direction. Someone else becomes the next Voss, and someone else after that."

"Cap doesn't think that way."

"Cap's an idealist. Idealists are dangerous. They make you believe in things that aren't true." Frank finished his drink and signaled for another. "You know what I learned in thirty years as a cop? The bad guys don't lose. They just get replaced. It's like cutting weeds. You pull one out, two more grow back."

Gator was quiet for a moment.

"So why are you here?"

"Because I've got nothing else." Frank's voice was flat. "No wife. No kids who want to see me. No career. No purpose. This is all I've got left, and I'm not even good at it anymore."

"That's not true."

"Isn't it?" Frank looked at him directly. "Name one thing I've contributed in the last month. One thing that actually mattered."

"You designed the disinformation strategy that took down Trevor Kline."

Frank blinked. He hadn't expected that.

"You read Eddie Reyes from thirty yards away when nobody else saw it. You analyzed the go-fast boat pilot's drift pattern on our first intercept. You showed up at the yacht with a gun when nobody asked you to and saved Luis's life." Gator's voice was steady. "Your hands shake. Your judgment is shit when you're drunk. Both of those things are true. But your brain—your brain is the best on this crew, and that's including Click, who has like four PhDs."

"Three. Click has three."

"Whatever. The point is, when you're sober, you're scary. And when you're drunk, you're still better than most people are sober." Gator paused. "I'm not saying you don't have a problem. You got a problem. We all see it. But the problem ain't that you don't matter. The problem is that you don't believe you do."

Frank stared at his glass.

"That's the most coherent thing I've ever heard you say," Frank said.

"Yeah, I been working on it. Click made me read a book."

"What book?"

"Some thing about feelings. I didn't finish it. But I got the basic idea." Gator took the whiskey out of Frank's hand and set it on the bar. "Come back to the meeting, Frank. We need you. The whole crew. But specifically the version of you that doesn't smell like this."

Frank looked at him for a long moment.

Then he stood up.

"Fine," he said. "But I'm not promising anything."

"Don't have to. Just have to show up."

Gator brought Frank back to the safe house an hour later.

Marcus met them at the door. One look at Frank told him everything he needed to know.

"Meeting's postponed," Marcus said quietly. "Everyone go get some sleep."

The others filed out. Dana lingered, watching Frank slump into a chair in the corner.

"This is going to get worse," she said to Marcus.

"I know."

"He's not operational. You can't take him on the Absolution in this condition."

"I know that too."

Dana shook her head. "Then what are you going to do?"

Marcus watched Frank staring at the wall, empty glass in hand, already reaching for a bottle that someone had left on the counter.

"I'm going to give him a choice," Marcus said. "Same choice I gave everyone else. Be part of this or walk away."

"And if he can't be part of it?"

"Then I'll find a way to help him anyway. He's crew. That doesn't stop because he's struggling."

Dana's expression softened slightly.

"You know what his problem is? He's never had anyone who didn't give up on him. His wife gave up. His kids gave up. The department gave up." She paused. "Maybe that's what he needs. Someone who doesn't." She walked out.

Marcus crossed the room and sat down across from Frank.

"Talk to me," he said.

Frank's eyes moved to him slowly.

"About what?"

"About whatever's going on in your head right now. The drinking. The despair. Whatever's eating you."

"Nothing to talk about." Frank reached for the bottle. "I'm fine."

Marcus took the bottle first.

"No," he said. "You're not. And pretending otherwise is going to get you killed."

Frank's jaw tightened.

"Maybe that's the point."

"I don't accept that." Marcus leaned forward. "I've lost enough, Frank. I've lost my marriage, my daughter, my career, my boat. I'm not losing my crew. Not to bullets, not to Voss, and not to a bottle."

"Some things can't be saved."

"Maybe. But I don't know that yet. Neither do you." Marcus set the bottle aside. "Here's what's going to happen. Tomorrow morning, 8 AM, we're having that meeting. You're going to be there. Sober. Present. Part of this."

"And if I can't?"

"Then we'll figure that out together. But you don't get to give up. Not while I'm still fighting."

Frank was quiet for a long moment.

"You really believe that? That people can change?"

Marcus thought about his daughter. About the phone calls he'd never made and the presence he'd never provided.

"I believe they can try," he said. "I believe trying is worth something, even when it doesn't work."

Frank's face softened—just the eyes, just for a second.

"You sound like a fortune cookie."

"I sound like a man who's made a lot of mistakes and is trying not to make more." Marcus stood. "8 AM, Frank. Be there." He walked out.

Frank sat alone in the dark room, staring at the bottle Marcus had left on the counter.

He didn't reach for it.

Not tonight.

But tomorrow was another question.

Frank showed up at 7:45.

He looked like hell—unshaven, hollow-eyed, smelling faintly of the mouthwash he'd used to cover the whiskey—but he was there. Present. Vertical.

It was more than Marcus had expected.

The crew gathered around the kitchen table. Luis spread out documents he'd been compiling for weeks. Click had his tablet running some kind of analysis that made everyone else's eyes glaze over. Dana stood by the window, watching the street.

"We need leverage," Luis said. "The evidence against us is planted, but planted evidence is still evidence. The prosecutors don't care about truth—they care about convictions. If we walk into that courtroom with nothing but our word against documented seizure reports, we lose."

"Trevor's communications," Marcus said. "The tracking data—"

"Illegally obtained. Inadmissible." Luis shook his head. "We need something the court will accept. Something that makes the prosecution more afraid of proceeding than of dropping the case."

"And you have that?"

Luis was quiet for a moment.

"I have one more contact," he said finally. "Someone I hoped I'd never have to call."

"Who?"

"Someone who knows where all the bodies are buried." Luis's voice was flat. "Literally."

The room went silent.

"There's a woman," Luis continued. "Elena Vasquez. She used to run logistics for three different cartels—not product, information. She kept records. Detailed records. The kind that show who paid who, when, and for what. Politicians. Judges. Prosecutors. Anyone who ever took cartel money and thought they were clever about it."

"Why would she help us?"

"Because I helped her once. A long time ago. Before I went away." Luis looked at Marcus. "She owes me. And she's the kind of person who pays her debts."

"Where is she?"

"Miami. She'll meet me tonight. Alone."

Dana turned from the window. "That's a risk."

"Everything's a risk." Luis stood. "But this is the only play we have left."

The meeting happened at 3 AM in a parking lot outside a closed Waffle House.

Luis went alone. The crew waited in the van—a rented vehicle because the Regrettable Decision was now evidence—watching through binoculars that Click had enhanced beyond their original specifications.

A car pulled up. Black sedan. Tinted windows.

A woman stepped out.

She was maybe sixty, maybe older, with gray hair pulled back and a stillness earned through decades of practicing patience in situations where patience was survival.

Luis and the woman spoke for seventeen minutes. There was no audio—Click's equipment wasn't that good—but their body language told a story. Old debts. Old connections. The kind of history that didn't end, only transformed.

When Luis returned to the van, he was carrying a manila envelope.

"What's in there?" Marcus asked.

"Insurance." Luis didn't elaborate. "We'll present it tomorrow. To the judge, directly. It won't make the charges disappear, but it will make them reconsider their approach."

"What kind of insurance makes federal prosecutors reconsider?"

Luis looked at him.

"The kind that reminds them how many of them are implicated in things they'd rather stay hidden."

The hearing started at 9 AM.

Judge Harold Whitfield—a severe man in his sixties who looked like he had never once in his life experienced joy—presided over a courtroom packed with reporters, lawyers, and federal agents who were very much hoping their involvement in certain activities wouldn't become public.

The prosecution presented their case: drugs found on the Second Chance, crew with questionable backgrounds, a pattern of behavior suggesting involvement in the very crimes they claimed to be fighting.

Patricia Reyes presented the defense: planted evidence, coordinated attacks from rival crews, a systematic campaign to destroy honest operators who threatened corrupt interests.

It was not going well.

Judge Whitfield was unmoved by arguments about rival crews. He was unmoved by claims of persecution. He was, based on his expression, unmoved by the concept of human emotion in general.

And then Luis stood up.

"Your Honor," he said, "the defense requests permission to submit additional evidence."

Whitfield frowned. "This is highly irregular, Mr. Calderón. Evidence submission deadlines—"

"This evidence relates to the integrity of the prosecution's case. And the integrity of certain individuals involved in bringing these charges."

The courtroom went silent.

The lead prosecutor—a man named Richardson who had been confident all morning—suddenly looked less confident.

"Approach," Whitfield said.

Luis approached the bench with the manila envelope.

Whitfield opened it.

He read for approximately ninety seconds.

His expression didn't change, but his eyes narrowed—a recognition that the game had just fundamentally altered.

"We'll take a brief recess," Whitfield announced. "Counsel will join me in chambers. All counsel."

What happened in chambers stayed in chambers.

But when they emerged forty-five minutes later, the prosecution's demeanor had transformed.

Richardson stood. "Your Honor, the prosecution moves to dismiss all charges against the defendants."

A gasp rippled through the courtroom.

"On what grounds?" Whitfield asked, though he clearly already knew.

"Newly discovered evidence suggesting prosecutorial error and potential contamination of the chain of custody."

Whitfield nodded. "Motion granted. The defendants are released. Bail conditions are vacated. This matter is dismissed with prejudice."

He banged his gavel.

It was over.

Outside the courthouse, surrounded by reporters shouting questions, Marcus found Luis standing apart from the crowd.

"What was in that envelope?"

Luis lit a cigarette—a habit Marcus had never seen him indulge before.

"Receipts," Luis said. "The kind that show who paid for what. The kind that show which prosecutors attended which parties on which yachts. The kind that make people very eager to cooperate."

"That sounds like blackmail."

"That sounds like leverage." Luis exhaled smoke. "I told you—information is worth more than product."

"And the woman in the parking lot?"

"Someone who's been collecting information for a very long time. Someone who understood, long before anyone else, that the real power in the drug trade isn't the drugs. It's knowing who bought them."

Marcus watched the reporters, the cameras, the chaos of a story that none of them fully understood.

"We're free," he said.

"We're released," Luis corrected. "Freedom is something else."

He finished his cigarette and crushed it under his heel.

"The charges are dropped. Our licenses are still suspended. Our boat is still impounded. Trevor is in custody but Voss is still out there." Luis looked at Marcus. "We won a battle. The war isn't over."

As if on cue, Marcus's phone buzzed.

Unknown number. He answered.

"Captain Hale." Anton Voss's voice was calm as ever. "Congratulations on your legal victory."

CHAPTER TWENTY-FIVE

THE SECOND CHANCE BURNS

They got the boat back on a Thursday.

The impound process took two weeks—paperwork, inspections, the slow grinding of bureaucracy processing a case it didn't fully understand. But eventually, the Second Chance was released from federal custody and returned to its registered owners.

Privateer LLC.

Still suspended, technically. Still not authorized to operate. But owners of a boat that was, for the first time in months, actually theirs.

Marcus stood at the helm and let himself feel it.

The wheel was the same. Slightly worn on the left grip where his hand always rested during long watches. The compass was the same—the one Gator had salvaged from a decommissioned cutter and installed with more enthusiasm than precision, so it always read three degrees east of true. The deck was the same, with the scorch mark near the bow where Click's "warning shot" had misfired during their first real engagement.

This was his boat. His command. His home.

After Laura left, after Sarah stopped calling, after the Coast Guard became just another institution that processed people instead of protecting them—this was what remained. Four walls that moved. A purpose that made sense. A place where being distant was called "command presence" instead of "emotional unavailability."

He'd thought, when he bought her, that the Second Chance was a boat.

Now he understood she was a second chance. The name wasn't clever wordplay. It was prophecy.

They spent the first day back aboard just existing. Checking systems. Assessing damage from the impound—nothing serious, just the general neglect of evidence lockers that weren't designed for maritime equipment.

Gator disappeared into the engine room and emerged hours later, covered in grease, reporting that the Caterpillars were "still beautiful, just needed some love."

Click rebuilt his surveillance equipment from components he'd cached in locations Marcus didn't want to know about.

Dana ran security protocols, checking for bugs, trackers, anything that might have been planted during their absence.

Frank sat on deck with a beer and watched the sunset like a man who wasn't sure how many more sunsets he'd get.

And Luis made calls. Always calls. Building something. Planning something.

Marcus stood at the helm, hands on a wheel that finally felt like his again, and allowed himself a moment of fragile peace.

It lasted about four hours.

The explosion woke them at 2:47 AM.

Not on the boat—nearby. Close enough to rattle the hull, far enough that the Second Chance herself wasn't hit.

Marcus was on deck in seconds, weapon drawn, scanning for threats.

The marina was chaos.

The boat three slips down—the Tax Write-Off—was fully engulfed in flames. The boat next to it was catching. Fire spread across the water where fuel had spilled, turning the harbor into something out of a nightmare.

People were screaming. Running. Some jumping into the water, some trying to fight the fire, most just fleeing.

"What the hell?" Gator emerged from below deck, shirtless, wielding what appeared to be a shotgun in one hand and a fire extinguisher in the other.

"Bomb," Dana said, appearing beside Marcus. "Professional. Shaped charge. Designed to maximize fire spread."

"Who—" The radio crackled.

"Captain Hale." Voss's voice. Calm. Unhurried. "I told you the war wasn't over."

Marcus grabbed the radio. "What did you do?"

"I sent a message. The Tax Write-Off was skimming from the wrong people. Now they're not." A pause. "Your boat is next. You have approximately four minutes to evacuate."

The line went dead.

Everyone stared at each other.

Then they moved.

They grabbed what they could.

Weapons. Documents. Equipment. The things that couldn't be replaced, the things that mattered.

Three minutes.

Gator was trying to start the engines, but something was wrong—the systems weren't responding. Click dove below deck to check, emerged with an expression of horror.

"They've disabled the fuel pumps. Remote kill. We can't move her."

Two minutes.

Luis was shouting coordinates into a phone, calling in favors, trying to arrange evacuation for a crew that was about to be homeless again.

One minute.

They piled into the marina's emergency tender—a small inflatable that was never meant to hold six people and definitely wasn't meant for a high-speed escape.

Marcus was the last one off.

He stood at the rail of the Second Chance, looking at the boat that had been his command, his home, his purpose.

The galley where they'd argued about money and morality. The deck where Luis had told him about Maria. The cabin where he'd lain awake at night, wondering if he was doing the right thing or just finding new ways to hide from the people who needed him.

Sarah had left a voicemail two days ago. He'd listened to it three times but hadn't called back. She was pregnant, she'd said. Due in February. She wanted him to know.

He'd meant to call. Tomorrow. When things settled down. When he had time.

There was never time.

"Captain!" Dana screamed from the tender. "NOW!"

Marcus looked at the Second Chance one last time.

Then he jumped.

Ten seconds later, the boat exploded.

They watched from a hundred yards away as everything burned.

Fire consumed the hull. The deck. The equipment they'd spent months acquiring. The compass that read three degrees east. The wheel with the worn left grip. The scorch mark from Click's first misfire.

The Second Chance burned like a funeral pyre.

Which, Marcus supposed, was exactly what it was.

Gator was crying. Actually crying—tears cutting through the grease on his face, his body shaking with sobs he couldn't control.

"My boat," he kept saying. "That was my boat."

Then, after a long silence, quieter: "There was a sandwich in the galley fridge. I made it this morning. Turkey and that good mustard. I was gonna eat it tonight."

Nobody said anything.

"Who the fuck," Gator said, to the water and to God and to the Florida sky, "bombs a boat with a man's sandwich on it."

Dana put a hand on his shoulder. She didn't say anything. There wasn't anything to say. A man's sandwich, in a man's galley fridge, on a man's boat—in the specific grammar of grief Gator was using, the sandwich was somehow carrying more of the weight than the boat, because the boat was large enough to be abstract and the sandwich was small enough to be real.

Click sat in the bow of the tender, staring at nothing, his mind processing a catastrophe it couldn't quite accept.

Frank drank from his flask with the methodical determination of a man who intended to finish every drop before morning.

Dana held her weapon, scanning the darkness for threats that had already done their damage and vanished.

Luis was still on the phone. Still working. Still building.

And Marcus watched his ship burn and thought about Sarah's voicemail. About the grandchild he might never meet. About all the tomorrows he'd wasted waiting for a better time that never came.

The Second Chance was gone.

But maybe—maybe—there was still time for a third.

They washed up on shore three hours later.

A marina they'd never used, far enough from the chaos that no one asked questions, close enough that they could see the smoke still rising in the distance.

Six people. No boat. No license. No authority. No legal standing. No plan.

Just each other.

CHAPTER TWENTY-FIVE

"What now?" Click asked. His voice was hoarse, empty.

Marcus didn't answer immediately.

He thought about the Coastal Compliance, burning on the water, the story that had started all of this.

He thought about Anton Voss, out there in the dark, patient and merciless and absolutely certain of victory.

He thought about Sarah's voice on the voicemail. The hope in it. The uncertainty.

"We rebuild," Marcus said.

Gator laughed, bitter and broken. "With what? We got nothing."

"We have us." Marcus looked at his crew—battered, destroyed, but still there. Still together. "We have what we know. What we've learned. What we've become."

"That's not enough," Frank said.

"It's going to have to be." Dana stood up.

"He's right," she said. "We started with less than this. We built something once. We can build it again."

"And Voss?" Luis asked.

Marcus thought about it.

"Voss thinks he's won. Voss thinks we're finished." Marcus felt resolve settle into his chest—cold, sharp, unbreakable. "That's his mistake."

"What kind of mistake?"

"The kind where you stop watching for threats because you think you've already eliminated them." Marcus looked at his crew. "We're not privateers anymore. We're not licensed. We're not official. We're ghosts."

Click's eyes lit up. "Ghosts have advantages."

"Ghosts can go places living people can't," Luis agreed.

Gator wiped his face. "Ghosts can fuck shit up."

Frank took one more drink, then capped his flask.

"I always wanted to haunt someone," he said.

Marcus allowed himself the ghost of a smile.

They had lost everything.

Which meant they had nothing left to lose.

And that, in its way, was a kind of freedom.

"Alright," Marcus said. "Let's go haunt someone."

PART FOUR

GHOSTS

INTERCEPTED COMMUNICATION—DECLASSIFIED

FROM: Trevor Kline (Federal Detention Facility, Coleman, FL)

TO: [Legal Counsel—REDACTED]

RE: Re: Re: Re: Appeal Status / Please Get Me Out of Here

Gerald,

Day 47. They make us wear jumpsuits. Orange. Not my color. Not anyone's color. Orange is the color of traffic cones and bargain cheese. I am neither.

The food is an atrocity. I've started a petition to have the cafeteria investigated for human rights violations. Seven people have signed it. Three of them are in for murder. They understand quality of life.

I understand you're "working on the appeal." You've been "working on the appeal" since I arrived. I pay your firm $1,800 an hour. That's $43,200 a day. For that money, I expect either my freedom or a compelling explanation of where the money is going. If the answer is "research," I want to see the research. If the answer is "meetings," I want to see the meeting notes. If the answer is "I'm playing golf on a boat I bought with your retainer," I want to see the boat.

I should note that Hale's crew is still operating. They've apparently become folk heroes. There's a documentary. A DOCUMENTARY, Gerald. About people who live on a shrimp boat and chase drug dealers with equipment from a pawn shop. And I'm in HERE.

The universe has a sense of humor. It's not a good sense of humor—it's the kind that pulls wings off flies and calls it physical comedy—but it's persistent.

Please accelerate the appeal. I don't belong here. I belong on a stage telling people how I survived this. There's a TED Talk in this experience. Maybe a book.

Working title: "From Piracy to Profit: Lessons in Adaptive Leadership."

Pre-orders are going to be strong.

—TK

P.S. My cellmate is a man named Darryl who was convicted of securities fraud. He's actually very pleasant. We've started a book club. Our first selection is "The Prince" by Machiavelli. Darryl thinks it's "a bit soft." I'm concerned about Darryl.

CHAPTER TWENTY-SIX

GHOST OPERATIONS

The first unauthorized operation happened because Gator couldn't sleep and Luis couldn't stop listening.

Three days after Frank traced the evidence chain. Two days after Click compiled the full data package from the yacht drives. One day after Marcus stared at the ceiling of the Lucky Lady's captain's quarters—a ceiling that had a water stain shaped like Florida, which seemed aggressive—and decided that waiting for the system to fix itself was the same as waiting for the system to finish killing them.

Their licenses were suspended. Their boat was ash. Their bank accounts were frozen. They were, in every legal sense, civilians. And civilians did not have the authority to intercept drug shipments on the open ocean.

Marcus assembled the crew at dawn.

"We're going out tonight," he said.

"We don't have authorization," Dana said.

"No."

"Without the license, this is armed interdiction without federal authority. That's piracy. Actual piracy. Not the cute kind with paperwork—the kind with twenty-year federal sentences."

"No."

"We don't have weapons." A pause. "Good weapons."

"We have Click's weapons."

"Click's weapons are not, strictly speaking, weapons. They're hypothetical devices that may or may not function as intended in conditions that may or may not resemble the conditions they were not technically designed for."

"They work," Click said.

"They've worked twice. Out of five attempts."

"The failure rate is trending downward."

"Trending downward from sixty percent is not reassuring."

Marcus held up his hand. "Here's the situation. We have Click's data. We have Frank's evidence chain. We have enough to destroy Half the Booty and Black Flag—but only if we can get it to the right people. The right people are currently not answering our calls because we're suspended and accused and nobody wants to be associated with the crew that got framed."

"So we need leverage," Luis said.

"We need a seizure. One more. Big enough that the press can't ignore it, clean enough that the documentation is bulletproof, and public enough that the people who want us silenced can't pretend it didn't happen."

"Without a license," Dana said. "Without legal authority. Without a functioning vessel."

"We have a functioning vessel."

Everyone looked at the Lucky Lady. The Lucky Lady looked back, in the way that fifty-two-foot shrimp trawlers looked at anything, which was with the resigned patience of something that had been through worse and expected worse still.

"She's a shrimp trawler," Dana said.

"She's a boat with engines and a deck and a crew that knows what they're doing." Marcus looked at each of them. "We don't have authorization. We don't have the law. What we have is each other and the knowledge that if we don't do this, the people who framed us win. The people who burned our boat win. The system that punishes honesty wins."

"That's a speech," Frank said.

"Is it working?"

"Little bit."

Gator raised his hand. "I got the engines running sweet. She'll do eighteen knots if I ask nice."

"You talk to this boat too?" Click asked.

"I talk to every boat. It's called respect."

"It's called anthropomorphization."

"It's called RESPECT, Click. The Lady can hear you."

The Lucky Lady creaked in the dock swell, which Gator took as agreement. Luis had the target.

Three days of calls, three days of favors burned like currency, three days of conversations with people who remembered the man he used to be and traded information the way other people traded baseball cards—carefully, with an eye toward future value.

"Mendoza cartel," Luis said, spreading a hand-drawn map on the Lucky Lady's galley table. The galley table was smaller than the Second Chance's and wobbled in a way that suggested one leg was shorter than the others, or possibly philosophical. "Major shipment. Twelve hundred kilos. Coming up the Yucatán corridor on a converted fishing vessel called the Santa María."

"Twelve hundred kilos," Click repeated.

"Approximately thirty-six million street value."

"And they're using a fishing vessel named after Columbus's ship," Frank said. "The irony is almost too much."

"The irony is intentional. Cartel logistics people have a sense of humor. It's terrible humor, but it's consistent." Luis tapped the map. "They'll run the corridor between 0200 and 0400, when Coast Guard patrols are thinnest. The route passes through a stretch of water that's currently unmonitored because—"

"Because the privateer crew that was supposed to be monitoring it got framed and suspended," Dana finished.

"Correct. The gap we left when we went down is exactly the gap they're using. Our absence is their opportunity."

Marcus studied the map. The route was thirty nautical miles offshore—deep water, dark water, the kind of open ocean where things happened that nobody saw and nobody reported and nobody remembered.

"We'll be completely exposed," Dana said. "No backup. No Coast Guard coordination. No legal standing. If they shoot at us, we can't even claim self-defense under the Lee Bill."

"We can claim self-defense under regular law," Frank pointed out. "Someone shoots at you, you're allowed to shoot back. That predates Congress."

"The legal nuances of—"

"Dana. Someone shoots at me, I shoot back. I don't need a bill for that. I need ammunition."

They went out at midnight.

The Lucky Lady moved through dark water with a practiced grace of a boat that had spent decades navigating without radar, without GPS, without anything except a compass and the accumulated knowledge of whoever was at the helm. She was slower than the Second Chance. Heavier. Less maneuverable. But she was also invisible—a shrimp trawler on the Gulf was as common as a pickup truck on a county road. Nobody looked twice. Nobody looked once.

Gator had the helm. He navigated by instinct and memory, reading the water the way other people read maps—the color, the texture, the way the current moved against the hull. He knew where the shoals were. He knew where the deep channels ran. He knew the Gulf the way you know a house you grew up in—every room, every hallway, every creaking floorboard.

"Two miles to the corridor," Gator said quietly. "Current's running south-southeast. Wind's at five knots, offshore. Good conditions for running dark."

"Good conditions for them too," Dana pointed out.

"Yeah. But they don't know the Lady. She's got a draft of four feet and a turning radius that'd make a sportfisher cry. Anything gets tight, I can put her in water they can't follow."

Click was running his equipment on battery power—the Lucky Lady's electrical system was not designed for surveillance technology, and the modifications Click had made were held together by optimism and marine-grade zip ties. The radar was a portable unit he'd smuggled off the Second Chance before it burned, repaired with components salvaged from a marine supply store that had been "very understanding" about the definition of "purchase."

"Contact," Click said. "Bearing one-nine-zero. Speed fourteen knots. Profile consistent with a sixty-foot fishing vessel."

"That's her," Luis said. He didn't check the radar. He was watching the horizon with eyes that had spent twenty years reading the ocean's handwriting. "She's running heavy. Deep draft. Engines working harder than a vessel that size should need for fourteen knots."

"How much product?"

"At that draft? Twelve hundred kilos is conservative. Could be more."

Marcus picked up the loudspeaker. Then he put it down.

He didn't have a federal authorization number to announce. He didn't have a license to cite. He didn't have the legal authority to order anyone to do anything on the open ocean.

He had a crew. He had a shrimp trawler. He had the accumulated evidence of a corrupt system and the stubborn certainty of a man who had been told, repeatedly, that honesty was a losing strategy.

"No loudspeaker," Marcus said. "We pull alongside. We board. We seize. We document everything—every gram, every photograph, every timestamp."

"And the crew?" Dana asked.

"Detained. Handed over to the Coast Guard with our evidence package."

"The Coast Guard that suspended our license."

"The Coast Guard that still has people like Vasquez. People who know our numbers are clean." Marcus looked at her. "We're not going to fight the entire system. We're going to find the people inside it who still give a damn and hand them something they can't ignore."

"That's optimistic."

"It's the only play we have."

Dana checked her weapon. "Then let's be optimistic."

They closed on the Santa María in darkness.

No loudspeaker. No warning. No authorization.

Just six people on a shrimp trawler, coming out of the dark like something the ocean had decided to send.

The boarding was fast and ugly and nothing like the clean operations they'd run from the Second Chance. The Lucky Lady didn't have a boarding platform. She didn't have tactical approach capability. She had a deck and a rail and Gator driving the boat close enough to the Santa María's hull that the two vessels scraped together with a sound that made every sailor present wince at the cellular level.

Dana went over the rail first—a six-foot gap between boats in a two-foot swell, the kind of jump that looked suicidal and was, in fact, suicidal, except that Dana had done it in places where the people on the other side weren't just carrying product but carrying grudges.

Marcus followed. Then Frank, who made the jump with the surprising athleticism of a man whose body remembered being capable even when his mind had stopped believing it. Then Luis, who boarded with the calm efficiency of a man returning to a world he'd left but never forgotten.

Gator stayed at the helm. Click stayed at the communications station, recording everything, jamming everything, doing seventeen things simultaneously with the manic focus of a man who had finally found a situation paranoid enough to justify his personality.

The Santa María's crew—seven men, young, armed, terrified—didn't fight.

They didn't fight because Luis walked to the center of the deck and spoke.

"Escuchen. Yo sé quiénes son. Yo sé para quién trabajan." His voice shifted when he spoke Spanish—softer, more musical, the voice of a man speaking the language he dreamed in. "No quiero hacerles daño. Pero ustedes saben cómo termina esto si no cooperan."

Marcus didn't understand every word, but he understood the tone—quiet authority, the kind earned by decades, not rank. Luis told them who he was. What he'd been. What he'd done. He told them, in specific terms, what would happen if they resisted and what would happen if they cooperated. They cooperated.

Twelve hundred and sixteen kilos.

Luis counted twice. Click photographed everything. Frank took statements. Dana secured the crew and the weapons and the boat itself, moving through the operation with the muscle memory of someone who had done this a thousand times in places where the rules were simpler and the consequences were worse.

Marcus documented.

He documented the way he'd always documented—methodically, precisely, with the obsessive thoroughness of a man who believed that paper was power. Every kilo. Every timestamp. Every name. Every detail that would make this seizure airtight, unassailable, impossible to dismiss as the work of a suspended crew with a grudge.

Because that's what they'd call it. He knew that. They'd say he was rogue. They'd say the seizure was illegal. They'd say the evidence was tainted, the operation was unauthorized, the whole thing was the desperate act of a man who couldn't accept that he'd lost.

And they'd be right about everything except the numbers.

The numbers would be clean.

They always were.

INTERCEPTED CORRESPONDENCE—DECLASSIFIED

FROM: Trevor Kline (Federal Detention Facility, Coleman, FL)

TO: [Legal Counsel—REDACTED]

RE: Re: Re: Re: Re: Re: Media Strategy

Gerald,

Day 83. I am writing in pencil. They took my pens after the cafeteria "incident," which I would like the record to reflect was not an incident but a vigorous stakeholder critique delivered through the only channel available to me, which was a bowl of mashed potatoes. My handwriting has regressed to what my third-grade teacher would have called "a concerning trend."

I am told Captain Hale's crew just seized twelve hundred kilos on a shrimp trawler with no license. No license, Gerald. They are technically, now, pirates. Actual pirates.

The press is calling it a comeback. The press is an idiot. It is a prelude.

They are going after Anton next. I can feel it in the shape of the questions federal investigators are asking—less about Half the Booty, more about Black Flag, more about who knew what about whom. This is, for the record, my plan. Anton makes a better villain on the courthouse steps than I do. He has the scar. He looks like what Americans think a criminal looks like. I look like a man who ran a marketing consultancy, because I did, because the marketing consultancy was real, it just also moved a non-trivial amount of product while being a marketing consultancy. Americans cannot convict a marketing consultancy, Gerald. They can only convict things that look like they belong on television.

Three years. A book. A stage.

Please continue to bill at the previously agreed rate. I understand the rate has increased. The rate has always increased. It is the nature of the rate.

—TK

P.S. Darryl was transferred for something he "didn't do." I have replaced the book club with a reading group called *Trevor Reads Moby Dick and Does Not Care For It*. The whale is late. This is, as I read it, a structural problem. I am taking notes.

[CORRESPONDENCE DESTROYED PER COUNSEL INSTRUCTION—TRANSCRIPT RECONSTRUCTED FROM INTERCEPT]

CHAPTER TWENTY-SEVEN

THE ABSOLUTION

The yacht was a fortress pretending to be a pleasure craft.

Three hundred feet of white fiberglass and black intentions, anchored where the only law was whatever Anton Voss decided it was. Four smaller vessels prowled the perimeter. Click's thermal imaging showed thirty-two people on board, at least twenty armed.

"We're in a shrimp trawler," Click said quietly. "With a creative approach to weapons law."

"We're not here to fight," Marcus said. "We're here to finish it."

The hours before midnight stretched like taffy.

Each crew member prepared in their own way. Click ran diagnostic after diagnostic on equipment that was already as ready as it would ever be. Dana cleaned weapons she'd cleaned three times already. Gator checked the engines, the fuel lines, the hull integrity—anything to keep his hands busy.

Marcus found himself on deck, watching the sun set.

His phone was in his pocket. He'd called Sarah two weeks ago, after the yacht heist. Told her he loved her. Heard her say it back.

Now, facing what might be his last night alive, he wondered if he should call again.

And say what? "Hey, remember that dangerous thing I mentioned? It's about to get more dangerous. Just wanted to say goodbye. Again."

She'd worry. She'd ask questions he couldn't answer. She'd hear the fear in his voice and know that this time was different.

He pulled out the phone anyway. Stared at her name.

Then he typed a text instead: *Thinking of you. Talk soon.*

Simple. True. Not a goodbye, but not nothing either.

The phone buzzed almost immediately. Her reply: *Love you, Dad. Be safe.*

Marcus stared at those words until the screen went dark.

Then he put the phone away and watched the last light fade from the sky.

Frank had been below deck for an hour. Dana found him sitting at the small galley table, his flask in front of him, untouched.

"You shouldn't be doing this," she said, sitting down across from him. "Any of it. The drinking. The mission. Being here."

"I'm fine."

"You're a liability." The words were harsh, but her voice was gentle. "I've seen it before. Good people who push too hard. Who get themselves killed because they couldn't admit they weren't ready."

Frank looked at the flask.

"My whole life," he said, "I've been waiting for something to matter. Something that wasn't just going through the motions. The job, the marriage, all of it—it felt like rehearsal for something real that never came."

"And this is real?"

"This is the first thing that's felt real in twenty years."

He stood up, walked to the rail, held the flask over the water.

"One night," he said. "I can give you one night. After that…" He shrugged. "After that, we'll see if there is an after."

"Frank—"

"I know what I am." He met her eyes. "I know what I'm not. Just let me do this one thing. Let me matter, just once, before it's over."

He opened his fingers.

The flask tumbled into the black water and disappeared.

Dana watched it go.

She didn't say anything.

She didn't have to.

Dana found Marcus in the wheelhouse ten minutes later. She closed the door behind her. Didn't sit.

"Don't bring him tonight," she said.

Marcus looked up from the charts he wasn't really reading.

"Dana—"

"I watched him pour the flask out. It was already half empty. He'd been drinking since noon. His hands aren't steady. His timing is gone. He's going to get someone killed. Probably himself."

"He wants to be here."

"Wanting isn't the same as being able." Dana's voice was level. Operator voice. The one she used for calls she didn't want to make and was going to make anyway. "You're the captain. Bench him. I'll tell him it was my call. He'll hate me for a week and then he'll get over it."

"He's earned this one."

"He's earned a better death than this one. That's what we owe him. That's what you owe him."

Marcus set the parallel ruler down. He looked at the charts. He looked at the door. He did not look at Dana.

"I need his gun in that corridor," he said. "We're four people going up against thirty. Luis is bait. Click's on comms. That's you and me and Frank. I can't do it with just you and me."

"Then we don't do it tonight."

"We don't get another night."

Silence. It was the silence of two people who had both already made a decision and were finding out which one of them had authority.

"That's not a reason," Dana said. "That's a rationalization."

"I know the difference, Dana."

"Do you."

He met her eyes. For a long moment he almost said yes. Almost said *you're right, pull him*. Almost said the thing he knew, underneath the tactical argument, was the actual truth—that Frank had earned a peaceful death in a Hialeah bar, not a loud one on a yacht, and the crew's numbers problem was Marcus's problem to solve, not Frank's to die for.

He didn't say it.

What he said was: "He's coming."

Dana stood there another second. Then she nodded, once, and walked out.

She closed the door with a control that was more damning than slamming.

Marcus sat in the wheelhouse alone and looked at the charts and waited to find out how much this was going to cost.

Luis took the inflatable across the dark water alone.

They watched him go—a small figure heading toward a fortress full of killers with nothing but words and hidden weapons. The yacht's searchlights swept the water in patterns Click had analyzed and predicted, and Luis threaded between them like a ghost.

"He's reaching the perimeter," Click reported. "One of the patrol boats is moving to intercept."

Marcus held his breath.

Through binoculars, he watched Luis raise his hands. Watched the patrol boat circle him once, twice. Watched men with guns board the inflatable and search him—finding nothing, because Click had built the ceramic rounds into the lining of Luis's jacket in a way that felt like fabric reinforcement.

"They're taking him aboard," Dana said.

"Now we wait."

The waiting was the hardest part.

Every minute felt like an hour. Every shadow on the yacht could be Luis being executed. Every radio silence could mean the plan had failed before it started.

The ocean rocked them gently, indifferent to their fear. Stars wheeled overhead in patterns that had watched countless men sail toward death and would watch countless more.

Frank stood at the rail, staring at the Absolution with an expression Marcus couldn't read. He'd been sober for two hours now—the longest stretch in weeks. His hands had stopped trembling, but his jaw was clenched tight.

At 11:23 PM, the yacht's lights flickered.

Once. Twice. Then darkness swept across the upper deck like a wave.

"That's the signal," Dana said, already moving. "Go."

Click's fingers flew across his keyboard, and somewhere in the digital realm, the Absolution's security systems began to lie to themselves. False contacts appeared on radar. Communications scrambled and unscrambled in patterns that made no sense. For fifteen precious minutes, the fortress would be blind.

Then Click froze.

"Wait." His voice was sharp. Different. "Wait, wait, wait."

Marcus turned. "What?"

"There's a signal I'm not blocking. Encrypted burst transmission. Outgoing." Click's eyes were wide. "They're calling for backup. Not yacht security—external. There's a patrol boat three miles out that wasn't on any of our scans."

"How did we miss it?"

"Because it was running dark. No transponder. No radar signature." Click looked up. "It's Black Flag protocol. They have a kill team staged offshore. If we go in now, they'll cut off our extraction."

Gator swore. "Can you jam them?"

"I can try. But it means splitting my attention. Security systems might come back online faster."

Marcus looked at the yacht. At Luis, somewhere inside, counting on them.

"Do it," Marcus said. "Jam everything. We'll move fast."

Click nodded and went to work.

Thirty seconds later: "Kill team's blind. But I'm losing the yacht's internal systems. You've got maybe ten minutes before they figure out what's happening."

"That's enough." Marcus grabbed his weapon. "Gator, get us in close. Dana, Frank—we're boarding."

Gator pushed the throttle forward.

The Lucky Lady surged toward the yacht, engines screaming, spray exploding from the bow. They came in fast and low, using the confusion Click had created, aiming for the stern where the disruption was greatest.

"Contact on the port side," Dana called. "Two hostiles."

Gunfire cracked across the water. Rounds punched into the Lucky Lady's hull—the junk armor Gator had welded on months ago doing its job, deflecting what would have killed them.

Gator swerved. Frank returned fire—surprisingly accurate for a man who'd just poured out his only comfort. One hostile went down. The other took cover behind a deck structure.

They pulled alongside the yacht's stern platform.

"Boarding ladder," Marcus said. "Go."

Dana was first—up and over the rail in one fluid motion, weapon sweeping the deck, dropping a guard before he could raise his radio. Then Marcus, slower but steady, covering her advance. Then Frank, breathing hard but moving, refusing to be left behind.

Click stayed on the Lucky Lady with Gator. "We'll be here when you need extraction. Just… try to need it soon."

The Absolution was built on four decks. Click had drilled this into them during the briefing: lower deck for service and engines; main deck for the salon, the grand staircase, the public spaces where the money showed; upper deck for Voss's office and private quarters; sun deck for the party. They'd boarded at the stern of the lower deck. The main salon was one flight up, directly above them. Voss would be higher still.

Between them and Voss: approximately thirty people, at least twenty armed, spread across three hundred feet of yacht.

Security personnel were everywhere—confused, reacting, but still dangerous. Click's electronic attack had knocked out their communications, but their training kicked in fast. They were forming up, establishing defensive positions, trying to figure out what was happening.

Click's voice crackled in Marcus's earpiece: "You've got four contacts on the lower deck moving toward your position. Two more on the upper deck. One of them appears to be carrying something very large. I'm choosing to believe it's a fire extinguisher."

"And if it's not?"

"Then you'll know before I do. Good luck."

Dana took point. She moved the way Marcus remembered operators moving in the service—fluid, controlled, checking corners with the methodical precision of someone who had cleared buildings in places that no congressional oversight committee would ever acknowledge. She signaled: two fingers, right side, moving.

Marcus stacked behind her. Frank behind him, breathing hard but present, his weapon up, his hands steady for the first time in months.

A guard appeared around a corner—young, tattooed, body armor that probably cost more than his annual salary. Dana dropped him before he could shout. One shot, center mass. He went down like someone had cut his strings.

Another came from a stairwell, this one faster, weapon already tracking. Marcus put two rounds in his chest. The body armor stopped the first. The second found the gap above the collar. Frank covered their six without being asked, the instincts of thirty years of police work operating independently of his conscious mind.

"Stairwell clear," Frank said. His voice was calm. Detached. He sounded like a completely different person from the wreck Marcus had recruited in a Hialeah bar. "Two more incoming from the service corridor. Twenty seconds."

"How do you know?" Marcus asked.

"I can hear their shoes." Frank paused. "Also one of them is wearing cologne. Who wears cologne to a gunfight?"

"Expensive mercenaries."

"Expensive stupid mercenaries."

They were right. Two guards appeared at the end of the service corridor. Dana took the first. Marcus took the second. Frank didn't need to fire, but his weapon tracked perfectly—covering the transition, ready for anything.

Click's voice again: "Updated count. Eight contacts between you and the main salon. Two appear to be arguing about something. Possibly whether to stand and fight or run. The smart money is on running, but nobody ever accused mercenaries of being smart."

"Main cabin," Marcus said. "Luis should be there."

They pushed forward through corridors that smelled like money and fear. Artwork hung on the walls—originals, probably worth millions—splashed now with blood and bullet holes. A Basquiat that had been acquired at auction for seven figures now had a 9mm hole through its center. Classical music still played somewhere, Vivaldi's "Four Seasons" providing a surreal soundtrack to the violence, which Marcus would have found darkly funny if he'd had time to find anything funny.

"Spring," Frank observed as they moved past the speakers. "Fitting."

"What?"

"The movement. It's Spring. The one about renewal." He kicked open a door, cleared the room. "Not a music guy, but my ex-wife played it a lot. Usually when she was pissed at me. Which was always."

"Frank, please focus."

"I am focused. I can focus and make observations simultaneously. It's called multitasking. Cops do it."

They reached the main salon.

He was standing in the center of the room, weapon in hand, blood on his face. Around him lay three men who would never get up again. His jacket was torn, his breathing heavy, but his eyes were clear.

And across from him, seated in a leather chair like a king on a throne, was Anton Voss.

Voss was not armed. Voss didn't need to be armed.

Two guards flanked him, weapons raised. Behind those guards were more guards. And behind those guards was the entire weight of an empire built on death and discretion.

But Voss himself sat perfectly still, watching the intruders with an expression of mild curiosity—like a man observing an interesting specimen rather than facing his enemies.

"Captain Hale," Voss said pleasantly. "I was wondering when you'd arrive. Luis has been telling me the most fascinating stories about your little crusade."

"It's over, Voss. The data is out. The network is collapsing. Your name is in every headline."

"Yes, it's been quite the news cycle." Voss smiled. "But you misunderstand the situation."

"Do I?"

"You think you've won because the truth is out. But truth doesn't defeat systems—it just forces them to adapt. The politicians who protected me will claim they were deceived. The businessmen who profited will rebrand as victims. The machine will continue. It always continues."

"Not with you running it."

"Perhaps not. But someone will." Voss leaned forward, his eyes bright with something that might have been amusement or might have been contempt. "You've inconvenienced me, Captain. You've cost me money and time and reputation. But you haven't changed anything. The demand exists. The supply will follow. The only question is who profits."

Luis spoke for the first time since they'd entered. "My daughter died because of that system."

Voss looked at him with something like curiosity. "Many daughters have died. Many sons. Many parents and siblings and friends. That's what a war on drugs produces—casualties. I didn't create the war. I simply found a profitable position within it."

"And now you'll find a position in a federal prison."

"Will I?" Voss smiled. "The evidence you've gathered is impressive. But evidence requires prosecution. Prosecution requires political will. And political will…" He gestured vaguely. "Political will is for sale, like everything else."

Marcus felt the weight of it—the sheer, exhausting certainty that Voss was right. That this would never really end. That whatever they did, whoever they stopped, the machine would grind on.

Then Frank stepped forward.

"You know what I've learned," Frank said, "in thirty years of chasing people like you?"

Voss looked at him with mild interest.

"I've learned that you're never as smart as you think you are. You make plans. You build systems. You surround yourself with protection. And then one day, some drunk with nothing to lose walks into your fortress and—"

Frank raised his weapon.

"Wait," Dana said.

The guard on the left fired first.

The bullet caught Frank in the chest.

Not the head. Not instantly fatal. Just a hole in his body that started leaking life before anyone could react.

Frank looked down at it with surprise. Almost wonder.

Then he fired.

His shot took the guard clean between the eyes. The second guard turned, too slow, and Luis dropped him with the ceramic rounds he'd been saving for three years. Voss dove for cover behind his leather throne. More guards poured in from the corridor.

And Frank was falling.

Gator's voice crackled over the radio: "Captain! That kill team Click spotted—they're moving! Two minutes out!"

Marcus caught Frank before he hit the ground. They were in the center of the main salon—thirty feet wide, paneled in teak, the grand staircase rising to their left. Dana had positioned herself at the forward corridor entrance, flanked by marble columns that gave her cover on both sides. From there she controlled the only approach from the lower deck, methodically dropping anyone who tried to push through. Luis had gone right—through a service door behind the bar, up a narrow stairwell toward the upper deck, pursuing Voss.

"Frank." Marcus pressed his hand against the wound. "Stay with me."

"Captain." Frank's hand grabbed Marcus's arm with surprising strength. "Go. Finish this."

"I'm not leaving you."

"Then we both die here." Frank coughed, blood on his lips. "And Voss gets away. And none of it meant anything."

The gunfire intensified. Dana called out: "They're flanking left! I need support!"

Marcus looked at Frank. At the wound that was too big, too central, too fatal. At the man who had finally found something worth dying for.

"I'll hold this position," Frank whispered. "Buy you time. It's the only thing I have left to give."

"Frank—"

"Go." Frank's grip tightened one last time. "Let me matter."

Marcus hesitated for one agonizing second.

Then Gator was there.

He came through a side door Marcus hadn't even seen, shotgun blazing, clearing the guards who'd been flanking Dana. He moved to Frank's position and dropped to one knee, weapon trained on the corridor.

"I got him, Cap." Gator's voice was steady. Certain. "Go get Voss. I'll keep Frank alive."

"Gator—"

"I owe him." Gator's eyes met Marcus's. "I owe all of you. For the skimming. For Eddie. For the boat." He fired twice, dropping a guard who'd appeared at the far end. "This is me paying it back."

Marcus looked at Gator—the redneck, the liability, the man who'd betrayed them out of misguided loyalty and spent every day since trying to make it right.

"Don't let him die," Marcus said.

"Not planning on it."

Marcus ran.

Behind him, Gator's shotgun roared, and Frank's rasping breaths continued, and two men who had nothing in common except this crew held a corridor against an army.

They found Voss in an escape pod.

Luis had disabled it before he could launch. Now Voss sat in the useless vessel, watching his empire collapse around him, and there was finally something other than confidence in his eyes.

Fear.

It looked good on him.

"Anton Voss," Dana said formally, her voice steady despite everything, "you're being detained under citizen's arrest for conspiracy, drug trafficking, and murder. You will be turned over to federal authorities upon arrival at U.S. territorial waters."

Voss looked at the zip-ties. Then at Dana. Then at Marcus.

"I could have left," he said quietly. "The escape pod was functional before Luis disabled it. I had a window. Forty seconds, maybe more."

"Then why didn't you?" Marcus asked.

"Because I don't run from people I built." Voss's eyes were steady. "Everything you have—the data, the evidence, the courage to be here—you learned from the system I created. You're not my enemies. You're my students. And a teacher doesn't flee his own classroom."

Marcus said nothing. There was nothing to say to a man who believed his own mythology.

Dana zip-tied his hands without ceremony.

They moved back through the yacht.

Marcus found Gator still at Frank's side. The corridor was littered with bodies—guards who'd tried to push through and failed. Gator's shotgun was empty. He'd switched to a pistol taken from one of the fallen.

Frank was still breathing.

Barely.

CHAPTER TWENTY-SEVEN

"Told you," Gator said. His voice cracked. "Told you I'd keep him alive."

They carried Frank between them, Marcus and Gator, while Dana covered their retreat and Luis kept Voss moving. Click had the Lucky Lady ready at the stern platform.

"Kill team's still three minutes out," Click reported as they boarded. "I've been feeding them false coordinates. They think we're on the other side of the yacht."

"How long will that hold?"

"Long enough." Click looked at Frank's pale face. "Is he—"

"Alive," Marcus said. "For now."

They sailed into the dawn, the Absolution shrinking behind them, Voss in custody, Frank bleeding on the deck with Gator pressing cloth against the wound and refusing to let go.

"Stay with me," Gator kept saying. "Stay with me, you drunk bastard. You don't get to die on my watch."

Frank lasted until they could see the mainland.

They were twenty minutes from the Coast Guard rendezvous when his breathing changed. Gator was still applying pressure, still talking, still refusing to accept what everyone else could see.

"Frank." Marcus knelt beside him. "Frank, can you hear me?"

Frank's eyes opened. They were distant now, focused on something no one else could see.

"Captain." His voice was barely a whisper. "Did we get him?"

"We got him. Voss is in custody."

Frank almost smiled. "Good. That's good."

"Stay with me. We're almost there. Twenty minutes and you'll be in a hospital."

"Not going to make twenty minutes." Frank's hand found Marcus's arm. "Listen. I need you to listen." Marcus listened.

"I spent my whole life afraid of dying," Frank said. "Afraid of what comes after. Afraid of mattering so little that nobody would notice I was gone." He coughed, wet and ugly. "But this... this mattered. Right?"

"It mattered. You mattered."

"Yeah?"

"Yeah."

Frank nodded, just barely. His eyes were starting to dim, but something in them had shifted—the restless, hunted look he'd carried for years finally easing into stillness.

"Tell my ex-wife she was right," Frank said. "About everything. She'll know what it means." He coughed, and blood flecked his lips. "And tell the crew... tell them I'm sorry I was such a pain in the ass."

"They know."

"Yeah." The ghost of a smile. "Yeah, I guess they do."

His breathing slowed. The grip on Marcus's hand loosened.

"Hey, Captain?"

"Yeah, Frank?"

"This was a good one. This crew. This mission. This..." He searched for the word, and when he found it, his voice was barely a whisper. "This family."

"It was," Marcus said. His throat was tight. "It is."

Frank nodded one last time.

"Good," he said. "That's good." His eyes closed.

His chest rose once. Twice.

And then it didn't.

Gator sat on the deck afterward, staring at his hands. They were covered in Frank's blood. He couldn't seem to stop looking at them.

"I tried," he said. To no one. To everyone. "I tried to keep him alive."

Marcus sat down beside him. Neither of them spoke for a long moment.

"You held that corridor for six minutes," Marcus said finally. "Against eight guards. With Frank bleeding out beside you."

Gator didn't look up. "He still died."

"He was going to die anyway. The bullet was too deep." Marcus paused. "But he died knowing someone was fighting for him. He died knowing he wasn't alone. You gave him that."

Gator wiped his face with the back of his hand, smearing blood across his cheek.

"That's something," he said quietly. "Right?"

"That's everything."

They sat together as the coast grew closer and the sun climbed higher and the world kept spinning despite all the ways it should have stopped.

CHAPTER TWENTY-EIGHT

THE LEAK

Dana sat on the deck of the Lucky Lady as the full light of morning broke.

Frank's body was below, waiting for the bureaucracy of death to process him. There would be paperwork. There was always paperwork.

Marcus found her there.

He didn't say anything. Just sat down beside her.

"I couldn't save him," Dana said.

"No."

"I couldn't save my brother either." She looked at her hands. There was still blood under her fingernails. Frank's blood. "I keep thinking if I'm good enough, if I'm fast enough, if I'm present enough—I can stop it. I can keep people alive. I can be the thing that makes the difference."

"Sometimes you can't."

"I know." Her voice was hollow. "That's the worst part. Knowing I can't doesn't make me stop trying. It just makes the failure hurt more."

They sat in silence for a while.

Dana reached up and touched the pendant at her neck. Her brother's dog tags, cut down and reshaped into something she could carry everywhere.

"David Kessler," she said. "My brother. When he died, I promised myself I'd make it mean something. That I'd turn his death into a purpose. That I'd hurt the people who hurt him."

"Did it work?"

"I had a chance last night." Dana's voice was quiet. "On the yacht. One of the guards had cartel ink. Stylized poppy—same organization that supplied the heroin that killed David. I recognized it from his autopsy file. I memorized every detail of that file."

She was quiet for a moment.

"I had his hands zip-tied. He was unconscious. I could have tightened them until he lost circulation. Could have done real damage. No one would have known. No one would have cared."

"But you didn't."

"No." She looked out at the water. "I wanted to. God, I wanted to. For about two seconds, I wanted it more than I've wanted anything. And then I looked at him—really looked—and he was just some kid. Twenty-two, maybe twenty-three. Terrible choices, terrible job, terrible life ahead of him if he keeps going. But still just a kid."

Dana touched the pendant again.

"Hurting him wouldn't bring David back. It wouldn't close anything. It would just mean I'd become the kind of person who hurts unconscious people because it makes me feel better." She exhaled. "And I decided I didn't want to be that person. Even if being that person would have felt really, really good for about five minutes."

Marcus was quiet for a moment.

"That's the hardest thing," he said. "Choosing who you want to be when everything is screaming at you to be someone else."

"Is that what you did? With the privateer program? With... all of this?"

"I tried." A rueful expression crossed Marcus's face. "I failed a lot. But I kept trying."

Marcus looked at the water for a while. Then: "You told me not to bring him."

Dana didn't move. "I remember."

"You told me he'd die. You were right." Marcus's voice was level. "And I heard you say it. And I brought him anyway."

"I know."

"That wasn't a tactical call. That was me choosing what I wanted to be true over what you were telling me was true. And Frank paid for that."

Dana was quiet for a long time.

"I know you heard me," she said. "That's what made it worse."

"Yeah."

"I wasn't going to ask you to say it."

"I know. That's why I did."

Dana looked at him.

"Do you think it's over? This thing with Voss?"

"Part of it is. The rest is just aftermath." Marcus stood, offering her a hand. "But we're still here. We're still crew. And that has to count for something."

Dana took his hand and stood.

She didn't feel better. She didn't feel healed or whole or any of the things that grief was supposed to give way to eventually.

But she felt less alone.

And for now, that would have to be enough.

The Coast Guard arrived with the full light of morning.

They took Voss. They took statements. They asked questions that Marcus answered with the flat precision of a man who was functioning on autopilot because the alternative was to stop functioning entirely.

Frank's body was transferred to official custody. There would be an autopsy. A report. A bureaucratic processing of one more life ended in the line of what some would call duty.

Click stood beside Marcus as they watched the Coast Guard cutter disappear over the horizon, carrying Voss toward a justice system that might or might not do its job.

"The kill team," Marcus said. "How did you spot them?"

Click shrugged. "I was looking for things that shouldn't be there. Signals that didn't fit the pattern."

"You saved us."

Click was quiet for a moment. Then he nodded, just once.

"Yeah," he said. "I guess I did."

Gator appeared beside them, still carrying Frank's blood on his hands. His face was hollow, exhausted, but he stopped in front of Click and just stood there for a moment.

"Hey," Gator said finally. "I never believed you. About the patterns. About the things you saw." He swallowed. "I called you paranoid. I thought you were crazy." Click said nothing.

"You weren't." Gator's voice cracked. "You were right. About all of it. And if I'd listened—if any of us had listened—maybe Eddie never gets close. Maybe we don't lose the Second Chance. Maybe Frank is…"

He couldn't finish.

Click studied him for a long moment. Then, slowly, he extended his hand.

"You're not the first person to call me crazy," Click said. "You probably won't be the last. But you're the first person who ever apologized for it."

Gator shook his hand.

"I'm sorry," Gator said. "I really am."

"I know." Click's expression warmed, just slightly. "For what it's worth, your faith in people isn't a flaw. It's just… dangerous. There's a difference."

"Yeah." Gator laughed, but it came out more like a sob. "I'm starting to figure that out."

Click walked away to check on the equipment, and Marcus stood alone on the deck, watching the sun climb higher over an ocean that had taken so much from him and given back just enough to keep going.

Frank was dead.

Voss was in custody.

And somewhere, the world kept spinning, indifferent to justice and sacrifice and all the small heroisms that would never make the news.

Then Marcus's phone buzzed.

A text from Chad: *Captain. I'm so sorry about Frank. I won't post anything. Just—I'm sorry. He was a good one.*

Marcus stared at the message for a long time.

Then he typed back: *Post the truth. All of it. Don't let his death disappear.*

Chad's reply came thirty seconds later: *On it.*

By that evening, the world knew Frank Mulligan's name.

The footage Chad had been holding—everything from the planning through the assault through Frank's last sober night—went out as a documentary special, three hours long, professionally edited overnight by Chad's team because, as Chad put it later, "I work fast when it actually matters."

Forty-eight million views in twenty-four hours.

It became the most viewed piece of content Chad Bryson would ever create, and the only one he never monetized. The ad revenue went to Linda Mulligan and to a foundation Chad set up in Frank's name for the children of police officers who died in the line of duty. Frank technically hadn't died in the line of duty, but Chad's audience didn't seem to care about technicalities, and neither did Linda when the check arrived.

The documentary made Frank Mulligan famous.

It also made Anton Voss radioactive. The footage showed him with absolute clarity, in his own words, calmly defending an empire built on death. Whatever sympathies any congressman might have had for him—whatever quiet deals might have been arranged in the background—evaporated overnight.

Voss would die in federal custody.

Not because the system had defeated him.

Because public opinion, weaponized through forty-eight million phones, had made him impossible to protect.

Senator Richard Lee held a press conference three days later.

Marcus watched it from a diner outside Homestead, surrounded by his crew—minus one.

"The revelations of the past week are deeply troubling," Lee said, wearing the expression of a man who had practiced "concerned" in front of a mirror until it had stopped looking like constipation. "I have always believed in oversight and accountability. I am calling for a full congressional investigation into how the privateer program was corrupted by bad actors."

"Bad actors," Marcus repeated.

On screen, Lee continued: "Those responsible will be held accountable. The integrity of our maritime security must be restored."

He didn't mention that his campaign had received contributions from three shell companies connected to Black Flag.

He didn't mention that his chief of staff had attended meetings on the yacht where deals were made.

He didn't mention anything that mattered.

"Think he'll survive?" Gator asked.

"Probably," Luis said. "Men like him always do."

Gator was quiet for a moment, staring at the screen, where Senator Lee was now performing a careful sequence of concerned nods toward an aide who had handed him a sheet of paper.

"Frank," Gator said, apropos of apparently nothing, "once told me that the only honest thing a politician could do was die in office, and even then half of 'em managed to spin it as a career move." He took a long pull of his beer. "I keep hearing his voice. Like he's still in the room, just back there somewhere, telling me the thing about the thing. I'm gonna miss that voice, man. That voice was a whole education I didn't sign up for."

Nobody responded, because there was no response. Dana's hand came to rest, briefly, on the back of Gator's neck—the kind of touch she almost never allowed herself to give—and then she withdrew it.

On screen, Senator Lee was now making a hand gesture that his communications team had probably rehearsed with him. It did not land.

Rourke called that evening.

"You did this," she said. She said it flatly, as established fact.

"We facilitated the release of information obtained by a confidential source."

Rourke laughed. It was not a happy sound.

"You've started a war, Captain. Not against Voss—that war was already happening. A war against the system that protected him."

"Good."

"Not good. Messy. Unpredictable." Rourke paused. "There are people who want you dead now. Not just criminals. People in agencies. People in government. People who built their careers on the things you just exposed."

"We expected that."

"Did you expect them to be competent?" Rourke's voice hardened. "Because some of them are. Very competent. And very motivated."

"What are you suggesting?"

"I'm suggesting you come in. Officially. Turn yourselves in, cooperate with the investigation, become witnesses instead of fugitives." A pause. "I can't guarantee protection. But I can guarantee a chance."

Marcus looked at his crew.

Gator shook his head.

Dana's expression was skeptical.

Luis said nothing, which was its own answer.

"We'll think about it," Marcus said.

"Don't think too long." Rourke hung up.

They thought about it for approximately thirty seconds.

"I ain't turning myself in to people who might kill me," Gator announced.

"Agreed," Dana said.

"The system had its chance to do the right thing," Luis added. "It chose otherwise."

"We finish this our way," Marcus said. "Then we figure out the rest."

CHAPTER TWENTY-NINE

TESTIMONY

Marcus testified before the reconvened subcommittee three months later.

The night before, Dana came to his motel room in Arlington with a legal pad and a bottle of water.

"Sit down," she said. "We're going to practice."

"Practice what?"

"Not being you." She sat across from him at the small table. "You have a tendency, when confronted by authority, to say exactly what you think in exactly the words you think it. This is admirable in a captain and catastrophic in a witness."

"I've testified before."

"In the Coast Guard, where everyone already agrees with you. This is Congress. Half of them are compromised, a quarter of them are stupid, and the remaining quarter are hoping you'll say something quotable enough to put on their campaign website." Dana flipped to a clean page. "So we're going to practice the art of being honest without being suicidal."

They ran mock questions for two hours. Dana played every committee member simultaneously—Morrison's surgical precision, Harmon's folksy ambushes (she was disturbingly good at this), Dawkins's earnest enthusiasm.

"When they ask about Frank," Dana said, and her voice changed slightly, "tell the truth. All of it. The drinking. The flask. The night he gave it up." She paused. "Don't protect him. He wouldn't want that. Tell them who he actually was, not who we wished he'd been."

"That's going to be hard."

"Most honest things are." She stood. "Get some sleep. You look like you've been awake since November."

"I have been awake since November."

"That tracks." She stopped at the door. "Marcus?"

"Yeah?"

"Whatever happens tomorrow—you did the right thing. Not the smart thing. Not the strategic thing. The right thing." She met his eyes. "Frank would have made fun of you for it. But he would have been proud."

She left.

Marcus sat in the motel room for a long time after that, staring at the legal pad full of Dana's notes, wondering when she had become the person he trusted most in the world and whether that said more about her or about how few people he had left.

This time, the room was different. The committee was different—half the original members had recused themselves after their names appeared in the leaked data. Congressman Harmon had announced his retirement "to spend more time with his family," a phrase that in Washington meant "to spend more time with his lawyers."

The gallery was packed. Chad's documentary had turned public opinion, and the cameras that had once been pointed at Marcus with suspicion now pointed at him with something approaching respect.

Representative Morrison led the questioning now. She had become, in the months since the data dump, the de facto leader of the privateer reform movement. Her staff had grown by twelve people. Her name was being mentioned for higher office. She was, in the way that occasionally happens in Washington, a competent person being briefly rewarded for competence.

"Captain Hale," Morrison began. "Thank you for appearing voluntarily."

"Thank you for asking instead of subpoenaing."

A few laughs from the gallery. Even Morrison almost smiled.

"You've been described as a folk hero. You've also been described as a vigilante. How would you describe yourself?"

Marcus thought about it.

"I'd describe myself as a man who tried to do the right thing within a system that punished honesty," he said. "And when that system failed, I had to decide whether to fail with it or find another way."

"And what did you decide?"

"I'm sitting in front of you. So I guess I decided."

Morrison nodded. "Tell us, in your own words, what happened. From the beginning." He told them.

All of it.

The clean numbers crusade. The first encounters with Trevor Kline and Anton Voss. The audit. The betrayal. The yacht heist. The destruction of the Second Chance. The ghost operations. The Absolution. Frank.

Especially Frank.

He talked about Frank for almost an hour. About the drinking. About the brilliance underneath the drinking. About the night Frank dumped his flask into the ocean and gave them the only sober night he had left to give. About how Frank had died the way he'd lived—reckless, brilliant, complicated, irreplaceable.

By the time Marcus finished, several members of the committee were not making eye contact with the cameras, in the manner of politicians who were experiencing actual emotions and were uncertain whether this would play well with their base.

Representative Dawkins—the young congressman with the anchor tie, who had been taking notes with increasing agitation throughout Marcus's testimony—raised his hand.

"Captain Hale, I have one question."

Morrison nodded. "Go ahead, Representative."

"You said your crew operated with complete transparency. Accurate seizure reports. Full documentation. Clean numbers."

"That's correct."

Dawkins held up a piece of paper. "I've reviewed every report your crew filed. Every single one. They're the most thorough, accurate, and well-documented reports in the entire privateer program." He set the paper down. "Why couldn't anyone else do this?"

The room was quiet.

"Because it's not profitable," Marcus said simply. "The system rewards the people who cut corners. It punishes the people who don't. We were punished."

Dawkins nodded slowly. Then he looked at the other committee members. "I think we need to reckon with what it means that the most honest crew in this program is also the one sitting at that table. And everyone else—everyone who skimmed, who lied, who 'optimized'—is still operating." He paused. "There's a word for a system that destroys its most honest participants. I believe the word is 'broken.'"

Someone in the gallery started clapping.

Then someone else.

Morrison let it go for five seconds before reaching for her gavel.

"What would you recommend, Captain?" Morrison asked.

"End the program. Shut it down. Fund the Coast Guard. Fund enforcement. Fund the things that work, slowly and imperfectly but honestly."

"And the crews currently operating?"

"Some of them are criminals. Prosecute them. Some of them are idiots. Educate them." Marcus paused. "And some of them—a very few—are people who genuinely wanted to do something good in a system that made doing good impossible. Don't punish them for trying."

"Including yourself?"

"Including all of us."

The committee voted unanimously to recommend suspension of the privateer program.

The vote was televised.

Senator Lee voted with the majority and gave an interview afterward about the importance of "learning from our mistakes." He was wearing boat shoes. He mispronounced "maritime" twice. Nobody asked him why he'd created the program in the first place.

Nobody ever does.

Six months later, he was appointed chair of the newly formed Senate Subcommittee on Maritime Innovation. His first act was to commission a study on "next-generation privateer frameworks." The study cost four hundred thousand dollars and recommended, in essence, doing the same thing again but with better PowerPoint.

He was re-elected by eleven points.

His campaign slogan was "Anchors Away!"—still misspelled. Nobody corrected him. Nobody ever would.

Outside the hearing room, Marcus nearly walked past a woman leaning against the marble wall. Tactical boots. Suit jacket. Arms crossed.

Rachel Okafor. Captain of the Sovereign Remedy. The woman from the yacht party who'd raised a glass to Luis with a half-smile that knew too much.

"Captain Hale." Her accent was precise, Nigerian-British, the kind that made everything sound like either a compliment or a verdict. "Good testimony."

"You were in there?"

"Front row. I wanted to see how it ended." She pushed off the wall. "The committee's going to suspend the program. You know that."

CHAPTER TWENTY-NINE

"That's what I recommended."

"I know. I'm not sure I agree." She studied him. "Some of us were doing real work out there. Not your way—I won't insult you by pretending I operated like you did. But real work. Disrupting supply lines. Recovering assets. Making it harder for the worst people to move freely."

"And skimming?"

"And surviving." She didn't flinch. "The difference between you and me, Captain, is that you believed the rules would protect you. I never had that luxury." She straightened. "If they shut the program down, the ocean doesn't get safer. It just gets quieter. And quiet oceans are where the worst things happen."

She walked away without waiting for a response.

Marcus watched her go. She moved through the Capitol hallway the way she'd moved through the yacht party—like someone who belonged everywhere and owed nothing to anyone.

He wasn't sure she was wrong.

He wasn't sure that mattered.

In the gallery, Chad filmed the entire proceeding. He posted it with a caption that, for once, didn't include a single hashtag: *Sometimes the good guys lose. But they tell the truth anyway. That has to count for something.*

It got twelve million views.

Chad donated the ad revenue to the families of privateers killed in the line of duty. He announced this on a livestream while visibly crying, wearing a "SENT IT" tank top, surrounded by scented candles.

It was simultaneously the most sincere and the most ridiculous thing Marcus had ever seen.

He was going to miss that idiot.

CHAPTER THIRTY

AFTERMATH

They buried Frank Mulligan on a gray Thursday in November, in a cemetery outside of Tampa that overlooked the water.

It wasn't a military funeral. Frank hadn't been military. It wasn't a police funeral, either—his department had sent a representative, someone who'd never worked with him, someone who read a prepared statement about "years of dedicated service" that could have applied to anyone.

Frank would have hated that.

What he might not have hated was who showed up.

Gator wore a suit for the second time in his life. It didn't fit any better than the first time, but he stood straight and kept his mouth shut and only cried a little bit when they lowered the casket.

Click had organized the whole thing—logistics, scheduling, transport—because organizing things was how he processed emotions he didn't know how to feel. He'd also hacked into the Broward County records system to find Frank's ex-wife and invite her personally. She came.

Linda Mulligan was a small woman with tired eyes and a posture shaped by years of waiting for bad news. She sat in the front row and listened to the ceremony without speaking, and when it was over, she walked to the edge of the grave and stood there for a long time.

Marcus gave her space.

When she finally turned away, she stopped next to him.

"You were with him at the end," she said. Not a question.

"Yes."

"Was he sober?"

Marcus thought about lying. It would have been kind.

"No," he said. "But he was himself. Fully himself. Alert and aware and... Frank." Linda nodded slowly.

"He called me, you know. Two weeks ago. Left a voicemail. Said he was finally doing something that mattered. Said he wanted me to know that I'd been right about everything, but that maybe being right wasn't the same as being happy." She looked at the grave. "I saved the message. I don't know why."

"He mentioned you. At the end. Asked me to tell you that you were right."

"About what?"

"He said you'd know." Linda almost smiled.

"I do," she said. "I always did."

She walked away without looking back.

Chad showed up. Of course he showed up. He'd flown in from Los Angeles where he'd been meeting with Netflix executives about a docuseries adaptation, and he stood at the back of the crowd in a black suit that probably cost more than the casket. He didn't film anything. He didn't take selfies. He didn't even bring Megan.

After the service, he found Marcus.

"Captain. I'm sorry."

"Thank you for coming."

"I never met him. Not really. He always avoided me." Chad's face did something Marcus hadn't seen before—genuine quiet. "But I felt like I knew him from your stories. From the documentary. From the way you all talked about him."

"He would have hated being on camera."

"I know. That's why I didn't bring one."

They stood in silence for a moment.

"I'm changing my brand," Chad said finally.

"What?"

"Sent It Maritime. The whole thing. I'm shutting it down."

Marcus looked at him in genuine surprise. "Why?"

"Because the documentary about you guys—about Frank—it's the best thing I've ever made. And it's the best thing because it wasn't about me. And I realized..." Chad trailed off, searching for words. "I realized that everything I've been doing for the last five years has been about me. The brand. The followers. The merch. Even when I was doing the privateer thing, it was about me being a privateer. And then I watched you guys actually be one—really be one—and I realized I'd been playing dress-up while you'd been doing the work."

"Chad—"

"I'm starting a foundation. With the documentary money. To help fund actual maritime law enforcement training. Real work. Boring work. The kind nobody's going to make a TikTok about." He paused. "I'm going to keep posting, but it's going to be different. Less dance, more substance. My audience is going to hate it and I'm going to lose like a million followers. But I think Frank would have appreciated it."

Marcus extended his hand.

"He would have." Chad shook it.

"I'm still going to call you 'bro,'" Chad added. "Just so we're clear. I can't change everything at once."

"I expected nothing less."

The crew gathered afterward at a bar that Frank would have appreciated—dark, cheap, the kind of place where nobody asked questions and the whiskey didn't pretend to be anything other than what it was.

They took the corner booth. They ordered drinks they didn't touch. They sat in silence because there was nothing to say that hadn't already been said.

"He died well," Dana offered finally.

"He died drunk," Gator corrected.

"He died saving us." Dana's voice was steady. "He was covering that doorway. If he hadn't been there—"

"If he hadn't been drunk, he would have reacted faster. He would have seen the guard coming. He would have—"

"He would have died anyway." Luis spoke quietly. "Different timing, same outcome. Frank had been dying for years. He just chose how it ended."

Gator stared at his untouched beer.

"I keep thinking about what I said to him," Gator said. "All the times I told him to lay off, or made jokes about the drinking, or called him a liability. And now…"

"And now he's gone and you can't take it back." Dana's voice softened. "That's how it always works."

"The last thing I said to him was 'try not to fuck this up.'" Gator's voice cracked. "That was the last thing. I didn't even mean it. It was just… what I say."

"He knew," Marcus said.

"Did he?"

"He knew you. He knew us. He knew the difference between how we talked and how we felt." Marcus looked at each of them—his crew, what remained of it. "Frank spent thirty years reading people. He wasn't fooled by our bullshit."

"Just by his own," Click murmured.

Nobody argued with that.

They scattered in the weeks that followed.

Not dramatically. Not all at once. But steadily, quietly, in the way that groups dissolve when the thing that held them together is gone.

Gator went back to the Keys. His cousin really did have a charter business that needed help, and Gator really did know more about boats than anyone had a right to. The work was boring. The money was legal. The worst thing that happened most days was a tourist catching a fish too small to keep.

He took the chicken with him. Patricia had, by this point, survived a federal fugitive operation, an unsuccessful Everglades relocation attempt by Click, and one confirmed encounter with a raccoon in which the raccoon had come out worse. Gator called her his emotional support poultry. The Coast Guard port authority in Marathon, confronted with a chicken on a shrimp trawler, eventually issued her a name tag that read PATRICIA—CREW and stopped asking questions. She continued to lay approximately one egg per month, always in inconvenient places, which Gator interpreted as a form of artistic protest.

He called Marcus once a week, at first. Then once a month. Then occasionally, when he was drunk and nostalgic and needed to talk to someone who understood. His voicemails followed a pattern: a long story about a tourist, a brief update on Patricia, and, at the end, the same sign-off every time—*Miss you, Cap. Miss all of it. Especially the parts I shouldn't.*

Marcus saved every one.

Click took the consulting jobs. Cybersecurity, mostly. Sometimes for companies that didn't ask too many questions about his background. Sometimes for government agencies that asked lots of questions but accepted the answers anyway because they needed his skills more than they needed him to be clean.

He started seeing a therapist. He didn't tell anyone about it, but Marcus found out anyway because Click's paranoia manifested differently when he was working through it—less frantic, more focused, occasionally even calm.

Mr. Whiskers, the orange tabby from the shipping container, moved with him to a small house in Coral Gables. The cat was now seventeen pounds and had developed what Click called "a pattern of strategic affection that I find deeply suspicious."

Dana went private. Executive protection, crisis management—work that paid well and kept her busy and didn't require her to get attached to anyone. She was good at it. She was always good at it.

The night she accepted her first contract—three weeks after the funeral—she sat in her car in the parking garage of her new client's office building in Miami and cried.

Not for long. Not dramatically. Just a few minutes of sitting in the dark with her hands on the steering wheel, letting it come. Frank's voice in her head: *Can someone please make the noise stop.* David's dog tags against her chest. The weight of being the person who held everyone together and never, not once, asked anyone to hold her.

She wiped her face. Checked her makeup in the rearview mirror. Walked into the building and spent the next eight hours protecting a pharmaceutical executive who had never once in his life needed to be as brave as the people she'd left behind.

She sent Marcus a card on his birthday. No return address. Just: "Still standing. Hope you are too."

She also, Marcus learned later from Click, had quietly sought out and visited David's old Marine unit. She'd talked to the men who had served with her brother. She'd learned things she'd never known—stories about David being kind to a kid who couldn't keep up, about David sharing food when supplies ran short, about David being the one his unit went to when they needed to talk about things they couldn't talk about with anyone else.

It hadn't fixed anything. But it had helped. Sometimes that was enough.

A year after the funeral, she took three weeks off and paid her own way onto a pelagic research vessel out of Hatteras, North Carolina. Not for work. For birds.

She had been keeping the list since she was nine years old. Six hundred and forty-three species. She wanted to see a white-tailed tropicbird before she turned forty, and the only way to see a white-tailed tropicbird was to get on the kind of boat Navy training had taught her to be afraid of for all the wrong reasons. The ornithologists on board did not know what she had done for a living. They talked to her about shearwaters. She talked back. She stood on the pitching deck with her notebook and her ancient Leicas and wrote *South Polar Skua* in her clean small handwriting at 7:14 AM on a Tuesday, and for three hours afterward her hands did not feel like anything had ever been wrong with them.

She sent Marcus a postcard when she got back. Front: a photograph of a storm petrel. Back: *Saw 31 species I'd never seen. Hands worked the whole time.—D.*

Marcus kept it on the galley shelf of the boat he didn't own anymore, which is to say, he kept it in a drawer.

Luis disappeared.

Not literally. He was still alive, still somewhere. But he didn't call. He didn't write. He didn't show up at reunions or memorial services.

Marcus heard from Click, six months later, that Luis had been spotted in Medellín. Back where it started. Click couldn't confirm what he was doing there, but he'd found a single data point: a wire transfer to a small veterinary clinic in the barrio where Maria had grown up. Monthly. Automatic. The clinic treated stray animals for free.

Maria had wanted to be a veterinarian.

Luis hadn't said goodbye. Hadn't explained. He'd simply gone back to the place where his daughter had been a child and started building something small and quiet in her name. Not revenge. Not redemption. Just presence. The thing he couldn't give her when she was alive, offered now to a neighborhood that remembered her laugh.

Marcus hoped that was enough.

He wasn't sure anything ever was.

CHAPTER THIRTY-ONE

HOMECOMING

Six months after the funeral, Marcus drove to Boca Raton.

The drive from Tampa took four hours. He could have flown. He chose not to. He wanted the time—the slow accumulation of distance between who he'd been and who he was trying to become. I-75 to Alligator Alley, the Everglades spreading out on both sides like the state's subconscious: vast, patient, indifferent to human ambition.

Outside of Naples, he passed a marina. A dozen boats, nothing special, but one of them was a fifty-foot patrol vessel that had been painted an aggressive shade of black, with "ASSET LIBERATION" stenciled on the hull in gold letters. Two men in matching tactical polo shirts were loading equipment onto the deck while a woman with a clipboard supervised.

New privateers. The program had been suspended, not terminated. Congress was still arguing about it. In the meantime, operators with existing licenses could continue to operate while the commission deliberated, which meant the ocean was still full of people with guns and laminated cards and varying interpretations of the word "authorized."

Marcus drove past without stopping.

He noticed, in the rearview mirror, that one of the tactical polo shirts was tucked in wrong.

Some habits died hard.

Halfway across Alligator Alley, his phone buzzed. A text from Gator: *Hey Cap. Caught a mahi today that weighed more than Click. Naming it Frank. How are you?*

Marcus typed back: *Good. Driving to see Sarah.*

The reply came instantly: *Tell her Uncle Gator says hi. And that if she names that baby anything stupid I'm filing a formal objection.*

Marcus put the phone down and smiled. Not almost. Actually smiled. Just him, alone in a car, crossing a swamp, heading toward a daughter he'd spent twenty years failing and was now—finally, imperfectly, stubbornly—trying not to fail anymore.

His daughter lived in a house that looked nothing like anywhere he'd ever lived—suburban, neat, a place where people mowed lawns and waved to neighbors and worried about property values. It should have felt foreign. Somehow it didn't.

Sarah met him at the door.

She was showing now. Seven months along. Healthy, according to the doctors. Due in February.

"You came," she said.

"I said I would."

"You've said a lot of things."

"I know." Marcus didn't try to defend himself. There was nothing to defend. "I'm trying to be different."

"I know." Sarah stepped back to let him in. "That's why I invited you."

The house was warm and cluttered and lived-in. Her husband, Matt—the accountant, the one who showed up, the one who remembered—was in the kitchen making something that smelled like actual home cooking.

"Mr. Hale," Matt said, extending a hand. "Good to see you."

"Marcus is fine."

"Marcus, then." Matt's handshake was firm, his eyes direct. He had the steadiness of a man who came home at the same time every day, who remembered anniversaries without reminders, who was present in the way that Marcus had never managed and was only now beginning to understand the value of. "Sarah's told me about... everything. The work you did. What it cost."

"Did she tell you I was a shitty father?" Matt blinked.

"She didn't have to," he said after a moment. "But she also told me you're trying to change. And that's worth something."

"Is it?"

"It's everything." Matt smiled slightly. "Anyone can be good when it's easy. It's what you do when it's hard that matters."

Marcus looked at his daughter.

She had her mother's eyes. Laura's eyes. The ones that saw through bullshit and pretense and all the ways people hid from the truth.

"I'm not going to be perfect," Marcus said. "I don't know how to be a grandfather. I barely knew how to be a father."

"I know."

"But I want to learn. I want to be here. Not just for the big moments—for the boring parts. The ordinary parts. The parts I missed before."

Sarah was quiet for a moment.

Then she hugged him.

It was the first time she'd hugged him in years. Really hugged him, not the obligatory greeting embrace that families performed when they'd forgotten how to be close.

For a half-second, in the middle of it, Marcus thought: *Frank isn't here for this because of a call I made in a wheelhouse.* The thought arrived uninvited and did not leave. He returned the hug anyway, because what else was there to do—but he understood, with a clarity that was going to stay with him, that some things were going to come home with him forever, and this was one of them.

"Okay," she said into his shoulder. "Okay. We'll figure it out."

He stayed for dinner. He helped clear the table afterward. He insisted on doing the dishes, which Matt tried to argue against until Marcus pointed out that he had spent two decades of his life refusing to do dishes for a woman who had loved him, and he had a lot of dishes to make up for.

Sarah laughed at that. Actually laughed.

It was the best sound Marcus had heard in a year.

While Marcus dried plates, Sarah leaned against the counter.

"Mom has a garden now," she said. "She's completely obsessed. She joined a community garden. She grows heirloom tomatoes and gives lectures about companion planting. Her friends only know her as 'the tomato lady.'"

Marcus tried to imagine Laura—precise, controlled, beautiful Laura—elbow-deep in soil, lecturing strangers about tomatoes. He couldn't picture it. And the fact that he couldn't told him everything about how much he'd missed.

"She sounds happy," he said.

"She is. She really is." Sarah paused. "She also said something about you. She hopes you're actually changing and not just performing change because you found a new audience."

The plate was clean. Marcus dried it anyway.

CHAPTER THIRTY-ONE

"She's not wrong to wonder," he said.

"I told her you're trying. Really trying." Sarah took the dish towel from him. "She said 'trying' was your favorite word. That you'd been 'trying' for twenty years. And that the difference between trying and doing was whether anyone noticed when you stopped."

"She's right. She was always right."

"I know." Sarah looked at him. "But she also said—and she'd never tell you this herself—she's glad you're here. That Sarah has you." A pause. "She used your first name. She hasn't done that in years."

"Tell her I said thank you."

"Tell her yourself. She's coming for Thanksgiving. If you want to be here."

"I want to be here."

"Then be here."

After dinner, they sat in the living room. Sarah on the couch, Matt in the armchair, Marcus in the spare chair that had been pulled in from the dining room because nobody had needed a third chair before he started visiting.

They watched a movie. He couldn't have told you afterward what movie it was. He spent most of it watching Sarah out of the corner of his eye, trying to memorize the fact of her, the reality of being in the same room as her without an emergency forcing it.

When she fell asleep on Matt's shoulder twenty minutes in—pregnancy exhaustion, Matt explained quietly—Marcus stayed quiet and watched her breathe.

He thought about all the times he hadn't been there. The nights he'd missed when she was a baby. The recitals he'd skipped when she was a child. The dinners he'd canceled when she was a teenager. The graduations and milestones and ordinary Tuesdays that had stacked up into a wall between them.

He couldn't take any of it back.

But he could be here. Now. For this Tuesday. And maybe the next one. And maybe the one after that.

It wasn't much.

It wasn't enough.

But it was a start.

EPILOGUE: COMPLIANCE

Statement of Trevor Kline, Founder and Former CEO of Half the Booty, Global

Submitted to the Federal Oversight Committee on Maritime Privatization

Six months after program termination

People keep asking how it felt when the reforms passed.

They expect me to say "relief." Or "vindication." Or maybe something performative like "gratitude."

The truth?

It felt like finally getting the software update we'd been beta-testing in production.

We were never pirates. Pirates are inefficient. Pirates wear skulls and pretend chaos is a strategy.

We were early adopters.

When Congress legalized private interdiction, most people heard guns. We heard workflow. They saw boats. We saw vertical integration.

Do people say we skimmed? Of course. That's what amateurs call margin control.

You think Amazon doesn't lose packages? You think governments don't misplace entire wars?

Loss is baked in. You just decide whether you're honest about it—or profitable.

There was a phase—very brief—where people thought the system was "out of control."

That's when Captain Hale happened.

Nice guy. Moral backbone. Terrible understanding of scale.

Marcus believed the law was a promise.

We understood it was a prototype.

And for that, we're grateful. Because after Hale, Congress didn't ask if privateering should exist. They asked how to professionalize it.

Black Flag?

They weren't villains. They were legacy hardware. Necessary, ugly, expensive to maintain.

Violence is bad branding.

Compliance kills cleaner.

I watched Marcus Hale testify once. Not live—live feeds are messy. I watched the recap. He spoke like a man who believed truth was a currency.

That's sweet.

Truth is content.

And content needs distribution, sponsorship, and legal review.

A thing I learned about Captain Hale, during all of this, that I find more interesting than anything he ever said at that table: he once made a tactical call that killed one of his own men. A good tactical call, by the way. Correct, even. The wrong moral one.

He knows he made it. He will know it for the rest of his life.

That is not a flaw. That is the *feature* he doesn't know he has. Because the people who make clean tactical calls without paying for them are the people I hire. The people who pay for their calls forever—the people whose faces do the bookkeeping the paperwork can't—those people are exactly who the system needs to grind down first.

Marcus will be fine. He'll have a grandchild. He'll do the dishes. He'll never be dangerous again.

That is, in its way, a kind of winning. Just not the kind he wanted.

Sometimes people ask me if I sleep well.

I do.

Because I know something Marcus never understood:

The world doesn't run on good or evil.

It runs on who fills out the paperwork last.

And I always do.

You're probably wondering: how is Trevor Kline sitting here when he should be in prison?

I cooperated.

Not because I felt guilty—guilt is an emotion for people who got caught doing things they knew were wrong. I cooperated because cooperation is just another form of optimization.

Voss didn't understand that. Voss thought he could fight the system from inside a prison cell.

Voss is going to die in federal custody.

I'm going to serve three years minimum security, write a book, and emerge as a cautionary tale people will pay to hear at conferences.

He thought he was above the system.

I knew I was the system.

Tomorrow I'm meeting with my publisher.

The book's called From Piracy to Profit: Lessons in Adaptive Leadership.

Pre-orders are strong.

I'll stand on stages and talk about "ethical navigation of challenging regulatory environments."

I'll smile.

I'll wear the suit.

And somewhere, Marcus Hale will watch a clip of me on television and know that despite everything he sacrificed—

I'm still here.

I'm still winning.

That's the real ending, if you're honest about it.

The good guys don't always win.

The bad guys don't always lose.

And the ones in between—the ones who understand that morality is just another variable to be optimized—

We adapt.

We survive.

We profit.

—Trevor Kline

Former CEO, Half the Booty, Global

Author (forthcoming)

Speaker, Consultant, Survivor

THE END

CODA

On a Saturday in June, Marcus took his granddaughter to the water.

Not the Gulf. Not the deep water where he'd spent his life chasing things and being chased. Just the Intracoastal—the calm, flat, sun-warmed ribbon of water that wound behind the houses of Boca Raton like a lazy afterthought.

He'd borrowed a skiff from a neighbor. Fourteen feet. Aluminum. A motor so small it sounded like an angry sewing machine. The kind of boat that couldn't outrun anything, couldn't chase anything, couldn't do anything except float and move forward at a speed that allowed you to notice the world going by.

Grace was five months old. She sat in a car seat that Sarah had strapped to the center bench with the particular engineering overkill of a first-time mother who had watched too many safety videos. The car seat was secured with four straps, two bungee cords, and a length of marine-grade rope that Marcus suspected was structural overkill but knew better than to argue about.

"Is she okay?" Sarah called from the dock, her hands making the unconscious reaching gesture of a mother watching her child move beyond arm's reach.

"She's fine."

"Is the car seat—"

"It's fine. Everything is fine. We'll be back in an hour."

"Forty-five minutes."

"Forty-five minutes."

He eased the skiff away from the dock. The motor puttered. The water opened up around them—flat, green, warm—and the houses slid past with their docks and their boats and their pelicans sitting on every piling like gargoyles on a cathedral.

Grace looked at the water.

She had never seen this much of it before. Her eyes—Sarah's eyes, Laura's eyes, the eyes that saw through everything—went wide with something that wasn't quite understanding and wasn't quite surprise but was somewhere in the territory of first recognition. The world is bigger than I thought. There is more of everything than I knew.

Marcus cut the motor near a spoil island where the manatees gathered. The skiff drifted. The silence was enormous—not empty silence but full silence, the kind filled with water sounds and bird sounds and the particular hum of a Florida afternoon being hot.

A manatee surfaced twenty feet away. Gray back, barnacled and scarred, moving through the water with the slow deliberation of something that had nowhere to be and all day to get there.

Grace made a sound.

Not a word. She was too young for words. But a sound—a vowel, long and round and full of the specific amazement that only belongs to people seeing things for the first time.

"That's a manatee," Marcus said. "Your Uncle Gator has some theories about them. You'll hear all about it when you're older. Probably sooner than you'd like."

The manatee regarded them with one small, ancient eye. Then it sank beneath the surface and was gone, leaving only a ring of ripples that spread out and faded and left the water exactly as it had been.

Marcus sat in the skiff with his granddaughter and watched the ripples disappear.

He thought about a lot of things. The Second Chance. Frank's flask tumbling into the dark water. Luis standing at the rail, counting. Click's napkin, pinned to the wall. Gator's hands, covered in someone else's blood, refusing to let go.

He thought about Dana, too. He thought about the door she had closed so quietly, that night before the yacht, that the closing of it had been louder than if she had slammed it. He thought about how many months it had been since then and how, still, he could not hear a door close carefully without hearing that door.

He thought about Trevor Kline, somewhere, giving a speech. Smiling for cameras. Winning in the way that certain people always win—not by being good but by being present when the music stopped.

He thought about Laura, who had been right about everything and had left before he could prove he'd heard her.

He thought about the ocean. The real ocean. The one that didn't care about clean numbers or dirty money or the distance between who you were and who you wanted to be. The one that took everything you gave it and gave back nothing except the chance to float.

Grace made another sound. Louder this time. She was reaching for the water with both hands, straining against the car seat straps, wanting to touch the thing that was everywhere and always moving.

Marcus dipped his hand in the Intracoastal and let a few drops of warm water fall on her fingers. She laughed.

It was the first time he'd heard her laugh.

It was not a profound laugh. It was not a meaningful laugh. It was the laugh of a five-month-old who had just discovered that water was wet and that wet was funny, and who had no context for anything beyond the immediate, overwhelming fact of sensation.

It was the best sound Marcus Hale had ever heard.

He sat in the borrowed skiff, in the flat warm water, with the sun on his face and his granddaughter laughing and a manatee somewhere beneath them, moving slowly through a world that was bigger and stranger and more beautiful than anyone who hadn't stopped to look would ever know.

He didn't reach for his phone.

He didn't check the time.

He stayed.

COMPLIANCE

Thank you for reading.

If you enjoyed this book, please consider leaving a review. It helps more than we are legally permitted to explain.

"There's a legal distinction."

"Paperwork."

www.ingramcontent.com/pod-product-compliance
Lightning Source LLC
Chambersburg PA
CBHW060632260626
47161CB00008B/2864